Into This Mind

Into This Mind

Lisa Nevin

Copyright © 2007 by Lisa Nevin

FIRST EDITION

ISBN
Hardback: 1-58832-186-X or 978-1-58832-186-2
Paperback: 1-58832-185-1 or 978-1-58832-185-5

Unlimited Publishing LLC
Bloomington, Indiana

http://www.unlimitedpublishing.com/authors

Author's web site:
http://www.lisanevin.com/

For my friend Karen and sister Diann:
Friends are found rarely.
Sisters are a blessing of birth.

Acknowledgments

To my husband, Nick: Thank you for supporting my endeavor.

To my sisters, Vicki, Judy, Diann, Rita, and, forever in our hearts, Jenny: You are all dear to me, and my source of encouragement and warmth.

To L. P. Sloan: Thank you for all the time you spent answering my many questions and helping me find my way.

To Jack Magestro: I will be forever grateful for the time and effort you put into my novel.

Table of Contents

3   Lisa Nevin

Chapter 1: Time to Explore

Excited that the long-locked gates have finally been opened, I leap out of bed to a gorgeous spring day and run outside to fetch the morning paper. Nature also senses that today is the day, offering a clear, blue sky, newly blossoming forsythia, a rainbow of budding tulips, and a light breeze that nudges me forward. Time is wasting. I'm expecting Katri and Adam Evers this evening, so I hurry to get ready for my morning hike. The day has finally come when I can legally enjoy a long hike around the newly opened Betta Conservation Land.

Before now, whenever I walked along the road that borders it, I always felt a strong desire to explore and to disregard the No Trespassing signs. On one occasion, I had ventured onto the trail entrance, but I stopped myself. As much as I tried to convince myself it was acceptable, I knew it was wrong so I turned back. I chalked up the incident to my overzealous urge to explore new places. So yes, today, I'm particularly excited to explore the land that has been taunting me.

The Betta Conservation Land is on the other side of the Betta River in Betta, Massachusetts—rolling hills, fields, ponds, and a side stream from the Betta River leading to a large lake, or so I've heard. In total, about two thousand acres have been unavailable to the public for nearly forty years.

My husband, Ben, is working from home today as he often does on the weekend when deadlines grow pressing. He promised he would take an hour's break and straighten up the house before our friends arrive this evening.

His office is in our loft above our family room. He walks over to the loft railing, looks down, and shakes his head as he watches me fuss with the harness on my cat, Sweetie Pie. Ben thinks I shouldn't bother with the harness. "Just use the smaller collar that he's wearing," he's said many times before.

I explained each time why it's important that the small collar be flexible and designed to come off easily, where as the harness is more secure.

Regardless, even now, he continues to laugh at my efforts. His pale green eyes dance as he snickers, watching my struggle.

Sweetie Pie growls and squirms, I curse while avoiding his

claws, and Ben looks on as if it's his personal comedy hour.

He brushes his sandy-red hair out of his eyes and walks off squeezing his own cheek, the gesture he uses to make fun of me when I'm angry.

Ben doesn't think I can make a proper angry face. No matter how I contort my face in anger, he laughs. One time, I told him about our hundred-thousand-dollar electric bill. Initially, he was mortified. As I explained, I got angrier as I remembered the cavalier attitude the customer support specialist had, and positively livid at what I had to do to fix their error. Ben had to leave the room because he was laughing so hard. With an oval face and puffy cherub cheeks, I guess when I'm angry I do look a bit like an inflated balloon with a scowling face drawn on it.

The intoxicating scents from the catnip satchel work wonders in distracting Sweetie Pie. I finally maneuver the harness into place and hook it and we head out. He, too, is particularly eager for a walk today. As usual, Sweetie Pie struts down the street oblivious that he's a cat. Although he's bigger than most cats, he's still smaller than most dogs, but it doesn't matter. He rules the street, the house, the chair, the lawn; wherever he is, he rules. Don't mess with Sweetie Pie when he's on a mission. Ben says the same thing about me.

Today we're both on a mission. Even if I didn't want to explore the Betta Conservation Land, I'd be hard pressed to convince my cat to walk in any other direction. Normally, he stops to observe the hopping bugs, butterflies, and darting chipmunks. Not today!

We cross Betta Bridge, then head down Dirt Road, the only road that borders the conservation land, and, yes, Dirt Road is its name. I've walked it many times before, desperately wanting to veer off, tear away, and run into the forbidden land.

To make things more complicated, people must leave their cars at the aptly named Dirt Road Parking Lot and walk along the road to get to the Betta Park Playground half a mile down the road. Dirt Road continues for miles beyond the park; eventually, it dead-ends beside another parking lot just before joining a busy paved road.

I've lived on the opposite side of Betta River for so many years that I've had numerous encounters with people asking for directions to the playground. Often, it's an impatient person who interrupts and we get into one of those ridiculous, back-and-forth name games.

"Where is Betta Park?" the person will ask.

"Go up and turn right on Dirt Road."

"What's the *name* of the dirt road?"

"Dirt Road."

"Yes, I heard that," the person will say, rolling his eyes at me. "What's the name of the dirt road?"

"The dirt road's name *is* Dirt Road."

Inevitably, the same impatient person asks me about parking. When I explain where to park, the person tells me how stupid it is that the parking isn't beside the park, as if I'd planned it that way.

My favorite question comes when I'm walking my cat. "You can walk your cat on a leash?" I know it isn't a rhetorical question because the person will pause, with arched brows, waiting for a response. Well, here I am, walking down the road, with a leash in one hand and a cat at the end of the leash. "Oh, he gets that all the time," I'll say, "because this dog species resembles a cat. But, no. He's a dog."

To which the person will nod, as if he knew that all the time. On one occasion, Sweetie Pie meowed, and the couple in question made it quite clear how displeased they were that I'd had the audacity to lie to them. When I said, "I was just kidding," they burned rubber and sped away.

In peak season, Dirt Road is still tranquil despite the heavy foot traffic. The gentle breeze, the river on one side of the road, and the tree-lined hillside on the other, are in themselves so serene that the crowds have no impact on their calming effect.

The spacious Betta Park Playground sits on the spot where part of Betta Train Station once stood. The playground has all the latest equipment: swings (both baby and full size), two merry-go-rounds, a jungle gym, monkey bars, a sandbox, four seesaws, and a multilayer plastic tunnel maze. After it rains, though, the tunnel maze turns into a mudslide. It was a nice idea on paper! Wooden benches sit around the perimeter of the play area and additional benches face the river.

Betta Train Station covered twice as much land as the playground, with buildings on both sides of the train tracks. I've heard that it even had a walkway over the tracks to connect the buildings. I thought it odd that the station was on both sides of the tracks, but who knows? Maybe people arrived at the station from the river. If the train tracks were here today, the playground would be on the river side.

Sweetie Pie and I approach Betta Park Playground, the widest section of flat land along Dirt Road. Some portions of Dirt Road are so narrow it's a marvel that the trains ever made it through without scraping against the hillside.

The trains stopped coming more than a hundred years ago, but when they were active, my small town was a popular vacation spot. The trains brought in wealthy vacationers, who rested and explored what was then called the Betta Grand. Years later, long after the train tracks were removed, it was renamed the Betta Conservation Land.

Being such a curious person, I often wonder about the history of the places I visit. Wherever I may be, I wonder about those who walked before me: where they came from, why they were there, what they did for a living, whether they had a family, and on and on. Pretty much everything about history fascinates me. Two minutes, a decade, a century—it's all the same to me. Each time I visit a new place, I think of the memories made there, which live there now and make up the history of that spot. How intriguing!

Not many people enjoy conjecturing about what happened at some spot at various moments in time, so I have to make do with friends and family. My favorite person to recreate memories with is my best friend, Katri Evers. Although she doesn't have my creativity when it comes to recreating what might have been, she adds an amusing twist. On one occasion, I pondered about the wealthy vacationers who arrived by train. "They might have been in this very spot, Katri, waiting to disembark."

"At this point?" she answered, sounding skeptical. "The end of the station? So the passengers were disembarking from the engine car?"

I sighed; she can be so literal sometimes. "The tracks could have been longer then. Who's to say it always ended here? In any case, before you interrupted, yes, as they stepped off the train, wearing their beautiful, billowing dresses, they surveyed the platform and then headed down to the Betta Train Station where they waited for transportation to the Betta Grand Hotel. Maybe it was their first time here, or maybe it was their last."

"*Billowing* dresses?" Katri laughed. "What? And the dresses swell up and get in their way, so they can't see that the step wasn't placed for their dainty little feet, resulting in their going *boom*, face down on the platform. You know, I can visualize that." She stood there, nodding at the spot where she believed it might have happened, not because she was really visualizing, but more, I suspect, to tease me. I'm the one who tries to visualize.

"I'm proud of you, Katri. I think I'm making some progress with you, but you need to work on visualizing happier memories."

"Thank you. After listening to so many stories from you, maybe it's rubbing off. In any case, I doubt that anyone could rival your imagination! I've never met anyone as intensely interested in the story in the trees as you are. Sometimes, listening to you, it's almost like a real scene from yesteryear." The "story in the trees" is what Katri calls my ever-wondering thoughts about who, what, when, and where.

Pointing at random spots in the trees, she added, "Oh, look, there goes a memory now! Get it, Jena, and bring it back to me!" She paused and looked at me thoughtfully. "You get so engrossed in your thoughts. Remember that time, a few years back, when you tripped on a stone? You were actually looking at it, but you were so busy describing this elegant trunk that might have been placed there, you didn't see the stone."

"Oh, come on, Katri. You must find it at least somewhat interesting, this very spot where we're walking. So much may have happened here before. Someone may have laughed, cried, thrown themselves in front of a train and . . . ."

"What? What did you say about happy memories?"

"Whatever! The point is the possibilities. Where we stand now, so much history has happened before. Each step we take, we stand where memories live on. You know, we're making more memories for this spot."

"Fascinating," she laughed. I think she was talking about me rather than the conversation, given how intently she listened. Even now, when we converse, it's almost as if she studies what I say, as if she's waiting for something: a key, a word, a phrase, a signal. Maybe it's the psychiatrist in her, and she just naturally studies people, looking for clues. I'm not sure. However, that particular day, I saw both concern and relief pass across her face.

Sweetie Pie and I turn onto Main Trail, the entrance to the Betta Conservation Land, which is across from Betta Park Playground. The same person who named Dirt Road must have named this trail. They won't win any awards for creativity.

We make our way to the top of the hill where the massive Betta Grand Hotel once stood. At the highest point on the conservation land, it would have had a breathtaking panoramic view of the countryside.

I pause to marvel at the memories that live in this area. This spot was once brimming with activity—guests coming and going, hotel staff bustling, children fidgeting. In spite of my fascination with this spot, the gentle breeze caressing my face is guiding me away.

Sweetie Pie's tail starts twitching; he's unimpressed by the view. No doubt, the memories that linger are of no interest to him. He can think of nothing other than chasing after the poor little creatures he sees in the distance. If he had his small collar on instead of his harness, he could easily twist and slip away. He makes chirping sounds; the same sound he makes right before he hunts down and pounces on any poor bug that gets into the house.

Sweetie Pie tugs me toward a hidden side trail. It's only about three feet wide and more overgrown than Main Trail. The overhanging tree limbs that were so carefully removed from Main Trail have been allowed to grow in all directions here. I find myself equally drawn to this path, and I allow my cat to lead the way. Occasionally, I must step around or under the limbs that block the path, but no matter; I feel content.

Sweet Pie disrupts my peaceful reverie as he uncharacteristically struggles to be free. He meows, contorts his body, lifts his paws in a peculiar way, and rubs against a fallen limb. As I wrestle with him, to my horror, his harness unhooks and falls off, and away he goes. Because it's early spring and most trees are either bare or just starting to show growth, I see him running into the distance and out of sight. My cat is on a mission.

I charge off after him. He's my cat and I have to find him. Unsure whether I'm running in the right direction, I'm propelled forward by a bizarre, uneven feeling, like a quiet battle within me. One side demands that I charge ahead, as if my life and well-being depend on it. The other side urges me to stop before I become terribly lost. I tell myself that the urge to continue is just a desire to find my cat. What else can it be? In any case, I'm relieved when the trees open up onto a worn-down gravel road.

Again the battling forces within me whisper. Turning left will almost certainly take me home, but the thought of heading home right now, without Sweetie Pie, makes me anxious. It's soothing to consider either heading into the woods on the other side of the road or turning right and heading up the gravel road. Uncertain what to do, I stand quietly, listening and looking around. I'm rewarded by my cat's distinctive meow, barely audible above the sound of my breathing.

Listening intently, I look in the direction of the meows. The leafless trees can't hide the shape of a large, weathered building. My heart beats with excitement. What memories live there? True to form, I'm easily distracted, and I remind myself that I'm looking for my cat. I'm impressed that Sweetie Pie had the good sense to run in this direction. Ben has always said to me, "You're just like your cats!" Maybe my cats are just like me!

"Sweetie Pie?"

His meows are definitely coming from the direction of the building, so I eagerly move along the road, which I assume will take me to the building. Why else would it be here? With a bounce in my step, I reason that this is the perfect place for me. I make a note to myself to give Sweetie Pie a nice treat for this find!

Bounding cheerfully up the road, I strain to get a better view of the building. As the trees start to thin out, I see a boarded-up front door.

Undeterred, I follow the road as it arches left, where, to my delight, I find a covered side entrance with granite steps leading to a spacious porch. A stone half wall prevents the overeager from entering anywhere other than the stairs in the middle of the porch. The steps are cracked and crumbled in some spots but otherwise sturdy. The reason for my excitement isn't the half wall, the granite steps, or the pillars. Alongside another boarded-up door is a window frame with neither glass nor boards.

Naturally, my cat sits poised on the windowsill, inviting me to check out the memories that live inside. Well, that's how I interpret what he's saying, anyway.

I refit the harness on Sweetie Pie, giving it a tug to make sure that it's secure, and then I pick him up. Poking my head through the window opening, I look around at the huge Christmas present that he's found for me. The floors are stable, and to my delight, light is visible from a room farther down.

I carefully step over the sill into the room, looking around in amazement at what was once a grand entrance. To my left is a boarded-up window, and to my right is a door-sized bookshelf. Dust-covered trim borders the bookshelf, doorway, and windows. I would have expected to see more cobwebs possibly because I've watched too many movies. No matter. I'm too enthralled by this building to care about bugs, cobwebs, or even a few rotten floorboards.

There's not much more to see in this room, so I proceed to the next one, which is two feet wider all around. It, too, has a window to the left, but the bookshelf is lying on the floor. The same wood trim, just as dusty, frames the windows, the doorways, and the place where the bookshelf would have been.

The next room is by far the largest. Ten feet into the room, on my left, there's a smaller window—again, with no boards and no glass—where the light is streaming in. Just beyond the window is the boarded-up door that I saw from outside. Another window, also boarded up, is on the other side of the door. The open window was obscured from view by the previous rooms. This room has a staircase set back into its own space opposite the front door.

The open window provides a scenic view of the surrounding countryside. The lawn slopes down from the front of the building, explaining why guests would use the side entrance if they were pulling up in cars or carriages. At the base of the lawn is a forest so thick that I can't see anything beyond despite the leafless trees.

Off this grand entry room is one last room. I pass through the doublewide doorway to look around. On my left is a picture window overlooking the front yard, and on the wall facing it, there's a built-in hutch with two doorways, one on either side of the hutch. No light is coming from beyond the doorways. I gingerly walk over to the doorway closest to me and peer into the darkness. The light from the grand entryway outlines what looks like a center island. This back room must have been a kitchen.

Sweetie Pie lets out a low growl and squirms, expressing his displeasure at being ignored for such a long time. I put him down, and he immediately heads for the staircase in the grand entryway. I follow him. The grand entryway is at least thirty feet high, and with the stairs on the back wall, not much of the light from the window shines in this area. Even in this dim light, the large carved railings and curved steps invite me to climb.

What sort of fancy events might have taken place in this building? Was it a party hall or a home? Did the wealthy vacationers from years gone by come here? The possibilities of yesterday shoot through my brain.

I snap back from my daydreaming and study the U-shaped staircase. The first step arches toward the wall, and the subsequent steps rise up along the back wall, turning left against another wall, possibly the wall abutting the kitchen, and turning left yet again above and behind me. In the black void above me, I can make out a balcony overlooking where I stand, but nothing else is visible.

No matter. Sweetie Pie insists that we go up, and since cats see better than people in dim lighting, I reason that it's safe to follow. Sweetie Pie leads the way up the first six steps, which are seven feet wide, ending on a ten-foot-by-ten-foot platform. We turn left and continue up the next six steps.

I start to dive back into the memories of those who have been here before. I'm barely aware of moving and unaware of my cat. I descend into my own thoughts of yesteryear, about the women with their lovely ball gowns, chatting with their friends, as they ascend the steps discussing trivial topics of the day. It was a party, after all—let's keep the conversation light! As I approach the final set of steps to the second floor, the stairway becomes less dark. My brain acknowledges that there are a few steps missing, but it somehow becomes irrelevant as something guides me forward.

With each step, I see more clearly, and I feel a pull to continue my exploration. The balcony overlooking the steps, once blanketed in blackness, is visible. Instead of being alarmed, I stare in awe at the staircase splashed in natural light, unveiling a glistening mahogany surface.

Sound pulses in my ears. I hear music, ballroom music. Rather than thinking it's odd to hear music in an abandoned building, I'm disappointed that it isn't techno or hip-hop. It's all so mesmerizing that I'm not thinking about how bizarre it is that this once dark and quiet room is now splashed in light and sounds. Rather, I critique the music, greatly admire the lovely staircase, and

I'm indifferent to the two missing steps.

More important matters are unfolding, preventing me from bothering with trivial details, like how I floated up two missing steps. Now I see a massive ballroom that spans the lower level. The wall in front of me has floor-to-ceiling windows that run the length of the ballroom and are the source of the natural light. The windows provide a breathtaking view of the countryside, but I'm not the only one admiring the view. There are men in tuxedos, and, more important, women wearing fancy, ball gowns. Ball gowns! I just knew it; wait until I tell Katri about this! Of course, I'll have to word what I say carefully so she won't think I've really become delusional.

Chapter 2: Discovery

Groups of people—women wearing a colorful bouquet of Victorian-style ball gowns with matching hats and men wearing tuxedos—are standing along the windowed wall, admiring the blossoming trees. One guest speaks and points and the others follow his hand, smiling in agreement.

If nature's beauty can be outdone, it's happening inside. A splendid chandelier in the center of the ballroom sparkles so much that I can't tell whether it's lit or whether the natural light is bouncing off it. Two smaller versions of this spectacular chandelier hang on either side. Sculpted-gold wall sconces are mounted all along the walls.

As I take in the sights, I'm given a jolt as I see my hand reaching for a glass of red wine and find myself taking a small sip. It's a smooth red wine, and I enjoy the taste, but my hand puts the glass down. I don't remember wanting a drink, and now I would like more, but my hands don't respond. More disturbing, my hands do things that I haven't directed, and I can't make my eyes look at my hands.

After surveying the room, my eyes pause on the wall to my right, the one that abutted the second set of steps. I didn't notice as I walked up the steps that the wall is a solid mirror. I gasp, but I don't gasp, because the expressionless face I see isn't mine. This woman looks away from the mirror before I can get a good look at her, so I tell her, *"Wait! Return to the mirror."* Apparently unaware of my request, she doesn't comply. I see with her eyes, I hear with her ears, and, yes, I even hear and see her thoughts, but she, it seems, is completely unaware of my presence in her mind.

Who is this person? How did I get into this mind? What's happening? Where am I? Am I dreaming? If this is all a hallucination, I'm pleased that I've managed to circumvent scary voices or crawling bugs. No, my first shot at insanity involves wearing a lovely dress at a ball! I decide to enjoy myself and see where it takes me.

I must have been distracted by these thoughts because now this woman has moved past the stair railing and is walking along the wall to the right of the staircase. The floor-to-ceiling mirror running the length of the ballroom has a dazzling effect since it faces the windowed wall. A guest whose back is toward the window sees the mirrored reflection of the blossoming trees, which form a colorful bouquet behind the twinkling chandeliers.

I finally get a closer look at this young woman, who looks to be in her early twenties. Her eyes are a deep, brilliant blue, their color a startling contrast against her black hair and golden skin. She wears a deep blue silk ball gown over layers upon layers of underskirts. The sleeves are draped with blue lace. Blue buttons going up to a sweetheart neckline and a blue lace waistline trim the bodice, with a large blue silk bow in the back. She's wearing a blue lace hat accented with white flowers, beads, and ribbons.

The woman is petite and delicately proportioned. She clearly hasn't enjoyed as many pounds of fine chocolates as I have, and, given her slender arms, isn't as athletic. Ha! I feel vindicated!

"May?"

I hear May's thoughts, and she, recognizing her sister April's voice, turns quickly.

They share the same shiny dark hair, striking blue eyes, and sweet-natured smile. April, who is just as lovely as May, is wearing a bright pink gown of similar design. April's lace hat has a colorful collection of ribbons trailing off the back.

"Hello, April. I was looking for you. I thought you were downstairs. I haven't seen August, have . . . ?" May stops speaking as a commotion at the far end of the ballroom gains her attention. She can't see the source of the disturbance, so she hurries to investigate

"I think it's August. Come on; let's not bother with that right now." April tries to pull May away from the commotion. "Mother will sort out August, not to worry; Jeffrey said that he'll settle the affairs and that I should find you. It's a ball; time to dance!"

I understand from May's thoughts that August is their brother. Musing over their names, I decide to call them the Calendar family.

I notice that I miss what happens when I go off into my own thoughts. It's like trying to follow two conversations at once. I can't listen to what May is thinking, saying, and doing and listen to myself! While I was busy making jokes about their names, May had moved closer to her brother. She has concerns that she wants to discuss with him, but April is trying to stop her. May, unstoppable, continues toward the commotion.

Perplexed, May observes her brother's strange behavior. Surely, she thinks, even a drunken person wouldn't dance around in such a way. She has wanted to talk to him all day, but something or someone keeps coming between them. Now, since he is dancing about in such a foolish way, she doesn't believe a conversation is an option. She needs the key. *"What's this key, May?"* I ask, but she doesn't answer.

We walk by a dessert table. The sight of creamy chocolate confections distracts me. I'm desperate to persuade this slender woman to eat a few. *"May? May? Have a few chocolate treats. Just one of those heavenly looking chocolate treats—just one?"* I say in vain. It was worth a try. After all, Ben is forever telling me to quiet down when I watch TV shows. I jump around and yell at the characters to get up, flee, fight, or look out. TV watching isn't sedentary for me.

Gently pulling her arm from April, May makes her way through the crowd, stopping not far from August. The uneasy feelings rise again, but she beats them down. She'll go along with him, but only because he said it's for Hannah, his daughter. *"May? Go along with what."*

As May's husband Jeffrey approaches August, she feels mixed emotions because she trusts and loves her brother, but she also trusts and loves Jeffrey. She believes that if one is telling the truth, the other must have misunderstood. She doesn't want to consider the possibility that she could have misjudged either of them. Such thoughts cause the uneasy feeling to swell. *"Misjudge what, May?"* Maybe if I try hard enough, she'll eventually hear me. If nothing else, for me, it's better than not trying at all!

After much hurried whispering between Jeffrey and August, August settles down. August, just a few years older than April, is an imposing figure. Watching Jeffrey's attempt to direct August out of the ballroom is much like watching a mouse attempt to push an ox.

Seeing his sisters, August looks hopefully at April, who looks away with bored disinterest. Crestfallen, he turns toward May.

They lock eyes. He holds her gaze with the same deep blue eyes while he approaches her as if he's trying to convey a message. She stares back, confused, remembering the many times that she's looked into those eyes and cheerfully followed his direction; he's always led her down a safe path. He bends close to her and whispers quickly, "Don't tell them anything. Remember May Bear." A look of alarm spreads across Jeffrey's face, and he hustles forward to jerk August away. August glares at Jeffrey with unveiled hostility as he easily twists his arm away from Jeffrey's grasp.

I sense that August's worries are well founded and I find myself trusting him. As for the others, Jeffrey, although his polished features are attractive, he reminds me of a crafty weasel, and I'm on the fence about April. My suspicions mount as I witness Jeffrey and April exchanging a smile. May is oblivious. She idolizes Jeffrey although she has some unfocused doubts. She's torn between wanting to be a good wife to her new husband and her loyalty to a brother she's loved and trusted all her life. *"May, I for one would believe your brother. Where there is warmth and caring in his eyes, I see only cool and calculating in Jeffrey's!"* I must try harder to get through to her. I'm sure if she could hear me I could help her sort out the difficulty.

May's mother and father approach, and her mother rattles off, "What has happened? Is August drunk again? Jeffrey thinks August's troubles at home are wearing him down. May, has August said anything to you?" Sarah struggles to speak August's name. So much venom laces her voice that it's hard to imagine that she likes her son, let alone loves him.

"No, Mother. I don't understand. This is so unlike August—I'm sure he would tell me if there were problems at home."

"Mother," April says. "Augy whispered something to May right before he walked by. What was it, May?"

"You saw him, April. He made no more sense to me than he did to you."

April and Sarah exchange glances, unnoticed by May who is struggling with her emotions. May's eyes see it, so I see it, but May's mind is elsewhere.

"May, did you save the first dance of the party for me?" asks her father. Wendel, May's father, is well over six feet tall and clearly the source of the Calendar children's' lovely blue eyes. Wendel has a gentle face, like a man who has spent more time smiling than not. Sarah stands erect beside him. She offers her daughters a seemingly warm, well-practiced smile, but genuine love seems missing in her cold beauty.

"Oh, Wendel, dear, I see Jeffrey returning, May should

dance with her husband. They're still newlyweds. Allow them to start off the first dance."

"Oh, no, Mother," May says reaching for her father's outstretched hand. "I'd be happy to start the first dance with Daddy."

Jeffrey approaches, flashing a quick smile at Sarah. She bristles with pride and then seems more relaxed than before.

Jeffrey, though not nearly as tall as Wendel or August, stands a head taller than May. His steely gaze rests on May as his lips form a victorious smile.

Sarah says, "Jeffrey, my darling, the first dance is about to start, and I thought it would be lovely for you and May to start the dancing off together." As she puts her hand on Wendel's hand to pull him away from May, she says to Wendel, "Let's not interfere with the lovebirds; you can dance with May later."

Jeffrey offers his arm to May. I suppose it could be love in his eyes, but I see something more sinister and when coupled with May's uneasiness, I conclude that all isn't all right with the Calendar family! Nevertheless, time for dancing. She takes his arm as they glide to the middle of the ballroom. They pause, then the music begins anew, a waltz. Soon, the entire ballroom comes alive with guests twirling and whirling. May and I forget our concerns as she, too, loves to dance. Around and around they go, with me on the inside watching out. I occasionally catch glimpses of May as she looks toward the mirror, but usually other guests are blocking my view.

While they glide around the dance floor, I weigh the pros and cons of my situation. If my delusions are the result of a brain tumor, I'll likely be dead soon. After all, how many cases of cured brain tumors with advanced hallucinations have I ever heard about? Of course, I haven't done much—okay, I haven't done any—reading about brain tumors, but that's not the point I'm making to myself. I could be mentally ill, in which case they could give me a few drugs and the delusions would stop. But do I really want them to stop? So far, I've been enjoying myself. No harm done.

When I come back to their reality, they've left the dance floor, a new song is playing, and Jeffrey is standing beside May, sipping wine as a man and woman approach. I nearly miss the introduction. No commercial breaks for me.

"May," Jeffrey says, "I want to introduce you to Lanlore International's new business partner, Michael, and his wife, Marla."

"I'm so pleased you could attend tonight," says May, extending her hand to each of them in turn.

"May, it's a pleasure to finally meet you," says Michael as he clasps her hand. "I've heard so much about you, especially some fond childhood memories from August. The two of you make quite a pair! Speaking of August, have you seen him?"

"Yes," Jeffrey responds, speaking for her. "He left not long ago. He wasn't feeling well."

"Have you spoken to him?" asks Michael.

"August?" May's stomach does flip-flops. She doesn't understand why all three of them would be in the same business venture. "Is August working with you now, Jeffrey?"

"No, May," he says, patting her on the shoulder. He turns to Michael to explain. "Michael, August runs the shipping branch of the family business, and I handle procuring new products."

"But earlier August said that he didn't . . . ."

Jeffrey interrupts Michael, waving his hand, "Actually, I had to escort August out because of his odd behavior. I hate to say it, but I think he was drunk. The family has been concerned about him for the past few months. Michael! Marla! Come on. This is a party. Time to dance and drink and enjoy—business can wait till Monday morning."

Michael and Marla exchange quizzical glances. Marla's face seems oddly familiar. I want to look at her more, but May frustrates my efforts as she looks away.

"I need to use the ladies' room. Mother, May, please join me," says April as she and Sarah swoop in and pull May with them.

"May, this is a fabulous location for parties," says April as she pinches a delicious-looking chocolate confection from a buffet table they pass by. "How did you ever find out it was for sale? Will you be moving here?"

Much to my dismay, May picks up some fish-looking snack that still has its head and actually puts it in her mouth, in spite of my telling her not to. She replies to April, "Marlene told me about it; and, yes, Jeffrey and I will move here after some renovations to the first floor."

The ladies' room is an elegant affair. Each stall has an attendant who provides napkins and toiletries and opens and closes a stall door that's worth more than my entire jewelry collection. The attendant takes May's gloves. *"Yes, that's right. Don't take them into the stall—they could get wet."* I laugh to myself. If Ben could only see me now; I'm in my element.

As May walks out of the ladies' room, she sees her father approaching, with Jeffrey following close behind him. Jeffrey nearly jumps in front of Wendel. "May, it's beautiful outside; join me on the balcony for some fresh air."

Looking at her family, May says, "That would be lovely. Would any of you care to join us?"

"No, thanks," says April as she tugs on her father's arm, "I want to collect on that dance that Father promised me."

May and Jeffrey walk off, and I delve into my own thoughts. April, Sarah, and Jeffrey are trying to keep May from spending any time alone with August and Wendel, and May isn't objecting. My mind jumps around, first to the chocolate desserts and then to August. What's up with him? Is he really having problems at home, or is Jeffrey up to mischief? Stay tuned for the next adventures of the Calendar family.

When I rejoin the Calendars, they're on a balcony off the second floor room, I call the ballroom, looking out over the yard. Jeffrey is nodding as if in response to some question that I didn't hear.

"Do you want to live here, May?"

"Oh, yes, Jeffrey, very much. This would be perfect. I think that with some renovations we could make it happen. I want the second floor to remain a grand ballroom, though. We can live on the first floor."

"Then so it shall be!" He holds her hands and pulls her close to him. "You know, May, August has been behaving strangely for months now. I'm worried about him. I'm not sure how we can help him. You know him best, and you know best how we can help. What did he whisper to you when we walked by?"

She pauses. I panic and yell with my voiceless voice, *"Oh, no! Don't tell him anything."*

May momentarily ponders why he's so eager to know but dismisses the question as nothing more than curiosity. "You saw him, Jeffrey. He was incoherent when you managed to pull him away. He made no sense to me. Did he get home safely?"

"Yes, darling, just fine. Tell me about the renovations," he says, searching her face.

"I have ideas on where to put the baby's room! We could add an extension. There's a clearing to the right of the ballroom, off the dining room, and I think that would be a good spot to add a new wing."

"Sounds wonderful. I'll leave the renovations to you."

May drops something that reminds me of the catnip satchel; I've forgotten all about Sweet Pie! My kitty, what happened to him? I remember walking up the steps; he was leading the way. Where is he? How were we separated? "Wake up? Wake up?" I scream at myself.

I hear urgent-sounding meows in the darkness. "My poor kitty, where are you?" I say. The light from the first-floor window outlines the staircase, but it serves as little more than a nightlight in the shadows. Slowly, I make my way toward the staircase and my meowing cat. I approach gingerly as I don't see the gracefully sculpted railing from May's memory.

Sweetie Pie lands with a thud on the top step, reminding me that the first two steps are missing even though I recall climbing up effortlessly. No matter; I managed to get up safely. I shrug off the incident and make my way down the steps out of the building.

Chapter 3: Finding Our Way Home

Sweetie Pie leads the way along the gravel road away from the ballroom. If he were a big dog, he would be dragging me along. I know his harness doesn't fit properly, so I don't want to fight with him.

Looking back at the ballroom as we round the corner, I see no signs of the balcony that May and Jeffrey walked out on or of the additions that they discussed. I wonder if they decided not to live there. Next, I wonder why I'm wondering about them to begin with. After all, it wasn't real, was it?

We keep a good pace and it doesn't take long before the dirt road dwindles into nothing but forest. Sweetie Pie, unfazed by the ending road, plunges ahead. I reason that since Sweetie Pie is hungry, it's safe to trust his sense of direction.

I mark the trees every few feet with my lipstick, so I can find my way back should I wish to return to the ballroom. If need be, I have my cell phone, so I can always call Ben as a last resort. Considering how often I lecture Ben on the importance of using a harness, I would never hear the end of running off a marked trail because Sweetie Pie's harness came undone. At least, I was right in that Sweetie Pie did run off!

Sweetie Pie sets out through the trees as if he believes the ground will swallow him up if he lingers. I try to follow quickly, but I'm not nimble enough to duck the overhanging limbs. Saplings and underbrush in early stages of growth scrape at my legs and arms. When I raced through the forest earlier, I'm certain that I didn't have this problem. I vaguely recall moving as dexterously as my cat does now.

I give him free rein to lead the way, so he doesn't try to twist free from his harness. I envision him breaking free and rushing home before me. He would run up to the door screaming for food, and poor Ben would get all concerned because I wasn't with him. Ben might try to take him back out to find me. No way will Sweetie Pie play Lassie and, in a few meows, communicate that Jena has spent hours daydreaming in a ballroom, that she's lost in the trees in the Betta Conservation Land, and that she needs chocolate.

The woods open onto, what I believe, is the same side path we were walking on earlier today. Sweetie Pie turns left on the path, just the way I would turn, and I quickly mark this exit point onto the side path with my remaining lipstick. Sweetie Pie is walking so fast that I'm nearly jogging to keep up with him. No more walks for Sweetie Pie until he has a new harness. I'll need to sneak out of the house tomorrow morning!

Finally, we arrive. I walk into the kitchen and call, "Hi, Ben. We're home!"

"Jena, finally!" Ben says, rushing out to greet me. "I've been worried. You left early this morning; I thought you'd return hours ago. Why didn't you call?" Years of living in America have faded his South African accent.

"Sorry, I didn't think about it. Besides, it isn't like you'd have rushed around to get dinner ready."

"Well, I did."

"You've dinner ready?"

"Not quite, but close. I wasn't sure what we were going to have for dinner tonight, so I picked up some chicken to marinate. On the way back, I stopped at the ice cream shop. Yes, I bought frozen yogurt for you."

"Ben, bless your heart! Thank you!" Not wanting to discourage future acts of helpfulness, I don't mention that I already have chicken marinating for dinner. I look in the refrigerator and can't help but smile. Ben's marinating chicken is in a plastic bag sitting on top of the plastic tub of marinating chicken that I prepared earlier.

Chapter 4: What Katri Knows

With little time to spare, I manage to shower, change, prepare the side dishes and pop them in the oven along with the chicken to broil.

"The Everses are here," Ben says, pointing at Sweetie Pie sitting on the rug by the family room door, where he expects arriving guests to pay their devotional to him. When they walk in, he rolls from side to side on his back, expecting them to stroke him. The guests must dutifully oblige or they'll find an irate cat batting at them when they walk by.

One night a man named Brian, whom Ben knew from work, didn't provide the required devotional. He was startled, as were the rest of us, when Sweet Pie jumped right onto Brian's plateful of spaghetti and meowed loudly in Brian's face. Before I or anyone else recovered from the shock of it, Sweetie Pie jumped down, leaving red paw prints trailing after him on our hardwood floors. All of us sat there stunned by his behavior, and then everyone, except Brian, burst out laughing.

"Hello? We're here," says Katri, as she and her husband, Adam, enter our house. We're good friends; we always just let ourselves in when we're expected. "I hear you went for a hike on the Betta Conservation Land. How was it?"

Katri and Adam are a well-matched couple and fun to socialize with since they share so many common activities with us. Katri is tall and trim, with short auburn hair and delicate facial features that often mask her feelings. Her rare smiles, when she's listening to my stories or just happy to be with Adam, are radiant. Occasionally, her eyes twinkle with delight, but she doesn't like having anyone see it. Some people have commented that we're an unlikely pair of friends, Katri and I. But under the thoughtful, analytical exterior, I see someone who is holding back a desire to express herself freely.

Adam has dark hair and is a foot taller than Katri. He's an intriguing cross between a bumbling scientist and a tea-toting aristocrat. I suspect he's read a book on etiquette and follows it to the letter. Maybe he's even used these books for pointers on smiling. It amuses me to watch Adam's attempts at smiling. Apparently, his face had to learn the art of demonstrating amusement. At times, it forgets and must struggle to remember which muscle should turn in which direction. I tease him about his challenges with smiling, and he reciprocates by telling me that I look like I'm perpetually wondering! I can't argue with that. I do wonder about everything.

"Great!" I respond to Katri. "Beautiful weather for a hike, but I never found the lake."

"All that time you were walking around?" says Ben, as he pours wine. "Didn't you leave early in the morning?"

"Yes. I was distracted by some problems with Sweetie Pie's harness."

"Problems?" Ben asks.

"It came undone and he ran off. Don't give me any grief, Ben. The harness latch is broken. We can't take Sweetie Pie out again until he has a new harness! Anyhow, I had to run into the forest after him. Yes, I know, never leave the trail, but what was I supposed to do? Besides, I had my cell phone, reception was good, and no blizzards were predicted. Heck, what's the worst-case scenario? I'd be late getting back to fix dinner! My cat, on the other hand, might not find his way back. As it happened, he was the one that led the way back to the trail. He made it in a straight shot, dragging me along."

"Dragged you along, did he? Guess the Sweets didn't trust your navigational skills!" Adam mumbles, his facial muscles struggling to remember where to arch and bend for a smirk.

Ben's eyes twinkle, and I can tell he's about to say something that he thinks is brilliant. "He's the cheekiest cat I've ever met. Look at how he always sets himself apart from our other cats. Like he's the lord and master of the house and the other cats are his humble servants. That's about right; the lords of the house have to stick together—don't we, Sweetie Pie? Keep the ladies in line!"

"Ben, delusions of grandeur don't suit you," I retort. "That's my thing."

"Anyhow," interrupts Katri, impatiently, looking at me. "And then what?"

Ben, being a superb host, pours more wine, and we make our way to the sunroom, which looks out over a bend in the Betta River. Our house is the last on the street, and it sits on a gently sloping hill.

"Well," I say to Katri as we walk, "I saw this old boarded-up building—actually Sweetie Pie found it—and he called me over and insisted that I join him. I found him sitting in a window opening."

"Oh, right," says Ben. "More likely you put him in the window. Wait a minute. Didn't you say it was all boarded up?"

"Some of it was boarded up, but I found two windows that weren't. Naturally, Sweetie Pie demanded that we investigate. What was I to do? He had his little heart set on it!"

Katri tilts her head and leans forward as I speak, her body tense, a reaction I usually only see when she's ready to spar.

Adam, on the other hand, huffs and puffs, and it's clear that a great deal of steam, in the form of preaching, is about to spew. "An abandoned building? Why, the floorboards could have been rotten. You really shouldn't have gone in." Adam knows buildings—builds them, destroys them, repairs them—he's done it all. Whether it's a simple cabin or a twenty-story skyscraper, he can design it and build it himself.

"I was careful," I protest. "I looked around."

"Really? How did you check the stability of the building?"

"Whatever, Adam! I'm fine. I made it out safely. Dinner is ready. Let's eat." I scurry away happy the timer went off at the perfect moment.

After dinner Katri says quietly, "Jena, let's chat some more about the walk today. I'm eager to hear about this building. Tell me more."

As we make our way back to the sunroom, I explain, "It must have been a party house. I walked around the first floor with Sweetie Pie where I saw several different rooms. The second floor was one huge, magnificent room."

As I take my seat she says, "Oh, jeez. Don't let Adam know you went up to the second floor!" Her face is alive with interest as she sits down next to me on the couch, her shoulders tense. She listens intently, putting on a pleasant smile, but I know my friend well enough to sense her disguised alarm.

"Oh, believe me, I have no intention of mentioning the second floor to Adam or Ben! There was a chandelier in the center, possibly five feet wide and five feet tall, maybe even bigger! It was crystal with gold-trimmed etchings, and there were two smaller chandeliers on either side of the center one. There were restrooms that had marble countertops and gold wall sconces. Each stall had a lavish wooden door with a gold pansy emblem in the middle. It must have been twenty-four karat. There were attendants to take the ladies' gloves."

"Attendants?"

"Well, yes, of course. I mean, there *would* have been attendants. I assumed that the space between each stall was meant for an attendant. I even saw a painting of a woman in a lovely blue ball gown."

"What? She didn't have any dirt smudges on her dress after falling off the train?"

"Yes, the painter thought to also add mud spots on the dress, with a big huge one on her face, and a bird flying over just about to torpedo her."

"Any dancing?"

"Oh, yes. I could see May, dance after dance, in her splendid ball gown, gliding around the dance floor. The room was big enough for hundreds of couples. My, Katri, look at you; you really seem more interested than usual. What's up?" I realize that I've actually blurted out May's name and wait for Katri to call me on it.

Smiling warmly, Katri replies, "Jena, I've always been fascinated by how you muse so much over times past. Sometimes, it seems like you go so deep into your imagination that you find yourself there."

Wondering why she says nothing about May, I respond, "That's an odd thing to say."

"Why?"

"Just is! How could I find myself there? People can't time travel or anything."

"Not time travel! More like an ability to see a story in a situation, which makes you a good storyteller. You've a way of putting others in the moment. When you described what you saw to me, I felt like I was seeing it through your eyes. Did you think about anything else that might have happened? Maybe what time period the ball might have occurred in?"

"I'm not really sure. The ball gown I saw at the, I mean, saw in the painting, could have been from a hundred or more years back, but, then again, people might well wear dresses like that to costume parties or fancy-dress parties today. I'd love to wear a dress like that. Her hat was definitely from a different era—but again—it could have been a fancy-dress party. I couldn't see into the kitchen well enough to make out any of the fixtures since the first floor only had two windows that weren't boarded up."

"What sort of light was there on the second floor? I mean, how could you see what was up there?"

"A few boards were missing on the windows. I'm not sure how many, but enough so that I could see the painting."

Katri walks over, closes the door between the sunroom and the family room, and sits across from me. With a fixed and serious look, she places both hands firmly in her lap, leans in toward me, and she says, "Jena, I've always thought there was something special about you."

Katri is a serious person; she always pauses to think through her actions, so a serious look in itself isn't unusual behavior. However, it's rare that I'm the recipient of such a look. Amused, annoyed, frustrated, captivated, astounded, perplexed—those are all possibilities. But in regard to me, and others close to her, a serious look masks fear and concern. I've seen this particular look only once when Adam's young cousin nearly fell off a cliff. I guess, in spite of all my antics, she's never felt I was in danger.

To break the chill, I smile. "You've been talking to Ben. He says the same thing. I agree. I'm special."

"Please, Jena, hear me out. I really do enjoy listening to the memories you bring forward from the past. It's as if you're telling a story—a true story. Like you said, you never know. I think there's something special about you that drives you to wonder so much about memories from times past. I think that some memories need to be heard, and you hear them."

"I'm not sure what you're getting at, Katri. Or, shall I say, Dr. Evers? If one of your patients told you that they hear memories, I'll bet you'd have them committed. And here you tell me that I'm special. I can somehow already do this amazing genius thing of hearing memories. I'm waiting for you to laugh, but instead you sit here listening to me. What gives?"

She chuckles obligingly. "Hearing voices is a problem. I'm not talking about my patients. I'm talking about you, and I think you know what I'm talking about, too."

"Okay, you've caught me. I hear voices. They say: 'Eat chocolate. Just one more piece won't matter. If you eat them quickly, the calories don't count.'"

I feel like I'm making suitably light of the situation but Katri isn't to be distracted by my flippancy and she persists, "Jena, please listen to me. Try not to wonder about things like chocolate or frilly dresses. If you really feel like there's something to be heard, try actually listening. If you're distracted, you could miss the message, and maybe those memories will only speak once, or someone special will walk by to hear them only once. Then what? I can understand if you don't want to talk more about the ballroom. I won't push it. I'll say just three more things that I hope you'll think about and take to heart. That is, you don't have a brain tumor, I'm sure of it."

I gasp. She raises her hand to silence me, and we eye each other suspiciously.

She continues, "You're not mentally ill—you could probably drive a few people nuts if given the chance, though. Lastly, Adam has heard of that ballroom you're talking about. Someone removed and sold the mirrors long ago. As to the chandeliers that you described so well? They were stolen years ago. Enough of that now. Tell me what's for dessert. Or, I mean, what sort of chocolate dessert will we be having?"

"Now, wait," I protest. "You can't say all that without some kind of response, so to the 'three things' that were more like four things, or five, depending on how you were counting. Regarding dessert, I had Ben run out late this afternoon because I was having a cake craving. He picked up a chocolate mousse cake! He also bought ice cream and frozen yogurt."

Katri and Adam are well on their way home, so I have a chance as I get ready for bed to ponder what Katri said tonight and what it means. Katri knows much more than she's telling me. I have little doubt that she wants me to pay more attention to what the Calendars have to say and wasn't just making sure I understood that I wasn't ill. I feel confident she was telling me it was all real, or real enough that I should be listening. She knew that I was lying about the cracked window boards on the second floor, but I was too baffled to ask her questions. I didn't know what to ask. I didn't want to admit that I was in May's mind. How can that be anything but fantasy? I honestly didn't think much about what happened today. I wonder so much about what goes on around me that I just pushed it aside. I thought it all rather amusing, more like a dream, a waking fantasy than some lethal disease or mental illness.

"Ben to Jena. Come in, Jena. Jena, are you receiving?"

"What?" I turn to see all four cats kneading, batting, and pouncing on Ben. Pookachoo makes a point to jump on his stomach, as if there was a mouse to be caught, then bounds off in hot pursuit. The cats learned long ago that the quickest way to get my attention is to annoy Ben. He's shoved me out of bed on many mornings because the cats' antics have awakened him.

"I'm glad you're amused. These cats. Your cats," he says, trying, without success, to push them away, "are disgruntled that you've been taking so long to get ready."

I get into bed, and all the cats settle into their sleeping spots while I cuddle up to Ben. "Sorry, Ben. I was deep in thought. I was solving world hunger, global warming, world peace, that sort of thing. I nearly had it all solved before you interrupted me!"

"Just as well. Chocolate for everyone won't solve world hunger!"

"Ben, about our walk tomorrow. Would you mind if I went out alone in the morning? I really didn't get to walk around as much as I would have liked today. Do you mind?"

"Not at all! Is the building calling you?"

"What do you mean by that?"

"Why so defensive? Just be careful in that old building. When you and Katri were so engrossed in your conversation after dinner, Adam had a lot to say about the dangers of walking around an abandoned building. He also had a lot to say about his new country club membership and he's invited me to go golfing with him tomorrow. I'll give Adam a call tomorrow and let him know I'm available. Do you want to skate in the afternoon? We can try out the Rail Trail that opened up last season. I'm not up for the twenty-two-mile distance just yet, but how about we skate it halfway and have lunch?"

"I'd like that. Good night."

31   Lisa Nevin

Chapter 5: Going Back

Walking down the stairs this morning is a challenge, with four hungry cats not only racing past each other but also stopping to make sure I'm still following. Fooffula stops right underneath my foot, nearly causing me to tumble down the stairs.

Despite my cat's best efforts, I make it to the kitchen safely. I fetch my water bottle, fanny pack, and cell phone. With my hiking supplies ready, I quickly feed the cats and run out of the house before Sweetie Pie realizes that I'm not taking him with me.

As I power hike to get to the ballroom, I think more about what Katri said, and I'm determined to follow her suggestion and focus more on what I see and hear.

Even with my musings, I easily spot the tree I marked yesterday. A string of similarly marked trees before me explains how I wore my lipstick down. I march quickly through the forest.

The forest edge opens up onto the gravel road leading up to the ballroom. It arches with the curve of the forest until it reaches a clearing, where I suspect the grass will grow several feet high by summer's end. However, it's now only about two inches high, with a few dead and dry heaps from last year's growth. Beyond the clearing are leafless trees, thick enough to hide the ballroom from my view. When I stumbled upon the gravel road yesterday, it was further up this road where the trees weren't quite as thick.

Just a few feet from the gravel road, I see an object protruding amid the grass. Naturally, I must investigate. Dead grass covers a stone base and two cracked stone pillars that lie toppled on either side of it. Face down between the pillars is a board. I wrestle it out of the dead grass to discover that the other side reads, "Dellner Ballroom, 1970."

I continue walking up the road, speculating on the age of the ballroom. Were May and Jeffrey the Dellners?

I reach the Dellner Ballroom and decide to walk around to the front to see what happened to the balcony. The lawn slopes gently and steadily down as I make my way around the building. I'm mesmerized by the beauty of this aged building. A granite arch over the entryway marks the place where the steps once were. Four stone pillars, two on either side of the granite arch, stand between the first-floor porch and the second floor. The porch, nearly fifteen feet wide, starts in front of the dining room and ends where the side entryway juts out. Because the lawn slopes, the porch is at least six feet off the ground in some spots.

This two-story building could easily pass for four stories. I walk backwards, tilting my head back to the point that I'm dizzy as I take in the height. The sheer size of the building astounds me, and I feel a crushing sadness that such a gem was allowed to fall into disrepair. I feel a profound sense of loss as I look at the porch. Dazed, I shake my head to get rid of the weighted feeling. It's only a building, I wonder, why does looking at the porch cause such feelings of sorrow?

I trudge slowly to the side window, still trying to shake off the gloomy feeling. I poke my head in and see that nothing has changed, so I step in. With eyes that now appreciate the magnitude of this building, I realize that I misjudged the inside dimensions. Maybe the darkness made it appear smaller.

I make my way to the stairs, hoping to see the first floor in May's time, but I'm not shifting into May's memory here. Since the memory shifting (that's how I think of it) started on the second floor, that's where I'll go.

Darkness hovers around the staircase, but the fragments of light from the window behind me entice me further. I walked up these stairs yesterday; I'm not shy about approaching them today. The mirror along the second set of steps is gone. As I turn left on the third set of steps, I realize that it isn't working. I'm not shifting.

It's peculiar that the top two steps are missing. I use the stair railing to hoist myself over the missing steps. I first walk to the right of the stairs, then to the left. Other than the bits of light that make it through some of the cracks, the light comes mainly from the window in the entryway below.

I sigh; I don't understand why May's memory is eluding me today, whereas yesterday it was so simple. I decide to go down to the first floor and start over, but, the same thing happens on the second trip. There's no memory available on these steps. I plod back down and vow to try one last time, but that fails, too.

Feeling frustrated and defeated, I go back down to the first floor and plop myself on the first step. I really don't understand what's happening. I didn't know anything about any memory yesterday. I just walked up the steps, and poof! I was there. The problem is that I have no clue how to walk up the steps as if I'm not expecting anything to happen. Maybe it was a waste of time to come back. Maybe I should enjoy a walk and possibly find the lake? Why am I even listening to Katri to begin with? What does she know, anyhow? So what? She knew that the chandeliers aren't there anymore and that the mirrors are gone. She could have read about it somewhere.

Our role reversal is another anomaly. Katri is encouraging me to indulge in an oddball fantasy, yet, I'm usually the one to seek out adventures and lead the charge in wild directions. Nevertheless, here I sit, considering giving up on this quest that Katri has recommended I pursue.

Wild directions. I have some fond memories of going off in wild directions. My fondest memory is of Ben, Adam, Katri, and I sharing a condominium on a cross-country skiing trip. We set off on a weekend when the ski conditions were awful. Many cross-country ski areas had temporarily closed, and I was the only one insisting that we should still go skiing. "So it's warm out," I said. "We won't need to wear our coats! It'll be fun, less crowded!"

Since the cross-country ski lodge had to close off so many trails because there was so little snow, they had to bus us to higher elevations where it had snowed more and rained less.

As we skied around, I saw an access trail that could take us down to the River Trail Bridge, which we could ski across to reach the River Trail, the only cross-country trail open on that side of the river. "Come on, you guys," I said, pointing at the trail. "It will be an adventure and much better than taking the bumpy bus ride back to the lodge. This side of the trail is all covered with snow!"

"Look! It isn't marked as open on the map," said Adam, unconvinced. He tapped on the map that I was holding so hard it nearly fell out of my hand.

"Well, it isn't marked as closed, either."

"If we could have come this way, why didn't they tell us at the lodge that we could take River Trail?" countered Katri. "I'm guessing it's probably because we shouldn't. They probably figured that people would have more common sense than to go off on their own."

"Oh, jeez, you guys. Whine, whine, whine; this trail isn't closed! The best things in life are the ones where you jump into the unknown, take a chance, follow the less-traveled trail. Look at all that untouched snow. We'll be the first ones to make tracks. How bad could it be?"

They all conferred and then Ben said, "We'll agree to go if you're willing to shop, prepare dinner, and clean up afterwards in the condo. Deal?"

"Deal!" And I made first tracks down the slope, much to their delight. The snow, a foot and a half deep in some spots, wasn't groomed. I remember thinking how silly it was that they hadn't groomed this hill when I fell face down in the mud. Skis don't glide very nicely across mud. Behind me, Ben, Katri, and Adam had already stopped and were removing their skis. Because they weren't enjoying the serene beauty as much as I was, they were paying more attention to the changing landscape, which allowed them to notice the little stream that cut into the trail.

"Excellent," laughed Adam. "Dinner and entertainment—brought to you by Jena! What will the encore be? You're right, Jena. What a great idea."

"I wear this mud proudly," I proclaimed. "I'm no whiny baby. I love the adventure. If I want to blaze a new trail, I have to get a little muddy."

It took nearly five minutes of listening to their laughter and recounting who saw what to stop before we could resume skiing. It was just as well. I needed the time to wipe the mud off my face and torso with the available snow, in as dignified a manner as I could muster. On several occasions, when we reached other thin spots, they teased, "Encore! Encore!"

However, the best of the adventure didn't end there, not for me, anyhow. When we got to the river crossing where the bridge was supposed to be, there was no bridge. We walked a good half-mile in both directions and saw no sign of a bridge or what should have been a bridge. There was no way to cross the river.

"I'll bet it's an ice bridge and it hasn't been cold enough yet to form," smirked Adam.

"And this explains why the ski lodge didn't recommend we ski this way," added Katri.

"Look," I said pointing down the river, "those stones are close enough that we can hop across, no problem!"

"Or we can walk back up the slope and not drench ourselves," added Ben. "Don't give me that bull about adventure again, Jena. I say we walk back up. Trust me, in my years of traveling with Jena, I've been caught in some really tight spots! Our best bet is to turn back."

"This is what memories are made of!" I said smugly. "The best ones, the ones we'll all keep talking about later, this is one of them! Ben says to turn back now, but if we'd turned back every time Ben suggested, we'd have missed out on a lot of special memories." Since Ben grudgingly agreed with me, I quickly added more ammunition. "Turn back? That won't provide a fond memory. No! The time we all hopped across a river on a cross-country ski trip, now that's a memory! Admit it, Ben, you love it— the unstoppable Jena! Follow me; I see an easy spot to cross. Once we cross the river, it's only three miles back. If we turn back, it's about six miles back up that long hill and another three to get to the bus. You know, we might not make it back that way before dark."

They reluctantly followed me as I led the way across the river. Everything was going well, we were hopping across just fine, but Katri pointed to the shore all excited about seeing a deer, and I had to turn to see it. She really should have known better. I was holding long, potentially lethal weapons. Well, like dominoes, my ski first knocked Ben. As he lost his footing, his ski hit Adam, and since Adam was helping Katri, he pulled her in with him. In spite of feeling mortified, I laughed so hard (nearly falling in myself) that they weren't convinced I was sorry. After I recovered, I made my way easily to shore. The only reason that they didn't kill me on the spot was that I had a backpack full of jackets. I was quick to point out that I'd insisted we bring our coats and offered to carry them.

Even though I'd redeemed myself some by providing them their dry jackets, they still demanded that I clean, cook, and do all the needed shopping for the rest of the trip. If someone wanted wine, it was, "Jena! I want a glass of wine!" If we were out of whatever he or she wanted, off to the store I went. It worked out, though. I needed to get away because every time I looked at them, I saw their bodies falling, their horrified expressions, and their hands frantically grasping the empty air. I didn't want them to see me laughing.

That was a great memory of my motivation to lead the way in wild directions, but here I am, wondering how to get back into May's memory and ready to give up. What was so different about yesterday? Energized, I bounce up. I think I've figured it out. Yesterday, when I made my way up these steps, I was thinking about what it must have been like to be in this building for a party and what the guests might have worn. I vaguely remember shifting into the memory on the way up the steps.

I start up the steps again, this time thinking of May, her dazzling blue gown swishing delicately around her as she talks with August or April or . . . . Oh, dear. This isn't working. I reach the top step and nothing has changed.

I sit on the edge of the top most step and feel around behind the stair frame of the missing steps. Other than some dirt, and a bit of change, there's nothing of interest. I surmise that the mahogany stair treads were probably worth quite a bit of money, but why did the thief steal only two?

Enough about stair treads! I tell myself. Back to May and her memories. I know I can work this through. I just need to focus. What's the difference today? Today I know the memory is May's, whereas yesterday, I walked into May's memory quite by accident while I was walking up the steps. That's it! I understand what I need to do now; I must move to where I last left May. Well, now, isn't this cool? I've hit a pause button on someone's memory. Shame the rewind doesn't work!

Yesterday, when I left, May was on the balcony. I head over to the balcony, but then I stop dead—there's no balcony. Thinking about the front of the house, I conclude that someone converted the balcony to part of the room and moved the wall farther out. Yes, that must be it; the balcony was over the first-floor porch. I start moving in the general direction of the balcony, thinking of May and how she felt about her brother, August, her sister, April, her husband, Jeffrey. I can feel it. The light is coming on. With each step, the second floor is slowly transformed from a dark, boarded-up room to the splendid and glorious ballroom of May's memory. I'm here again.

Chapter 6: Keeping Secrets

May and Jeffrey are walking through the crowded ballroom, mingling with their guests. She's distracted and not listening as guests talk to her about the weather, the party, the trees, and what have you. I can't hear what these guests are saying because May's thoughts are confused and filled with doubt. She mulls over what has happened so far today, trying to neatly label and categorize.

Jeffrey won't explain the problems that August is having, insisting that men will talk more openly with each other. May finds this idea somehow unsettling since she believes that August talks to Marlene about everything that troubles him. It doesn't make sense to her that her brother would suddenly find Jeffrey a more agreeable confidant. Jeffrey's claim that he and August are actually planning a hunting trip after the baby is born is especially unsettling. August doesn't like to hunt, or so May always thought. Could August have changed? When she tried to push Jeffrey for more information, he became irritated and impatient. He even implied that she isn't mature enough to plan their period costume party since she wasn't tending to her guests. Jeffrey told May that if she were older and more mature, she wouldn't forsake their marriage for her family. But she doesn't see any conflict between wanting to help her family, in particular her brother and her sister, and her commitment to her marriage. August is committed to Marlene and Hannah, yet, he has time for his sisters and their father. It's peculiar how August has been at odds with their mother. Maybe Jeffrey is right. If she were more mature, she wouldn't spend so much time fretting over her family. Instead, she would spend her time being a good hostess to her guests and a good wife to her husband.

She thinks she has it all sorted out, but then she remembers that, earlier, Jeffrey accepted April's offer to speak to August. Why did Jeffrey believe it was acceptable for April to speak to August but not for her? She felt irritated when her mother nudged her back into the ballroom to allow Jeffrey and April to speak alone. She remembers that April seemed rather upset by what Jeffrey was saying, but when they noticed that she was watching, both of them acted more casual.

Then, again, she rationalizes; she needs to eat something. She tends to forget to eat, and she's pregnant now. Maybe her mother really was only looking out for her earlier.

May's thoughts are hard to follow as she bounces between maybe this and maybe that. Now she questions why her mother insisted that they go to the buffet at the opposite end of the ballroom, the one away from the windows. May wanted to look out of the window to see when her sister left. What possible reason could her mother have for stopping her from looking outside?

May's awareness returns when she notices that Jeffrey (who had joined them soon after April left the party) is no longer by her side and that her mother is involved in a conversation with Michael. Seeing a chance to escape, she decides to stroll over to the windowed wall. She realizes that she won't be able to see her sister from this vantage point because the trees are too thick, but there's a large window overlooking the parking area on the opposite side of the room. In front of the window is a small buffet table that will give her an excuse to stand in front of the window and give her the food she needs at the same time.

May mingles with a group of young women making their way toward the table. She nods and seems interested as they chatter about who is doing what and going where with whom. May looks back and notices her mother's displeasure as she moves farther and farther away.

Something moves at the end of the clearing, catching May's attention. There's no mistaking April's bright pink dress. Transfixed, she numbly stares out the window, watching April's alarming movements. April's back is to the ballroom, but her sharp, angry hand gestures indicate that she's arguing with someone I can't see. April steps backwards, away from a man advancing toward her. The man, still partially obstructed from my view by April, points to the ballroom with dramatic gestures. He tries to take April's arm, but she shakes it off. They both move farther into the woods and out of sight. May continues walking along the windowed wall toward the table, desperately looking for further signs of April.

She catches sight of her mother trying to advance toward her, but Sarah is constantly waylaid by guests, who prevent her from reaching May's side. May seems convinced that her age causes her family to exclude her from important matters. She is tired of being treated like a child. She finally reaches the buffet table.

Sarah comes up to May, insisting she needs her help in the ladies' room and claiming that she doesn't feel well. May takes one last look out of the window, not really wanting to leave her post but feeling obligated to help her mother. Sarah doesn't look ill, and she finds it curious that her mother walked past the ladies' room, past her father, and past others who could help, just to fetch her.

On the way to the ladies' room, Peter, one of the guests, approaches them. Suddenly, her mother no longer seems so ill, and she starts telling Peter about May's plans to renovate the ballroom. Peter, a short, stocky, rather jolly black man, is an architect and is very keen to hear the details. Seeing a chance to get free of her mother, May says, "Peter, so good to see you. I'd love to go over my plans. Let me take you around the first floor and point out the areas I'd like to renovate."

He takes her arm and says, "I'm flattered that you'd like to discuss them with me. I'd be happy to accompany you downstairs and admire more of this charming building's architecture. It's nice to finally speak to you."

"I'm sorry Peter; I haven't been making the rounds as a good hostess should. There was an incident earlier with August. Were you here then?"

"Yes, I was. I was close by when he and Jeffrey were whispering."

"Oh, really? What did they discuss? I was pleased that Jeffrey was able to calm him and convince him to leave!"

"Calm?" Peter says as they walk down the stairs together. "I'm not sure any of Jeffrey's words had a calming effect on August."

The wall across from the stairs has a mural of a neatly trimmed multi-colored pansy-lined pathway through the forest opening onto the lake. A wood bench with wrought-iron arms and legs sits to the right of the trail opening. May wanted this mural painted since guests couldn't see the lake behind the ballroom. As May looks at Peter, she sees the reflection of the mural in the mirror.

The chandelier in the main entry, a duplicate of the largest one in the ballroom, hangs over a Queen Anne center table with fresh flowers. A Persian rug lies under the table, more likely placed to protect the marble floor from the legs of the table than as an accent piece.

Oblivious to these details, which are already familiar to her, May asks, "Why do you say that?"

Peter seems distracted by the ballroom and doesn't answer. He gazes around at the amazing architecture and says, "Do you know that this ballroom was built over one hundred and fifty years ago? It's had many renovations. Guests of the Betta Grand Hotel used to come here for the fanciest balls in Massachusetts. You're fortunate to have had this property in your family for so long!"

"Oh no, it was Marlene's family that owned it. I bought it from her grandparents."

Peter continues to talk about the renovations and what he thinks will and won't work. May listens halfheartedly, fretfully scanning the room for her sister.

They enter the dining room, which has the same crown molding and sculpted wood trim as the other rooms, along with a much smaller version of the grand chandelier. The room has wine-colored walls trimmed with chains of hand-painted golden ivy leaves. Between the two doors to the kitchen is a built-in mahogany hutch with a mirrored back panel, filled with fine china. Someone in the kitchen pulls open the back panel and fusses around with the china.

Peter looks around approvingly and asks, "You say you want to add onto the dining room?"

May is about to answer, but her eyes are drawn to the enormous kitchen, bustling with servants preparing trays of food to carry upstairs. Cabinets circle a huge center island where two chefs are busy with preparation. I catch sight of April's pink ball gown through the kitchen window overlooking the backyard and understand what has distracted May.

May politely excuses herself from Peter and makes her way through the kitchen and into the hallway behind the stairs, which leads to the back door. As she steps out the door, her sister, seated alone on a large rock, looks up, alarmed by the sound. May is about to speak when she feels a hand grabbing her arm from behind, and she turns to see Jeffrey's scowling face. He glares over at April as if she's a leper come to infect them all. His nostrils flare. April rises; she looks ready to bolt, yet, too terrified to move.

Jeffrey holds May still, commanding, "I need to speak to you."

"Jeffrey, it will have to wait. April is upset. I have to go to her. Let me go, Jeffrey! Why are you holding me?"

"I must speak to you now!"

"Speak to me later," May insists, struggling to get free of Jeffrey's steel grasp. "April? Did you speak to August?" Just as she breaks free, she falls backwards. She sees April running toward her, and then I feel, see, and hear nothing. It's all black.

May opens her eyes to find herself lying on a couch in an ornately decorated room. Large family paintings hang on all four walls. One painting is of May and her brother and sister as children, their clothing from the 1960s. On another wall is a recent family portrait of May, April, August, Sarah, and Wendel wearing '70s clothing. Hanging on the third wall is a painting of August and Marlene with Hannah, who looks about a year old. The fourth painting is a family portrait. Hannah, who looks about two, is sitting on Marlene's lap; August is standing behind Marlene, with his left hand on her left shoulder and his right hand on her right upper arm. April is seated between Marlene and May. In the back row, beside August, are Wendel, Sarah, and Jeffrey, who is standing behind May.

The real May's eyes move back and forth between Sarah and Jeffrey, who are standing over her, along with the rest of the family.

April is the first to see May's eyes open and rushes to her sister's side. "May, we were so frightened! Are you okay?"

May, unconcerned about herself, blurts out everything on her mind. "April, have you spoken to August? How did you get there and back so quickly? How is he? What's wrong? What's that scratch on your face? I thought I saw you in the trees earlier, talking to a man. What were you doing there? Who was he?"

April touches May's face and smiles warmly. "My dress is a little too long, so I stumbled—nothing, really! I did see August. He's fine. Our conversation was short, and he's just grumpy about things not going his way. You know how stubborn August is. He told me he realized he's behaved badly and he'll apologize to you later. I told him how he's worried you. He's sorry! Really, May, all of us are surprised at how you've worried and fretted about August so much."

Disregarding April, May says to her father, "Daddy, did you speak to August? Do you know what's troubling him? And what about the business dealings with Michael?"

Wendel clears his throat. A look of alarm appears briefly on his face at the mention of Michael, but he merely smiles and says, "Darling, you worry too much! I haven't spoken to August. Given how fiercely he would fight for the rights of a fly who 'needs to eat, too,' I suspect his outburst this evening was a combination of drinking and misplaced concern. I think with the party, August's behavior, and your pregnancy, the entire affair has been blow up to be something much bigger in your mind than it really is."

"Yes, listen to your father!" Sarah pats May's hand. "You have many guests now and more will arrive later. Do you feel well enough to continue with the party? We can send the guests home if you like."

"No, Mother, I'm fine. But there was a point when I started feeling like everyone was keeping something from me, and I felt like I was being pushed and pulled around like a doll."

"What do you mean?" asks Jeffrey.

"First, I wanted to talk to August, and later when I tried to talk to April, you stopped me, Jeffrey."

"You're right, May," Jeffrey says, holding May's hands in his own. "I think we're guilty! I see now how our attempts to shelter you have only caused more problems. Darling, why don't you speak to August tomorrow? Tonight, if you're up to it, we can enjoy our first party. We'll give you space to move freely, without all of us always hovering around to protect you. How does that sound?" Jeffrey assists her as she stands up, and she leads the way out of the room into the side entryway.

Rows of expensive automobiles line the driveway. Just at the top of the hill, under a covered tent, male attendants wearing pressed white-collared shirts and black jackets stand waiting for further instruction. A covered walkway connects the tent to the side entrance. I'm impressed with May's planning!

May stops. "I could do with some fresh air and some time alone to clear my thoughts." She turns to the door, satisfied that if they're being honest, they won't follow her. I also welcome the chance to think if May can just sit quietly. In the seconds it takes me to think how much I'd enjoy some quiet time, I realize that May is scheming something and I missed her plan! *"Jeez, May. Give me a chance for some quiet time. No, never mind that. I'm in your memory. Let's not argue semantics."*

Jeffrey looks around, right through the attendants. They don't exist to him. Sarah, looking rather contented, nudges Wendel and April away. April grudgingly follows her mother, not only avoiding eye contact with May but also making a point to walk on her father's outside arm, away from Jeffrey. This feat requires her to take a few steps backwards, going behind both her mother and father. They walk off and, incredibly, leave May in peace.

May steps out onto the side entrance porch and nods at the attendants, who nod back. The oldest one, who is attending the key station between the covered tent and the walkway, calls out, "Mrs. Dellner, I hope you're feeling better! I heard you had an accident."

"Yes. Thank you, Jameson. I feel fine. It's so good to see you here today. I hope that's a sign that your daughter's health is improving?"

He hesitates, taking a deep breath before responding carefully. "Annie's holding her own, Mrs. Dellner. Thank you for asking. If you're still feeling tired, I can have that bench brought over here; you can sit in the shade." Jameson is an imposing figure with broad shoulders. It would be more fitting if he were a quarterback rather than the lead parking attendant, but he carries himself well and doesn't seem out of place.

May, focused on her plan, doesn't notice he hesitates before speaking of his daughter. She says, "Of course not. I look forward to feeling some sun on my face. Oh, and Jameson, have you tended that post for the last four hours?"

"Yes, I have. We also keep full logs as guests come and go. How may I assist you?"

"Excellent! What time did August leave and who drove him home?"

Looking down, Jameson checks the log. "Mr. Lanlore left at 2:30, but no one drove him home; he drove himself."

"Himself? My God, Jameson, he was drunk! How could you?"

"I assure you, Mr. Lanlore was not drunk! I remember it clearly because he and Mr. Dellner exchanged some words before Mr. Lanlore asked for his car."

"'Exchanged some words'? August was dancing around like a fool earlier. Jeffrey spoke to him and escorted him out. I hope he wasn't too harsh with August. Did you hear what they said?"

"Not really."

May notices Jameson flinch and worries that Jeffrey and August got into a fight. "Jameson, please tell me what you heard. Small things can sometimes lead to big rifts in families. If you heard something that my brother and husband said, I really need to know. I won't repeat where I heard it."

He motions to a sunlit bench facing the front yard. "Please sit down. I'll join you."

"No!" May says forcefully, pointing up toward the ballroom window. "They'll see us talking."

"I can't have you standing there. Please sit down, and I'll speak from here."

"Thank you!" May walks over to the bench and positions herself with her back to the window, but not before she looks up and sees Jeffrey and Sarah staring out the window.

"I couldn't really hear what they said, Mrs. Dellner. Most of their discussion was in angry whispers. Twice they raised their voices, and once I heard your name, something like 'not May,' and . . . ."

"Yes. Why are you hesitating?"

May, living a sheltered life, believes that they were talking about her involvement in the family business. She knows that Jeffrey shares her mother's view that she shouldn't be involved. August has always encouraged both May and her sister's involvement with the family business. Based on the memory flashes, August has butted heads with Sarah many times on the issue of his sister's involvement.

"I don't think I should say any more."

"Jameson, you may be the only person speaking honestly to me tonight."

He looks at her for a moment and then nods. "You've always been dear to me and my family. My little Annie loves you so! She often asks when she can visit with Auntie May again."

"At least Annie listens when I tell her to call me May though I've never heard her call me 'Auntie May' before. How sweet! And August and April? What does Annie call them?"

His voice trembles. "She calls Mr. Lanlore 'Augy' and Ms. Lanlore 'Pril.'"

A memory of Annie flashes into May's mind—a sweet,

bright-eyed little girl of about three saying to May, "I have your eyes."

"Please, Jameson, tell me! What did Jeffrey and August say?"

"I heard August say, 'don't threaten' and the rest was muffled. Then Mr. Dellner stormed back into the ballroom. Mr. Lanlore walked over to me and requested his keys, and I sent a man down to fetch his car. While we were waiting, Mr. Lanlore said, 'That man will be the ruin of us all or the death of me.' Then he gave a weak sort of smile."

May gasps. "August," she whispers. Trying to rationalize that it's nothing more than August being overly defensive, she sits for a while longer to compose herself. When she rises to return to the party, she sees Jeffrey and Sarah still standing at the window.

As May steps up to the porch of the covered side entryway, she turns back and asks, "Jameson? Did April send for her car?"

"No, Mrs. Dellner. But I did see Ms. Lanlore and Mr. Dellner out walking earlier." Jameson pauses as if to say more. May waits. He quickly shakes his head, hastily walks up to her, takes her hands gently in his own and says, "May, please be careful." He raises his hand up to silence further questions. "The Lanlore kids have always been good to me. You've helped so much when Annie was in the hospital. She loves all of you."

"And Mother, Father, and Jeffrey? Does Annie love them?" she asks, hopefully searching Jameson's face.

He looks at May sadly, as if he's apologizing for his daughter's misdeed. With one last firm squeeze of May's hand, Jameson returns to his post. He stands with a stiff back, as if to draw strength from his erect posture. May watches him walk away, both touched and perplexed that he's finally called her by her first name.

"May, listen to yourself! Your body screams 'flee or fight,' but you just sit and take it." To no avail. She doesn't hear me.

I have to talk to Katri about this! May's love for her husband is preventing her from seeing the truth. Creeping concerns rise up in her mind, and she works furiously to trivialize their meaning. I desperately want to grab her and tell her to open her eyes!

Chapter 7: Back to the Ball

May walks slowly through the entryway and into the next room. Closets take up all the available wall space. Glass doors allow me to see that these closets are deep enough to hold two full rows of coats. As it's a spring day, there's only one coatroom attendant and very few coats in the closet. A window on one end faces the front yard; a doorway to the painting room is on the opposite end.

May sees her sister in the painting room, looking up at their childhood portrait. Her hopes soaring, she walks over and stands quietly beside April, who stares with vacant, cloudy eyes at the painting of May, August, and herself when they were children.

"Do you remember how hard it was to sit still for that portrait?" asks May.

April jumps, her eyes damp. "May, you scared me. I thought I was alone."

"Are you crying?"

"I, well, no. It's just some dust in my eyes."

May looks around at the dust-free tables and desktops, then closes all three doors in the painting room—one from the side entry, another from the coatroom, and the last from the kitchen hallway—and returns to her sister's side. "Dust? April, I saw you outside earlier today at the bottom of the hill, almost hidden in the trees." She raises her hand to protest. "Don't deny it! Look at your dress! You're the only one wearing a bright pink dress with a matching hat. I also saw a man with you; it looked like he made you angry, then both of you went off into the trees. What's going on?"

April says angrily, "I'm worried about you, May. You should focus on taking care of your health rather than spending so much time worrying about others. I heard you fainted last week because you forget to eat and today it happened again!"

"Today, I tripped! Last week, well, you're right, I forgot to eat. It has nothing to do with today. Are you telling me you're keeping the truth from me because you're worried I somehow can't handle it? That's absurd! April, tell me honestly. Did you really talk to August earlier today?"

April looks down, shaking her head.

"Why tell me you did, then?"

"Because this scene will blow over, and I want us to enjoy ourselves. I did fully intend to talk to August, but I . . . well . . . ."

"Yes, but you what, April?"

April stands erect, biting her lower lip, and replies, "I just didn't feel like going. Do I need an explanation? Big deal; August had another outburst. He acted up. Do we have to stop everything? I decided to go for a walk, instead. August will be around tomorrow."

"I suppose you're right. Talking to August can wait till tomorrow. Maybe I've been overly suspicious about small things. Before you told me that you spoke to August, Jeffrey told me that August had confided in him about some 'problems.' If that wasn't unusual enough, Jeffrey said that he and August were planning to go on a hunting trip together!" They look at each other, and they both burst out laughing.

April perks up and claps her hand together. "Can you see it, May? First, August would have his hunting 'costume' neatly ironed. Then he'd find the hunting stand poorly constructed and would need to change into work clothes so he could 'build it properly.' By the time he'd finished putting in a few nice shelves, a bench or two, and possibly a small table, he'd have scared all the deer away!"

"And the idea of August actually shooting an animal for sport!" laughs May.

"Really! Tell me about it! Remember when we were kids and that little dirty boy who used to show up occasionally in our neighborhood tried to chase me with a big black spider? I had good reason to run!"

"Oh, yes! We thought August was rushing out to rescue his sister from the 'dirty boy.' He was livid, screaming at the kid, to 'put that spider down' or he would 'beat him to Jupiter and back.' When the kid put the spider down, August rushed forward, carefully carried the big ugly spider to the woods, charged back, and slugged the kid anyhow! Don't kill spiders or bugs around August, we learned!"

May stops and studies her sister. April laughed along as May recounted the story, but April's eyes, weighted with hidden sadness, revealed her true feelings. "April? There's a drastic difference from the sad April I see now and the peppy, happy April who arrived earlier. What happened? What has changed? Maybe I can't do anything, but at least I can listen!"

"I suppose we've never been good at keeping secrets from

each other. It might have to do with Mother, but I don't really know. I haven't spoken to August yet, but I have the situation under control. One of the reasons I can't say much is that I don't have enough specifics. I'm afraid it won't make much sense yet. I need time to sort it all out. I really need you to let me handle it."

"And Jeffrey? Is he working with you?"

April steps back, holding her hands in front of her as if to push off an attacker. "No! Why would you . . . ?"

"Jameson saw the two of you walking outside. What were you talking about?"

April quickly averts her eyes to the painting of herself and her brother and sister where August looks to be about ten years old, April about nine, and May about seven. She takes deep thoughtful breaths, biting her lip, starting to speak, and stopping. Finally, she starts to say, "Whatever you do . . . ."

Jeffrey and Sarah burst into the room. "Here you are!" Jeffrey says. "My wife and sister-in-law hidden away from the guests, behind closed doors, and looking much too serious!"

"We were just remembering how difficult it was to sit still for this painting of us," May responds. "The painter was a nasty, grumpy man, wasn't he, April?"

April nods emphatically, "He was!" Then she looks quickly away.

"Come on, April," May says. "I've only danced once this evening. This may well be the last party before I'm too big to dance. April, let's do the sisters dance!" She grabs April's hand and, in a grand show of cheerfulness, bounds from the room, dragging her sister behind.

May motions to the DJ. Much to the apparent horror of Sarah and Jeffrey, they hear "Cotton-Eyed Joe," and the elegant ball turns into square-dance/line-dance mayhem. May and April prance to the center of the ballroom. One demonstrates a step, which the other copies. The sisters spin, jump, tap, do-si-do, and whirl around the dance floor.

Many guests stand aside politely, smiling and whispering to each other. Finally, Peter takes his wife's hand and Michael takes Marla's, and they join May and April. Soon other guests join in on the mayhem, which results in an occasional woman's hat sailing through the air.

A jubilant round of applause follows the song. Jeffrey

scurries up to May's side and announces, "I'd like to thank all of our guests for attending tonight. It's a pleasure to have you here this evening. After that hopping dance, I'm ready to slow it down to music fitting our party theme." Jeffrey signals to the DJ and a waltz begins. Jeffrey and May gracefully waltz among the throngs of guests. Slowly, Jeffrey dances May over to the balcony where he whispers, "I need some fresh air."

They stand arm in arm, gazing out over the clearing, then Jeffrey pulls May to a tight spot between a large potted flowering shrub and the balcony rail. Both May and I are perplexed at this maneuver.

May is just about to ask why he's chosen to stand there when Jeffrey asks, "Are you happy?"

"Yes. Very!" Believing that he wanted a romantic spot, she thinks back to the night he proposed to her. He had scattered red roses all over the lawn of her family home and knelt on one knee in the middle of them. He called to her, "The roses represent my heart. When we're together, love feeds my heart. When we're apart, it's like these roses scattered on this lawn. Gather these roses, May, and show me you want my heart to be whole. I've removed the thorns to show you that my heart beats to protect you and keep you from harm. May, will you marry me?"

The memory flash was when she was only sixteen. She was leaving on a three-month trip to Europe with her brother and sister. After he asked her to marry him, she jumped out of the car, had her luggage removed, and ran to him. He even had the audacity to "remind" her to gather the one hundred or more roses on the lawn before she ran to him. She laughed at this tactic. Reliving her memory, I see a sly and manipulative man preying on the innocence of a young girl.

"May? May?" says Jeffrey. "May, you looked so far away! It was like when I saw you and April in the painting room. What were you so sad about?"

"Oh, no! Just now I was thinking of when you proposed to me!" She smiles adoringly at Jeffrey. Her vision, clouded by the romantic gestures from yesterday, prevents her from seeing the deceit in his eyes.

"Why were the doors shut?"

"What doors?"

"Just now, when we found you and April talking. All the

doors were shut."

"Shut? I didn't realize they were."

"May, either you or April must have shut them. They didn't shut themselves. When we left that room earlier, all the doors were ajar."

"Well, I don't know. Maybe others had been in there since? Really, Jeffrey, I'm surprised. Shut doors, open doors—I don't know that it matters. Why do you ask? Why do you care? Why even do you notice?"

Jeffrey responds with a mind-numbing monologue about how he's trying to keep their family together and May doesn't support and trust him. He even implies that their marriage is in danger. May's protests only give him fodder to support his arguments. It seems to me that having failed to control her actions, he's trying to control how she thinks. He carefully constructs his words so that poor May thinks she's acting for the future of their unborn child. I too find myself confused. Could Jeffrey be sincere? He concludes his monologue, commanding, "So, then, tell me what you discussed with April. No more secrets, May!"

"She didn't say anything to me, Jeffrey. She's worried about Mother. She didn't have any specifics, but she said that she can handle it. You see, my love. I haven't kept anything from you. She really didn't say anything of interest."

Anger flashes across Jeffrey's face. May sees the anger and believes that Jeffrey is just upset because she had held back. Jeffrey takes May by the shoulders. *How black his eyes are*, May thinks. *So like my mother's.*

"May, I'll confide something to you. But it will be difficult to believe; you must trust me. You must not speak of this to anyone! Your mother was the first to notice that there have been some questionable business dealings, some money missing, and she confronted August. He was angry and defensive and didn't own up to gambling, but we're sure he lost a lot of his own share of the family fortune. We believe he's trying to win it back without caring whom he destroys. You see, for the sake of our family, we can't allow August to drive a wedge between us."

Distressed that she has angered Jeffrey, she says through her tears, "I won't allow it, my love. I won't!"

Sarah walks out onto the balcony. "Look at you two lovebirds behind that shrub," she says, her smile fading as she sees their faces. "Not more serious talk! Need I remind you? This is a party, your party?"

Dabbing at her eyes, May says, "Jeffrey has just confided to me what August has been up to."

Jeffrey adds, "I confess, Sarah. I told May the truth. May understands now and won't allow August to come between us. I know what I need to do now."

Smiling, Sarah gives an approving nod and says, "May, I'm relieved that my daughter has married such a devoted and supporting husband. He's so concerned about protecting you and our family! He's done so much for all of us. The business will grow to fortunes far greater than ever before in the Lanlore lineage! If it weren't for Jeffrey, we wouldn't be where we are now." She smiles again. "Enough of this serious talk. Let's rejoin the party!"

Jeffrey straightens triumphantly; is it because he has successfully turned May against her brother?

Chapter 8: Needing a Break

I'm back in the dark ballroom. It was easy to exit the memory, as I only needed to think it, and I was out. There's no lovely chandelier or mirrored walls, just a big dark room. I need a break. I never realized until now just how much I need my hands and my voice! It isn't enough to think, "Gag me." I also need to put my finger in my mouth and demonstrate it—and emphatically so! I'm shocked that Jeffrey so easily swayed May's allegiance. She's never questioned her brother's integrity before as far as I can tell from my short time in her mind. Jeffrey's carefully chosen words succeeded in stabbing, beating, and hacking away all her reservations.

The time! I think, as I rush outside to check my watch. When I entered May's memory, it was sometime in the afternoon, for her, that is, but when I finally left her memory, it was evening. Quite a bit of time had passed in her memory. I worry that the same amount of time passed for me.

All that listening without thinking was driving me mad! I felt like her thoughts were overrunning mine. It was almost as if I was losing my own identity in her mind. To release steam, I dash down the gravel road, screaming, "I can talk. La, la, la, la, I'm Jena. There's no silencing me now! I'm Jena. Jena!"

I quickly look around and don't see anyone. What a relief! They wouldn't understand how difficult it is being cooped up in someone else's mind. I'd be better off not telling them the truth! How would I explain how I came to be an observer in her mind in the first place? Or that Katri convinced me to silence my own thoughts, which is why I feel so out of sorts.

Oh, yes, the time. I forgot to check it earlier because I was too intent on screaming the silence out of me! It's late morning, and I'm relieved that the passing time in May's memories isn't exactly equal to the passing time in real life. I'd have been terribly late meeting Ben if it were. Yesterday, the passing time in May's memory was equal to my own time, but I had interjected my own thoughts on many occasions. I don't fully understand the relationship between actual time and the time in May's memory, but if this test run is any indication of how it works, removing my thoughts makes the time difference smaller. Yet another good reason for me to pay more attention! If only I could perfect this memory-shifting skill! Oh, I wish! Oh, dear. Ben and Katri are so right. I overanalyze just as I'm doing right now! Never mind. I don't care. I have some time, and I want to check out the lake that I saw in the mural.

Bursting with energy, I sprint back up to the ballroom and into the backyard. I can see an entry into the woods farther down. Beyond that entrance is the same large rock that April sat on so very long ago. It dawns on me that I've never been back here before, and I didn't know that rock was here. It's just another reminder to me that these memories are real. And I don't know how to explain it.

It's a lovely day, and I want to relax. I peer down the well-maintained trail leading to the lake, which looks much like it did in the mural. Some newly planted pansies line one side of the trail. The sight stirs up peculiar feelings of unrest in me. I fight hard to disregard my feelings. Maybe someone likes to walk to the lake and plant flowers—so what? I bound down to the lake.

The lake is large. The unspoiled, tree-lined shore extends beyond my view in both directions, so I can't fully grasp the size. Although I can see the other side, it wouldn't be an easy swim, with today being a possible exception. I feel so bottled up that I half-believe I could actually make it there and back with energy to spare.

My cell phone rings, disturbing nature's tranquility.

It's Katri calling. "Hi, Jena. Ben said you went for a walk today. Adam told me to tell you, 'Stay out of that building.'" Her voice imitates Adam's stern directives.

"Okay. I'll stay out of that building today. What's up?"

"Ben and Adam didn't get their tee time this morning, so they only just started their round of golf. Ben said that you two are planning to go skating. I thought if you still had energy, you'd like to join me kickboxing? They're having a special kick-butt class today."

"Kickboxing? That would be perfect for me. I really need to kick and hit something. You have no idea!"

"Why is that? Have the trees been disagreeable to you? What? They didn't clear themselves out of the way as you walked through?"

"Exactly! And when I arrived at the ballroom, the tea was cold, the cookies were stale, and no one was there to open the door for me!"

"You poor baby. Well, your chariot awaits you. I'm at the Dirt Road Parking Lot now. How long will it take you to get here?"

"I have a lot of energy to burn; I'll run it!"

"Don't burn yourself out. Save some energy for kickboxing!"

"Okay!" I start jogging down the lake trail, picking up the pace down the gravel road. Once I reach the forest, I charge in, nimbly moving through the trees, effortlessly jumping logs and ducking limbs—if my Sweetie Pie could see me now! In no time, with little effort, I find myself at Katri's car.

Standing by her car, stretching, Katri says, "You made really good time!"

"I told you. I had a lot of energy to burn off! Say, did I already tell you I saw the lake? It's behind the old ballroom."

"No, you didn't mention a lake before. Was the tea service suitable there?"

"No. It was slow. I finally left without any tea! I want some now. Let's stop for a fix on the way back."

"How about lunch and tea?" Katri asks, eyeing me warily. "I'll be hungry by then."

"That's a great idea. I'm starving!"

On the way to our kickboxing session, Katri glances at me frequently.

"What? Why do you keep looking at me like that?" I ask impatiently.

"You weren't even winded when you reached the car, and look at you now, bouncing all around my car like a wind-up toy. I'm a little concerned, that's all. Anything you want to talk about?"

"Like I said, I have a lot of energy to burn!"

We arrive to a full classroom. There aren't enough kick bags, so Katri and I share one. I like sharing bags since it's easier to pause and chat (or yell) in between kicks! We also get a better workout. We have to keep pace with each other so that we don't accidentally kick each other doing some of the punch/kick routines. Often, Katri can set a more grueling pace; I smile happily to myself. I'll give her a good run today!

Master Kicker, as Katri calls him, sees us together and says, "Well, Katri, Jena will stop your bag from moving very far. She'll just kick it back to you."

She stares at me aghast when the music starts and I plow

my gloved hands into the bag with such force that the bag nearly tips over. "People really piss me off!" I explain.

"What? Is this the same Jena who tells me when I'm driving and someone cuts me off that the other driver could be having a bad day and I should give them a break?"

"I think it's gullible people that really piss me off. Someone who can stare at the face of danger and believe it when someone else tries to say there's no danger. Being gullible is the sort of thing that pisses me off!"

"Gosh, Jena, if you hit this bag any harder, it might just fall over!"

"These bags aren't going to fall over," interrupts Master Kicker. "That's what they're designed for. The two of you need to chat less and kick and punch more! There will be no butt-kicking going on in here if the mouths are moving. I knew I should have separated you two!" He laughs. "Come on, Katri. For once, Jena looks like she's hitting harder than you are."

"You bet, Master Kicker. I really need this today."

He shakes his head, smirking at Katri.

"His name isn't really Master Kicker, is it?"

"No," says Katri, laughing, "What did you say about gullible?"

"All this time you've been leading me on?"

"Revenge for that swim in the river a few years ago."

"If you hadn't allowed Adam to help you across, you wouldn't have fallen in! You know, there are names for people like you."

"Yes, we're good and tolerant friends. And, besides," she adds cheerfully, "it makes Adam feel good when he can help other people."

Master What's-His-Name turns up the music, so no more chatting with Katri! For a year, I've been coming here with Katri and I believed his name was Kicker. Katri swore it was his real name and he always answered to it. He must have been in on the joke! A person can get away with a lot when other people support them.

This thought makes we wonder about Jeffrey. Was someone helping him? That might make him look more believable. Is that why May was so easy to deceive? There was a point where I thought April wasn't to be trusted, but now I'm not so sure. Could

I be wrong about Jeffrey? Sarah seems to care more for Jeffrey than she does her own son, August! How sad. Could August really be having problems? Naturally, it's possible that a sister wouldn't know everything about her brother. I'm so confused. Oh, dear. Listen to me. Am I doing the very thing I thought May was doing? I'm providing reasons to explain why something I thought was wrong isn't really so wrong after all. I never thought our instructor's name was really Master Kicker but since Adam knew him and he used the name, too, I was successfully misled. They were all in on it! Numbers can support the credibility of a lie. Gullible? I never really thought of myself as gullible, and yet . . . .

A hand touches my shoulder. The image of Jeffrey holding May back flashes through my mind. "Fight back, May! Fight back!" I say aloud to a room blasting with music.

I return to reality in time to see Master What's-His-Name ducking from my swing at him. "I'm so sorry!"

Shell-shocked, Katri tries to speak but laughs instead. He signals her to continue and says to me, "I was trying to get your attention because the rest of the class has moved on and you didn't hear me. That would have been a knock-out punch if it had hit me."

"I was distracted. I'm so sorry! I'm glad you're fast on your feet."

After class, Katri inquires, "What happened to you today?"

"I was just so deep in thought that I didn't hear Master What's-His-Name; he startled me when he touched me."

"His name is *Kigger*, not Kicker. Sorry. I really should have corrected you earlier, but Ben discouraged me because he thought it was funny. You really are distracted today. What's the problem?"

"I'm feeling much better now. There's nothing like kicking and hitting a bag as hard as you can to get some frustration out."

"What frustration?"

"Just thinking about how easily people can be led on. Don't you think it's odd when you read stories about people who are swindled?"

"It isn't so odd. I think we want to trust each other. It's natural to try to find some good reason why someone, especially someone we love, is behaving in a way we think is contrary to how we think he should behave. We want to believe in others."

We shower quickly and change. Although Katri didn't

wash her hair, it still has a clean, fresh shine. I would never have guessed that she'd just spent an hour kicking and punching a bag at one hundred miles an hour.

Katri usually can match me chocolate for chocolate, but no one can tell looking at her that she eats anything other than lean meats, fruits, vegetables, and whole grains. I suspect that her daily "warm-up jog" helps her maintain her muscle tone. I, on the other hand, could stand to lose a few pounds even though many people call me physically fit. Sometimes, clothing is a blessing since it allows me to hide so many of my flaws. I do overindulge in junk food at times, and I don't always compensate with enough activity. Not that Katri snacks often; it's just that she plans her snacks. For that matter, I'll bet that she could tell me how many fruits and vegetables she'd had so far on any given day if I asked her. According to Katri, she even sends Adam to work with fruits and vegetables, and he retorts that she's trying to "kill him with fresh fruit."

Katri and Adam have known each other since they were both ten-year-olds. Katri told me that she "observed behavior in Adam that required some adjustments and I had just the fix for him. Adam was trying to build a bridge over a small stream. I asked him why he was building a bridge when we could just jump over it, and I demonstrated how easy it was to jump over the stream. After a thoughtful pause, he said quite seriously, 'I'll make it better.'

"He worked diligently each day, but he could never get the bridge done. You see, after Adam went home, the neighborhood kids knocked it down. Adam would lecture and threaten and fume."

I laughed heartily, imagining this scene. What were the odds that Mr. and Miss Fix-It would come together? And yet the story was perfectly in character for the couple I know.

"I told him that the lectures made the kids laugh," Katri continued. "His threats only made them more determined to show him that they weren't scared. That was why they continued their destruction."

As she spoke, it was easy to visualize a levelheaded and eager Katri explaining to a frustrated and irate Adam that if he looked up from his work, he would see that the other boys were amazed by what he was doing. They probably felt excluded. "Ask them to help you," advised Katri. Adam took her advice; by fourteen, he was running a workshop with a loyal following of neighborhood children eager to help him with his "projects." He and Katri were friends, but their relationship didn't blossom into romance until college.

I met Katri when she was in graduate school working on her Ph.D. We ran into each other as I whipped around a corner, and the ice cream cone she was eating flew into the air, scaring away a bunch of pigeons as it plopped down in the spot where they had been pecking crumbs of food off the sidewalk.

"Damn!" she said. "Almost got them back!"

"A premium ice cream is hardly payback for pooping on your head," I said. "Quick, take it back before they think this is the new trade-off. This could be an epidemic if word gets out they get chocolate ice cream in exchange for pooping on us." I swung my arms around as if I was battling a volley of pooping birds.

We laughed, and then she noticed my nearly new pair of inline skates and asked what they were. I explained that they were a new type of skates and that they were an excellent form of transportation, as well as exercise. She seemed fascinated yet skeptical about skating. I persisted, explaining the importance of learning how to brake. When she expressed interest in learning how to inline skate, I offered to give her a few pointers. We've been skating, biking, hiking, and skiing friends ever since. She and Adam introduced me to Ben. They said that I needed some sort of calming balance, and they thought Ben was perfect for me.

"Jena? Jena?"

"What?" I answer, coming out of my reverie as we walk to her car.

"I said, are you hungry?"

"Yes, very hungry and I'm in dire need of tea!" I say, pretending that I have the shakes.

"I don't think you need any caffeine! You've been so wired today. What's wrong? Did you go *into* the ballroom today?"

"Yes."

"In spite of Adam's warnings?" she says, trying to appear disapproving.

"I'm quite good at tuning out Adam when it suits me."

"Yes. We're all quite good at tuning out what we don't want to hear or believe."

After lunch, she drives me back to my house, talking about

the weather, planting vegetables, movies, trips she plans to take, and the new pair of inline skates that she wants to try out. My energy levels are through the roof as I listen, barely able to stay seated.

As we pull up to my house, I quickly gather my things together and say, "Thanks for the ride. That was a good class. I'd invite you in, but I have some chores to get done."

"No problem. I want to get back, too. Are you going to the ballroom tomorrow?"

"Yup!"

"Jena? Call me anytime if you need anything, or even if you just want someone to talk to."

"Sure, whatever," I respond hastily. In spite of the run back from the ballroom and kickboxing, I find myself still brimming with energy. Long before Katri pulled up to my house, I had a laundry list of other things to do. Today will be a good day for chores and refining some inline skating moves. First, I'll hone my curb-jumping skills so I can move more easily from the sidewalk to the road. After skating, I'll rip out some weeds in my garden, clean the basement, hose down the garage, stain the deck, and if the sun is still out, I'll wash the outside windows.

Chapter 9: Supporting Jeffrey

Walking back to the ballroom, I remember what Katri said about tuning out what we don't want to hear. I'm kicking myself for not pushing her for more information. Her behavior is similar to when we're watching movies that she's seen and I haven't. Even though I've told her that I like to know what's going to happen in movies and in books, she still won't tell me. She always has this wait-and-see look. I've explained that I'll read the last chapter of a book and fast forward to the end of the DVD, yet, each time, she looks ever so amazed that I would do that. "Won't it spoil it for you?" If she's seen a movie that I haven't seen and I ask any questions, her response is always something like, "Oh, I don't know," or "You'll see." I've given up trying to pry information from her. Maybe that's why I didn't push for more information. I've been Katri-programmed not to ask!

I can't find the shortcut that so easily took me to Dirt Road yesterday. I'm stuck going the long way around, but I welcome the exercise especially since I don't know what my body is doing when I'm in May's mind. For all I know, this might be the only exercise I'm getting, so I'd better make the most of it.

Once I'm at the ballroom, I know the drill, so I hop in the window and make my way toward the stairs. As I approach the main entryway where the stairs are, something moving catches my eye in the dining room.

"Anyone there?"

I realize that if someone who meant me harm is lurking there, he won't likely be volunteering any information. "Yes, I'm here. I'm waiting for you to turn your back so I can stab you a few times. Could you pretend like you didn't notice me? I have a schedule to keep, you know." To which I, not to be outwitted with sarcasm, would respond, "Oh, excuse me! My humblest apologies, but I have May's memories to shift to today and don't have any time to spare for robbers, murderers, and mayhem in my real life or May's." I laugh as I realize that I just said that aloud! If a killer is lurking in the shadows, I've probably scared him away!

No more chasing shadows. Memories are waiting. I shake off the silliness, glad that no one is observing me since I seem to be adding a completely new dimension to what Ben calls my "nuttiness factor."

I bound up the steps and hop up to the second-floor landing. I'm getting good at this. I haven't even really started thinking about May, and the changes are already starting.

It's exciting! Where's the popcorn? If I could only figure out how to bottle and sell this technique, I'd be rich. Parents would have a new way of telling their stories to their children. People terrified of trying new activities could experience them without fear, through others. Well, with the small caveat that they only experience the memories that have pleasant outcomes. It would be terrible to experience someone plummeting to his death parachuting.

May is standing between Jeffrey and Sarah, all three proudly surveying the contented guests. I'm surprised to realize that it's dark outside. When I left her memory yesterday, it was evening, but the sun had not set. In spite of my efforts to be more focused, I feel like I've allowed time to pass unaware. Or could it be that I'm entering her memory at a later time today than I left it yesterday? There are more guests than I remember.

May is the first to see August and Marlene step onto the second-floor landing. Soon Jeffrey and Sarah see them, too. Sarah gives Jeffrey an anxious look, but Jeffrey looks confident—too confident—and Sarah soon relaxes. Oblivious to their reactions, May struggles with her own demons. She's happy to see her brother, but she's worried about what might happen if he makes further efforts to pull her into a conversation. She works hard to convince herself that the truth will come out later and everyone will laugh about it. The only real danger, she reasons, is losing her husband. She's resolved to prevent August from causing any further disruptions.

She smiles at Jeffrey. "Would you like me to speak to August and tell him he needs to behave himself?"

"We can speak to him together, dear, but first let's invite him to dance! This is the first we've seen of Marlene this evening. I didn't think she was going to attend."

Sarah, Jeffrey, and May make their way to the staircase where August and Marlene are conversing with other guests. Jeffrey, spotting April, nods in her general direction. Sarah follows the direction of his nod, then separates from the threesome. May sees Sarah approach April, recognizing the "my stomach hurts" gesture. May becomes suspicious and wonders if Sarah is preventing April from approaching her. She shakes it off and instead thinks of more important matters, her baby's future and the future of her marriage. She won't allow her family's foolish antics to destroy her marriage.

The ballroom is crowded, so it takes some time for Jeffrey and May to reach August and Marlene. The Dellners exchange pleasantries as they walk by their guests, many of whom are dancing, since Jeffrey elected to cross the ballroom rather than going around. All the while, Jeffrey's eyes remain fixed on August.

"August!" he says as they reach the stairs. "May and I are pleased that you returned and this time with Marlene and in costume. Now that you're here, we must have a Lanlore and Dellner dance!"

August barely glances at Jeffrey; instead, he searches May's face hopefully.

May doesn't allow August to hold her gaze and instead looks fondly at Jeffrey, saying, "I can fetch April, Mother, and Daddy."

"No need. The four of us can dance."

Both Jeffrey and August offer their hand to May. Jeffrey gives May an indignant glance. May rolls her eyes and smiles at August. "Silly brother! Dance with your wife. I want this dance to be with my husband."

Aware that August is trying to get her alone, May doesn't want to upset Jeffrey any further. She noticed how August searched her face as if seeking some sign, some recognition. May holds his gaze again briefly. But, as earlier, she sees something desperate, something frightening, in his look. She again shakes off the worries that start to creep into her mind and again she rationalizes them all away. May takes Jeffrey's arm, pained at disappointing her brother but feeling that she must be firm.

Jeffrey twirls his arm above his head and the music stops. The dancing stops, too, as the guests look around. Those standing closest to May and Jeffrey step aside, opening a pathway to allow May and Jeffrey to lead the way to the center of the ballroom. May glances back, expecting to see August and Marlene cheerfully following them, but instead sees them exchange an ever-so-subtle look of disappointment. Then August offers his hand to Marlene. Marlene lifts her hand, as though weighted, and drops it, with a sigh, into August's extended hand. May swallows hard and quickly faces forward.

As May and Jeffrey prepare to dance underneath the grand chandelier, May, holding her head high, looks out over the front yard. The yard is entirely lit up. White lights shimmer all around the perimeter. Floodlights on the building shine down on the yard. The entire front lawn is crowded with people, more people than could possibly fit in the second floor of the ballroom. All of them are looking up.

Guests are standing ten people deep all around the perimeter of the ballroom, except along the windowed wall, where no one is standing—not so that May and Jeffrey can see out but so that those outside can see up.

Marlene and August's grace on the dance floor far exceeds May and Jeffrey's. August gently lifts and twirls Marlene, capturing the eyes of all onlookers. Jeffrey leads May to the side so they can watch August and Marlene dazzle their guests, but their position blocks the view of the guests on the lawn. May looks behind, uncomfortable because she's standing in front of the window. She's reluctant to point out this indiscretion to her husband, especially after he raised so many doubts about her devotion to him. She looks at Jeffrey, who looks captivated watching August and Marlene, and decides to stand quietly beside him. Jeffrey squeezes her hand.

Marlene is stunning—tall and slender and oddly familiar-looking. Her long blond hair cascades in gentle waves, bouncing toward her waist. As they whirl around the dance floor, the lights glisten on her hair, showing traces of red and brown. Unlike the other female guests, Marlene isn't wearing a hat to match her gown, which is made of the same material as the red silk vest with black lace paisley overlay that August wears under his tuxedo jacket. Folds of black lace layer their way down from Marlene's waist over the red silk gown. Matching black lace borders the bodice and ties in a large bow in the back.

Watching August and Marlene dance, May relaxes, reasoning that whatever caused the disagreement this afternoon has blown over. She hopes that she won't have to draw any lines between her family and her husband. Then she sees April leaning against the wall, making no effort to join the family. May wants to signal to April to join them, but she can't get her attention. May sighs, wondering why April and August chose this day to take turns with moody behavior. Nothing can be so pressing, so urgent, that it must disrupt her first party in the Dellner Ballroom.

The song ends, and August and Marlene make their way over to Jeffrey and May.

"August, my good man," says Jeffrey, "May and I were talking about you just before you appeared. Your timing, well, it's almost like you were listening." He attempts to put his hand on August's retreating shoulder.

"Really?" August greets Jeffrey with a dull glance and then says to his sister, "I owe you an apology for my earlier behavior." Before anyone else can interfere, he steps forward, secretly places a key in her palm, kisses her cheek, and whispers, "For Hannah. Remember our promise." He steps back as quickly as he stepped forward.

Afraid that he's about to start another scene, May steps back and forcefully proclaims, "Apology accepted, August, and let this be the end of any disruptions. This evening has had too many, and I've had enough!"

Jeffrey warily watches August, then bends close to May and asks, "What's the matter, darling? Has he upset you? I'll have him thrown out if he's upset you again!"

She shakes her head, clenching the key tightly in her fist. "Nothing, darling. He just said that he wants me safe, which is a silly thing to say. Of course, I'm safe!"

Jeffrey smiles jubilantly as he watches August retreat, defeated. He bellows, "Please drink, eat, mingle, and enjoy. This is a truly momentous day."

May doesn't see August leave. She clutches the key tightly in her hand while anger, sorrow, and fear battle within her. She stands wondering what to do with the key and finally tucks it into the little pocket in her dress.

Guests start rushing around them. One man slaps Jeffrey on the back and demands, "Jeffrey, join us for a drink; you've been hiding yourself away." Ignoring Jeffrey's protest, the man leads him away. Jeffrey looks back at May. She puts her hands on her heart, and then opens her hands out to him as she thinks, "My heart is yours." Jeffrey relaxes, apparently confident that he's won her allegiance.

August tries to approach May, but Sarah quickly steps

between them and says to May, "August and Marlene looked dazzling out on the dance floor."

Sarah continues talking while May occasionally nods and pretends to listen. She knows that Sarah likes Jeffrey. He's always been an attentive son-in-law, even during their long engagement. Maybe that's it! Her mother is merely looking out for her!

August arrives and kisses his mother's coolly offered cheek. "Good evening, Mother. How are you?"

"Splendid, August," she replies coldly. "I trust you already apologized to your sister for the disturbance today? We can't have anymore outbursts!" When August nods, she takes his hand and demands, "A dance for your mother."

Sarah and August exchange pleasantries as they walk away like mere business acquaintances. May catches a glimpse of a pink dress bobbing toward her and knows that it's April, who is pushing her way through the crowd toward May. Just as April reaches out for May's hand, Jeffrey appears and takes April's hand. May encourages her sister to go with him. As she studies Jeffrey walking away with April on his arm, she convinces herself that he only wanted to dance with his sister-in-law when the opportunity presented itself. After all, April hasn't been around much that evening. For that matter, May wonders, where has April been?

She steps out onto the balcony, now filled with guests, looks out over the yard, and pulls the key out of her pocket. Anger rises in her at August's audacity in giving this key to her here, at the party, right in front of Jeffrey. Surely, it could have waited until tomorrow. After all, it was just a childhood hiding spot. And what was that about May Bear? May visualizes Hannah holding a stuffed animal that Hannah named May Bear. She feels guilty for not telling Jeffrey about the key earlier. She knows that he'll be furious with her for not confiding about the key and the secret place. If Jeffrey sees the key, he'll demand to know how she came by it that evening. How will she explain why she lied about August's sneaking the key into her hand? Her heart races as she envisions her marriage ending over this key. She must get rid of the key! She holds it in her hand on the rail, then casually lets it drop down into the shrubs below. There! If someone finds it, there will be no connection to her. She feels confident that she's done the right thing.

Peter steps onto the balcony, lighting a cigar. When he sees

May, he approaches her, saying, "Glad to see August returned after all!"

"Did you think he wouldn't return after his drunken outburst?" asks May.

"Drunken?" Peter looks at May, puffing on his cigar and pausing as if waiting to be told that she's only kidding. When she says nothing, he continues, "August wasn't drunk. Looked to me like a bit of teasing on Jeffrey's part. August didn't want any such playfulness from Jeffrey."

"What do you mean?"

"From what I saw, Jeffrey bumped into August like he was having a bit of fun. I suspect that August thought it was intentional and pushed him back. Jeffrey laughed it off and told August that he was being bullish, but August only became angrier. Jeffrey told August he should leave if he didn't know how to conduct himself at parties and walked away. Jeffrey was laughing, so I thought it was all fun and games. When Jeffrey was out of sight, August acted in the bizarre manner you witnessed."

"You're sure he wasn't drunk?"

"Yes, I'm sure. I'd been speaking to him for an hour before the incident between him and Jeffrey, and I never saw him have a drink, not even water. You know, now that I really think about it, I saw August looking around the ballroom. It wasn't until he saw you and April that he started doing those oddball dance moves. I figured he wanted your attention or something."

"I see. Yes, well, August has been known to be rather dramatic in his attempts to get attention!" May says nervously as she tries to explain, more to herself than to Peter, that the incident was nothing more than a misunderstanding.

"Yes, I know." Peter changes the subject. "It was nice seeing Marlene this evening. She's looking much better."

"Better? What do you mean?"

"I went to visit with them before the party today since they live so near the ballroom. I had some questions concerning their home expansion. When I arrived, both she and August were out front. She was very pale and left quickly after she greeted me. When I asked August if she was ill, he said that she'd heard some distressing news."

"So she wasn't ill, just upset?"

"Yes, that's right."

"I see."

May turns and looks out over the yard, grabbing the rail tightly to steady herself. Panic rises as her mind races over all the small, small incidents that have happened today. She fights to prevent them from coming together to form a picture that frightens her. The key? Marlene? Too many rushing memories, too many thoughts, then nothing. It's black.

I can't see or hear anything. "May?" I hear my own voice saying.

Chapter 10: Losing Jena

Again I call out, "May?" but there's no answer. My head feels foggy. It seems right that I should speak and hear myself speak. Yet, it seems wrong. I have a mouth; of course, I should be able to speak. But for some reason I couldn't speak before. Now, suddenly, I have a voice. It seems right that this room I'm in is windowless and dark, but also wrong. I feel like I've been in this dark windowless room before. But still I wonder, where are the lights? Where are the guests? I can't even say why I think there should be guests. Both a brightly lit room filled with guests and this dark, empty room seem right. How can the same thing be right and wrong? "May?"

"Is something wrong?" says a voice in the darkness.

"Can you help me? I can't find May."

"You shouldn't be up here. You need to come downstairs."

"Where are the guests?"

I hear footsteps approach. Then someone touches me. "Jeffrey?" I ask him. Why did I speak that name?

"Not Jeffrey. My friends call me Sonny. Come on; let me help you out of here. Can you get up?"

I'm lying down and I'm not sure why. "I think so." I struggle to move at first because I feel like I won't succeed, but I find that I can move this body, the body that's mine.

"Do you know where May is?" I ask as we walk toward what must be the stairs.

"No, I don't. Come on, now. Be careful. There are some steps missing. You really shouldn't be up here. Wait a minute. I'll help you down."

As I follow him down the steps and through the building, I continue to have a sense that this situation is both right and wrong. I even marvel at how I can walk. I raise my hand and watch in amazement as it moves when I command it.

"Is there someone I can call?" Sonny says as we step through the window.

"I don't know. Do you know May?"

"I don't know any May now," he says sadly. "What's your name?"

"Maybe it's May?"

"You think your name is May, and yet you're looking for May, is that right?" He looks at me with a confused expression, slowly shaking his head. Then he sees the cell phone attached to my fanny pack that I have in the front. He makes a gesture that I think means he'd like to use it, so I motion him to go ahead. When he shakes his head again, I realize that he might have been telling me to use it. I guess that makes more sense.

"Let's see if we can find someone to help," he says. "I'll redial the last number you called."

He says, "Hi. You don't know me, but . . ." Pause. "Well, Sonny." Pause. That's why I'm calling because of this woman. You say her name is Jena?" Pause. "No, no, she's right here. I didn't steal her phone." Pause. "Look, man, just be quiet and let me speak," he says defensively. "I found her here . . . at the old Dellner Ballroom." Pause. "Oh, getting here can be tricky, so I'll walk her out and we can meet out on Main Trail." Pause. "She was asking for May. Do you know who May is?" Pause. "May. She said May." Pause. "When I asked, she said that she thought her name was May." Pause. "She's really confused and scared." Pause. "Sure, no problem."

He hands the phone to me. "The man on the phone would like to speak to you."

I put the phone to my ear. "Jena? Jena?" says a voice that sounds both strange and familiar.

I look at Sonny. "He's asking for Jena. Who's that?" All the while, the man on the phone speaks the name Jena more frantically.

"The man says that's your name."

"I'm Jena?" I say to Sonny and the man on the phone.

"Stop it, Jena!" says the man on the phone, his voice jumping to new levels of concern and fear. "This isn't funny. Who is May?"

"Do you know May?" I ask. "Are you Jeffrey?"

"Who the hell is Jeffrey?" he bellows into the phone as his voice shifts quickly from concern to anger.

Handing the phone back to Sonny, I say, "He's yelling at me. I don't want to talk to him."

Sonny listens for a bit, then hands the phone back to me. "He says he's sorry but he's just really scared. He knows you. He says he's your husband, Ben, and that your name is Jena."

He's scared? I don't know who or where I am. I thought the person on the phone was Jeffrey. Even as I thought it, it also felt wrong, as if the person on the phone couldn't possibly be Jeffrey. Then there's the problem of May. I think I'm May, yet, at the same time, I feel like I should be looking for May. That would mean I'm not May, because then I'd be looking for myself, which doesn't make any sense. I just know there's a May and there's a Jeffrey. I don't know where they are, I don't know how I got here, and he thinks he's scared! "I'm here," I say at last.

Ben says, "Good. The other line should be ringing. Be sure to answer it."

The cell phone makes beeping sounds. Sonny explains, "You have a call on another line coming in. Here. Answer it." I like this Sonny guy. He's nice, and he towers over me in a protective and comforting sort of way. He's an older man, maybe seventy or so—hard to say. Looks like he's spent a lot of time outdoors and keeps active. He has smile lines around his mouth and a deeply furrowed brow. So he smiles a lot while he thinks?

"Hello," I say.

"Jena?"

"So they say. Who are you?"

"This is Katri. We'll be with you soon. Okay? Just follow Sonny and he'll lead you out. We're going to fix this."

"Katri? Do you know who May is?"

"Yes, Jena, I know who May is. You told me all about her. But don't mention May to Ben."

"No problem. When I asked him if his name was Jeffrey, he got really bent out of shape!"

"Oh, I'll bet he did! We'll be there soon."

I put the phone away and continue walking alongside Sonny through the woods. He isn't following a trail, so I ask, "Do you know where you're going? I don't see any path."

"I sure do."

"That's good! At least one of us does. Thanks for helping me."

"No problem," he says.

As we step out onto a wide trail. "This is Main Trail. Your friends will be meeting you here. Yes, I see two people in the distance there. I'll leave you to meet your friends. It was a pleasure to finally meet you, Jena." He turns away and walks back off into the woods.

"Finally?" I call after him. He doesn't turn back.

Ben and Katri run over to me, along with a very unhappy, growling cat. "Sweetie Pie?" I ask as I reach for my cat.

"Good grief, how can you know the cat's name and not mine or your own?" Ben's eyes are weighed down with sadness. "Katri here hasn't been any help. She insisted that I bring the cat."

"I'm not really sure, Ben, but I have an idea what happened," Katri says. "Probably won't make any sense." Ben glares at Katri as she tries to explain. "I think that Jena just lost her sense of self, which is why I wanted you to bring Sweetie Pie. I thought it would help to jog her memory. The attachments we form with animals are more unconditional than our attachments to people."

Ben, his face contorted with worry, gives me a tight hug. I like this Ben; he's rather cuddly. I look at Katri and say, "Is he really mine?" To which she nods. "Lucky me! I really have good taste."

They both laugh, and Ben adds, "That sounds like my Jena. Now, Katri, what do you mean by 'sense of self'?"

Katri, who is standing behind Ben so that he can't see her, nods her head rapidly, signaling me to agree that I'm back to myself. "Yes, Ben," I say obediently. "I'm feeling better. I'm sorry I just got really confused with losing my, um, 'sense of self.'" Katri appears relieved. I'm glad because I don't know what she means by "sense of self." I lost my sense of self, the cat brought it back, and these strangely familiar people are happy that a cat can do such a thing. In any case, Ben seems to trust Katri's opinions. He doesn't press her for further information.

We all continue down Main Trail until we reach a children's playground where Katri and Ben lead me to a bench overlooking the river. I point to a house across the river and say, "Oh, now, that's a lovely house." Katri pinches me, alarmed. "We know." Then she and Ben say in unison what I was just about to say, "I love my house!"

"Ben? How about you take Sweetie Pie back and I'll sit here with Jena? I can talk to her and try to sort out what happened."

"I want to know what's going on. I was scared. Katri, you didn't hear her when I first spoke to her. She sounded like a different person."

As Ben and Katri converse, I study their familiar faces. Even more familiar is the feeling that Katri knows more than she's confessing to know. This feeling doesn't worry me; rather, I find it to be an endearing quality in this Katri person.

"Ben, Jena and I talked about some things a few days ago. I don't have enough information to explain. Once we figure it out, we can try to explain it to you. Just give me some time alone with Jena."

Ben hesitates, clearly unsure what to do. I give him a huge smile, which seems to convince him. When he's far enough away that he can't hear me, I say to Katri, "That Ben guy is a lot nicer than Jeffrey."

"Jena? What are the names of your other cats?"

"I have others?" She nods, so I think for a minute. "Well, the names Fluffy, Fooffula, and Pookachoo come to mind. Am I close? Pookachoo is a stupid name; well, actually, they're all stupid. Please tell me I didn't think of all of them."

"Those are their names, and yes, you named most of them. But there's a story about how Fooffula got her name. Can you tell it to me?"

Rather like water being poured into a bowl, a story pools in my mind. "When Fooffula was a kitten, she used to sit on my chest. She laid her furry head close to my ears as she cleaned her outstretched paw, which rested on the side of my face. From that angle, she reminded Ben of Dracula, so he called her Fooffula. It was a combination of Dracula and her original name, Fooffy." The bowl isn't full, though, and I struggle to remember more about Ben, Katri, the house, and the cats.

Katri nods approvingly. She unwraps a candy bar, handing me a piece of chocolate. "Yum, I love chocolate." I take a bite and spit it out as a cardboard-flavored abomination assaults my tongue. Almost immediately, I feel a surge of recognition. "What's this crap you've given me? Tell me, Katri. What happened today?" I know who I am, why I'm here, and, more important, that my good friend just tried to give me cheap chocolate. Kick me when I'm down. She was probably trying to distract me and prevent rising panic, but cheap chocolate? That's a low blow! What if I hadn't fully recovered? I might have eaten it!

Now I remember being in the ballroom in May's memory.

She was worried about her brother when I left her memory. I understand now. I lost my identity.

"Jena is back! Recovery is complete!" she says, hugging me with unusual exuberance.

"And do you think I'm going to forget that imitation chocolate you just gave me? Do you have any real chocolate?" Thankfully, she redeems herself by handing over a quality chocolate bar, which I cheerfully eat. Yes, in spite of my ordeal, somehow this chocolate soothes me. I ask her, "How did you know how to help me?"

"Like I told Ben, I don't really understand all the details myself, but I was pretty sure that if we could carefully make you see who you really are, your own thoughts would return, and, well, it's no secret that chocolate, cats, and Ben are your anchors. You really have a strong sense of self, of who you are. Usually, that is. When I'm not interfering.

"Do you remember when I told you that you needed to really concentrate when you're in the ballroom? I'm sorry. I was wrong. You need to maintain your own identity when you're there, and I believe you do that by just, well, being you."

"Wrong? Katri is wrong? I need a bullhorn! I need to share this." I get up, pointing my hands here and there doing my little victory dance. "I must mark this day in history when Katri Evers admits she's wrong. It's time to buy lottery tickets! We could win millions! Woo hoo!"

Katri is seldom wrong because she thinks almost everything through before acting, mulling for days over the pros and cons of a trip or a purchase. This habit has the disadvantage of being time-consuming and causing some opportunities to be lost. That's where I come in, charging ahead to seize the moment. I'm all for careful deliberations of major purchases, but when you're trying to decide if you should have a nonfat latte or a mocha latte, for heaven's sake, just go for the mocha!

"Yes, I'm glad you're amused. Honestly! I'm happy to see you smile. I was worried when Ben called. So, please, Jena, you must maintain your sense of self. Be yourself, wherever you are. Get lost in thought—naturally, not when you're driving—but always be yourself."

"Oh, yes, now that makes a huge amount of sense to me! How exactly do I 'maintain a sense of self'?" It's exasperating listening to Katri. Although her words are guarded, the truth is in her eyes, and it isn't what she's saying.

"When you're thinking about May's memories, remember yourself. Don't allow May's thoughts to be the only thoughts in your head. Go ahead; throw in that cheerful Jena commentary."

"So you're telling me to pay less attention?" She nods. "To allow my own thoughts to stray while others are talking?" She nods again. "To add in my own view and to . . . ."

"Yes! Enough already. I got the point, and you got the point, too." Katri doesn't laugh or smile. Instead, she looks out at the river. In a rare unguarded moment, her face is showing the pain of moments she's never spoken of before.

Hopeful that she may be willing to share more information, I ask, "Katri, do you know who May is?"

"Not really, but I know that you need to go back to the ballroom and figure it out."

"I don't know. That Sonny guy said I shouldn't be in the ballroom."

"And am I to believe you're going to stop and listen? Like you listened to Adam? Hey, why did Sonny run off?"

"He didn't say; I didn't ask. He was nice. I think he knows who May is, but he wouldn't admit it. You know, there was something even more unusual about him. Right before he walked away, he said, 'It's a pleasure to finally meet you.' He looks sort of familiar, but I don't recall ever meeting him."

"Maybe you've seen him at the supermarket or somewhere like that?" Katri says, jumping up as the fog of yesterday's pain clears away. "Let's go back to the ballroom. I'll go with you."

"What about Ben? Isn't he expecting me back?"

"I never said how long we'd be talking. He won't know."

"If Adam knew you were encouraging me to go into an abandoned building, he'd get bent out of shape about it."

"Not nearly as much if he realized I was going to go into that building, too."

More seriously, I add, "We really need to talk more sometime. I need to know what you know."

"I agree, but later, okay? Back to the ballroom." She walks off, thrusting her arms in front.

"Back to the ballroom," I repeat.

Chapter 11: Realization

We walk in silence to the ballroom. Katri is preoccupied, taking frequent long, deep breaths. I've never seen her so out of sorts and disengaged with her surroundings. For all my teasing, I'm always aware of what's happening around me. Katri isn't. I wish she would tell me what she's thinking. I'm beginning to realize that what's happening isn't just some Jena-type fantasy. The writing was on the wall and I saw it, but I didn't want to read it. Isn't that what May is doing? She isn't reading the writing on the wall, either. I don't know yet why I'm involved, or even whether Katri knows, but whatever she knows is deeply troubling to her.

I recall that Sonny knew a different path to the ballroom, which connected with Main Trail, but I'm not in a frame of mind to remember it, so I'm leading us my roundabout way. At some point, I'll have to look at a map of the Betta Conservation Land and see if I can figure it out. Since the ballroom is near the lake, I might be able to determine its general location on a map.

"Here! This is how I get to the ballroom."

Katri only nods and continues silently through the woods, her face reflecting a mixture of emotions fighting to express themselves. She bites her lip. Is that an attempt to keep the expressions at bay? Or is the bit lip one of the expressions that fought free?

Even though she's quiet, I'm glad she's come with me. I'm nervous about going back to May's memory. It was nice in the beginning when it was pretty dresses and fancy snacks, but now it's too intense, and I find it difficult to shake off the sadness.

We reach the gravel road and Katri stops, surveying the field and asking, "Is this the ballroom?"

"The ballroom is beyond those trees. This is an empty field. What are you talking about?"

"I don't know what's real in your memories."

"Remember the abandoned building? I mentioned it. That was real!"

"Well, you also said you saw a painting with May in a blue dress and that wasn't real," she says defensively, walking quickly past me.

I stare after her, feeling a combination of shock, surprise, and irritation. "Katri?"

"Come on, Jena. We don't have a lot of time today. I promise that when I understand more, I'll explain more." She sprints ahead, leaving me little choice but to follow her. How can I stare at her with my hands on my hips and demand to know what she knows if she's gone?

When I finally catch up with her, she's approaching the side entrance to the ballroom. She looks more enthralled with it than I was when I first saw it, that rather nostalgic look of a walk down memory lane. She sees me approaching, then bounds up the steps and jumps through the window with renewed energy.

I follow her. "Have you been here before?"

Her voice wavers and she says as she leads me to the stairs, "Maybe. Come on. Let's go up to the ballroom."

When we reach the top step, I ask, "Katri, when I step into May's memory, I don't know what my body does. Could you let me know? And try not to talk to me or make noises because it might pull me out."

"Sure, I can do that. It's dark up here." She climbs up and turns left while I follow her up, stopping to look into the darkness she walked into. I hear a click, then I see a dim light. "There," she calls down. "Some light."

"Well if I'd known there was a switch down there, I'd have turned the little light on, too!"

"Did you try feeling around for it?"

"What was that you said about being wrong again? I was way too busy with more important things, and besides, there are a lot of lights where I'm going!" Odd, whatever made her check for lighting in an abandoned building? For that matter, why does this building have power?

"Well, off with you. Don't swing from any chandeliers."

I walk toward the balcony, dreading what I'll discover and shift easily into May's memory.

May is standing where I left her when Sarah walks up. "Oh, here you are! I've gathered the entire family for a dance."

May smiles weakly and follows her mother. The Lanlores and the Dellners walk to the middle of the ballroom. All the women are lined up on one side and all men on the other. They approach their partners and walk around each other and back to their original spots. As May looks up at Jeffrey, her heart melts. She longs to find more reason to make sense of everything, so that it isn't so frightening. I say to her, "*May, haven't you learned anything? No wonder you caused me to lose my sense of self. Don't trust that guy.*" It makes me feel better speaking to her, even if she can't hear my words of wisdom.

The song seems to end rather quickly. More likely, I've spent a fair amount time amusing myself with unrelated thoughts, anything I can think of to distract myself from the anguish brewing in May. The lights, the dancing, the architectural details no longer enthrall me. The only thing left to feel is May's numb, melancholy mood. She repeatedly fails to find a nontrivial explanation for what's happening. With a heavy heart, she dances and smiles. I catch glimpses of her in the mirror. She looks lovely; no one would guess the torment she feels.

Sarah scurries around, chatting happily with their guests and giving May some freedom. May perks up when she spots April's pink hat bobbing down the stairs. Seeing a chance to have some time alone with her sister, she waves at Jeffrey and points to the front lawn. He nods and smiles. Apparently, he didn't see April. May reaches the bottom of the steps in time to see April turn left. Her heart racing with the prospect of finding some answers, she follows April until they both reach the painting room. April opens the door and walks in. As she starts to close the door, May stops it. April shakes her head to May and whispers, "We can't be seen talking."

"Then hurry so I can shut the door! Walk through the painting room and go out the back door to the lake. I have to tell you something that Peter told me." May takes April's hand and leads her to the far door and then into the hallway. They pass a large double door on the left, which I suspect opens onto a stairway to the basement, and the open door to the kitchen, where the cooks are still busy preparing food. May steps out of the back door with her sister's hand in her own, they follow the path to the lake, and then sit down on the bench overlooking the lake.

May asks, "Do you remember ice-skating on the lake, April?" She thinks back to when she was six and April held her hand, offering instructions on how to skate. The sweet memory brings back times when my sisters have helped me. I snap out of my own thoughts, worried that I might miss something important if I don't pay attention.

"Yes! Like the time Augy pulled us, zooming around in a snake chain on the lake, and he thought we were screaming with delight. Remember how sorry he was when he realized how much he'd scared us?"

May's eyes tear up as she remember. "Yes, we milked that for weeks. I had him sit down to tea with me and my dolls. He spoke to each of the dolls and poured their tea! Naturally, I didn't laugh, I was so happy to have my big brother for tea. I remember introducing each of my dolls to him, and he said to each one, 'Pleased to meet you.' Not many brothers would have done that."

"Yes, we could always count on Augy to be the defender of weak, the silent, the injured, and the sad. Augy to the rescue. This lake is where he first met Marlene. Do you remember that?"

"Yes, I do! He was about sixteen and was dashing around from child to child, providing first aid and skating tips and wiping away their tears. Marlene glided gracefully up to him. I remember him looking up and falling backwards because she was so pretty. Naturally, he denied it for years; he didn't admit until his wedding day to me that he was literally knocked over. He recovered quickly and said, 'Oh, good. You can skate, so you can help me.' He didn't ask her. He just assumed that she would help. Fortunately for him, Marlene eagerly twirled and whirled herself over to the group of children by the shore. I was sitting right here when August approached her to thank her for helping. Before he could speak, she raised her hand to stop him and said, 'I'm glad to help. It's the reason God gave me hands.' I think August was hooked right there. I don't think I've ever seen Marlene behave crossly with anyone." The images pass through May's mind, allowing me to see them, much like seeing through her eyes. I even get a sense of the crisp chill in the air.

They both look toward the lake. May thinks back to when they were preteens, taking turns doing a swizzle or a twirl and waiting for the other to imitate it just as they'd done in their ballroom routine that evening. April, being older, was more skilled in some steps than May and helped her learn them. After they managed to execute a series of steps each created, they would put them all together. Her memories drift over many different skating sessions where I see many steps that didn't fit together, resulting in clunky moves, tangled sisters, and much laughter.

May breathes in deeply and says, "I need to tell you what

Peter told me."

"I think I know. I spoke to Peter earlier today. That was why you noticed a change in me. I also thought August had too much to drink, which was why he acted up. Mother told me about some problems he was causing with the family business. She wanted me to keep him away from you; she felt that it wasn't a real concern and thought you might not handle it well. She told me how you fainted a week ago. I was convinced that you weren't well enough to handle any stress. I really thought I was protecting you." She shakes her head as May tries to speak. "Please let me finish, May. I also felt special to be included in the family business. You know how Mother always argued that we women shouldn't be involved. She even told me earlier that I should be more like you.

"Peter and I started talking about Augy by accident. That was when I learned that Augy wasn't drunk. What really upset me was when I learned that he didn't start his weird dance moves until after Jeffrey walked away and he saw us." April holds her hands to her heart as if that will ease its aching, her young face now a sorrowful display of remorse.

She gazes out over the lake, where the moonlight glistens off the water, and faint shimmers of light make their way through the trees from the ballroom. The subtle lights surround April's face as if to comfort her.

With each breath, her voice wavers, and she struggles to continue. "Then I remembered something Augy and I said would be our secret, just between the two of us. He said that if he ever felt like we were in danger, he would do what he called the 'danger dance.' He said that if one of us was scared enough to act so silly, dance around and say nonsense, that the other should come running to help. I agreed. A family always stuck together. We were kids!

"After talking to Peter, I finally started putting all the pieces together. When Jeffrey suggested that I go to Augy, I jumped at the chance. It hurt to know that Augy thinks I let him down! When he needed me the most, I failed him."

"Why didn't you go to August?"

"I tried. Someone stopped me."

"The man I saw in the trees? He pushed you, didn't he, April?"

"Yes. May, you must not breathe a word of this to anyone!

Anyone!"

"Who was it? Who was out there? I'll tell Jeffrey! He was out there, too! Maybe he saw who attacked you! He'll help!"

Has May gone mad? How can she not be aware that Jeffrey is part of the problem? Is she listening to her sister? If only May could hear me, someone with an unbiased opinion could shed a reasonable light on this situation. *"Listen to me! Don't trust Jeffrey."* It's frustrating to sit silently by.

"May! No! No! Tell me you haven't spoken to Jeffrey! Oh, no. When we spoke in the painting room earlier today, I wanted to say, 'Whatever you do, don't repeat this to anyone, not even Jeffrey or Mother.' But that's when Jeffrey and Mother walked in. What did you say to him?"

"There wasn't much to say! You didn't tell me anything in the painting room."

"What did you tell Jeffrey?"

"I only said that you'd take care of it."

April gasps, "That's enough! May, you must go back inside and not let anyone know that you've spoken to me."

"Jeffrey will help you."

"May, listen to me! Listen to me! Jeffrey is too close to the problem to see the dangers. Whatever he hears, he repeats. The Lanlores have enemies, May, and Jeffrey has unwittingly sided with them. You have a chance, May. You must look out for your baby and Hannah."

"Hannah? The baby? What are you saying? Do you think Jeffrey would allow anyone to hurt us?"

April hesitates, "No! No! I really must find Augy and warn him. I'll walk through the woods, make my way to his house, and wait for him there. I can't be seen leaving. No one can know I've left the party. No one can know that we spoke!"

"If I hadn't been kept in the dark to begin with, this wouldn't have happened."

"I'm not blaming you. I should have told you! Please don't blame yourself. We aren't sure who we can trust. The innocent look guilty, the guilty appear innocent. Mother thought her actions were for the good of the family, but she doesn't know. If we try to warn her, she'll tell Jeffrey, and we know where that will go." April takes May's hands. "Don't blame yourself, May. I should have gone to Augy. He was counting on me to go to him."

"The key! Oh, no. The key!"

"What key?"

"August and I had our secret, too, in case of danger," May wails. "It was our secret place. He knew the location and I had the key. We would keep special toys there. Before the ball, he asked me for the key. He told me he had very important business papers that he needed to put away. At the ball, when he returned with Marlene, he put the key in my hand, and I threw it away. Oh, April, he tried—he tried to talk to me, but I wouldn't allow it."

"Don't worry, May. The location is more crucial than the key. We can always break in or beat it open! Do you have any idea where the hiding place is?"

"No, but can't we ask him tomorrow?"

"Oh, May, don't blame yourself. No one knew this was coming. I had no idea of the danger. Your only hope is that Jeffrey doesn't know we spoke." April's eyes are cloudy with tears as she stands up.

"April, we can ask him tomorrow!"

"There may be no tomorrow for August. May, you have to go back. I'll go through the woods on the other side, so we're not seen leaving the same area."

As they hug, May whispers in April's ear, "April, May Bear knows where it is." April nods to show that she understands and the sisters run off in separate directions.

"Jena?"

I'm watching April run into the forest and I hear my name. May sighs and turns toward the ballroom. As she makes her way down the path, I not only hear my name but I also feel something touching me. Not May, but me.

"Jena, it's late. We need to go."

I jump, startled that I can hear and feel when I'm in May's mind. My hearing is different, as if the person speaking has her hands tightly over her mouth, but the oddity of someone touching me when I'm in May's mind is even more disconcerting.

Katri is standing beside me in the dimly lit ballroom. She says, "It's okay. It's just me. Sorry I scared you, but we need to go. Are you okay?"

"I'm fine now. It was rather freaky, though. I heard you while I was still in May's mind."

"That explains it."

"Explains what?"

"You came out ready to fight. I'll remember next time to avoid touching you! Ben called several times. He wants to know what we're up to. We have to agree on what to say. Let's go."

"How long have I been out?" I ask as I follow Katri out of the ballroom.

"About four hours."

"I've noticed that when I interject my own thoughts while I'm in May's mind, more of my time passes than if I remain quiet." She gives me a warning look, so I raise my hands in protest and say, "Yes, I know. I'd rather lose a few hours than my mind, or, as you say, my 'sense of self.' So tell me, did you see what my body was doing in the ballroom?"

Katri looks puzzled, and I can tell she's weighing her words carefully. "You were mostly in the darkness and I couldn't see very well. You moved around some and I thought you . . . I'm not sure what it was . . . you rather faded, but it probably had to do with the dim lighting. A few times, you spoke aloud, but I couldn't hear what you said from where I was. I went outside for a while, too."

She looks content with her response. I can tell that further questions won't lead to further answers, so instead I say, "I see. Thanks. Back to our 'what's our story?' That is, what are we going to tell Ben?"

"I don't think we should tell Ben any of this because it's a little out there, you know!"

"But you believe me. Why wouldn't Ben?"

Katri bites her lip. "We're walking slowly. Let's try to pick up the pace."

I persist, "Katri, Ben needs to know something. Remember what happened earlier today. I even called him Jeffrey. Oh, was he livid about that."

"I have an idea."

Katri's ideas usually involve blaming me. Well, to her credit, I'm often the one that gets us into tight places like the time I convinced her to skate the twenty-two-mile rail trail. I figured she was in such good shape that she could easily handle the round trip. After all, I can, and I don't jog every morning! Naturally, I conveniently didn't consider that my muscles are far more accustomed to inline skating than hers. Wouldn't you know that had to be a day when we had a steady supply of light sprinkles while we were skating back? She was tired and eager to get back, so she kept trying to push herself to keep her momentum going. I did tell her not to push off so hard since her skates could slip out from under her! She didn't have any kneepads on—again, not my fault. I always wear protective gear. Back then, Katri wore only a helmet and wrist guards. To make a long story short, she took a long, hard slide on her bare knees, and we had to call Ben to come pick us up to take Katri to the hospital. Everyone blamed me even though she had a hand in her own fall. Now, here we are again. She encouraged me to go back to the ballroom, strike one. She discouraged me from being me, strike two. No way am I going to take the fall!

"No! Absolutely not! We're not putting this all on me!"

"Why not? It's more believable. He already thinks you're a little nuts to begin with. I, being a doctor, can be the one helping you. It's a perfect plan . . . ."

"Yeah, for you! He thinks I'm 'cute nuts,' and you're suggesting 'certifiably nuts.' No way, because then you escape unscathed. In this plan of yours, there's nothing about what you encouraged and put me up to! I'm not so sure I'd have even gone back to the ballroom if it weren't for you. Your plan won't work. There have to be some mind-altering drugs. We just need to figure out how I got this drug and how I accidentally took it. Do any of them look like chocolate? That might be believable. Anything on the news about crazed people drugging tea at coffee shops?"

"The mood-altering-drug idea has some potential, but not having it slipped in your drink at a coffee shop. Drugging drinks might happen in a crowded dance club but not at a coffee shop over tea and latte."

"But the being-drugged idea has potential! Hey, do you carry any on you? Could one have fallen out of your purse, say doing kickboxing? I thought it was a pain reliever, I had a headache, and that was that. No, a better idea, and one that doesn't involve my doing something stupid. I asked you for a pain reliever, and you handed it to me. Yes! Bingo! It's your fault."

"I don't really like that idea."

"Well, tough. You know a lot more than you're telling me, so you can start taking some of the slack, too. I'm not going to have my good name tainted anymore."

"What about *my* good name?"

"It's so clear and unmarred that this will barely scratch the surface."

Chapter 12: Human Nature

Having sorted out the details for the story we're going to tell Ben, Katri and I walk silently back to her car. I've been holding my tongue, distressed that she's even more sullen than when we walked here. As I study her face, I realize that I don't want to push her too hard on what she knows because I think she's hurting. I must choose my questions carefully. I think she isn't speaking up because she honestly doesn't know how it all fits together, and she's afraid that her words could jeopardize the very progress and answers she seeks. It pains me to see such a distant look on my long-time friend's face. She isn't daydreaming or contemplating what chores to do next. She's thinking of banished moments from her tormented life; moments that are now fighting and clawing their way back in.

"Katri?" I venture tentatively. "Earlier today, on the phone, you said you know who May is. What do you know about her?"

"You mentioned her at dinner two nights ago. Remember? The blue dress and the painting."

"But do you know who she is?" I repeat.

She shrugs, which could mean a yes or a no.

"Have you heard of Jeffrey, April, or August?"

Another shrug.

"How about instead of me playing Twenty Questions and you giving open-air shrugs, you volunteer all the information you're willing to share. I, in return, won't keep prodding you for more information. How does that sound?"

"I know who August is," she answers.

That's it? I have to fight hard not to say that aloud because I can see how difficult it is for her to speak.

She adds in a quiet voice, "Tell me what you've seen."

"Oh, man, don't get me started! I'm irritated with the entire Calendar family."

"Why do you call them the Calendar family? Aren't they the Lanlores?"

"Well, yes, they are," I say, eyeing her suspiciously, "but I adopted Calendar as their last name when I, ah, first, ah, met them." I look at her with a big smile but she's not watching me. It makes my heart ache to see Katri, who's usually so strong and so vocal about the silly things that I do and say, so unresponsive. I'm determined to cheer her up. "When I learned their names, I had to ponder what would happen if the twelfth child was a boy and the only name left was June. Would they name him June? Then the days of the week could be the grandkids. Naturally, they'd be limited to seven. The great-grandkids would have a huge pot of names to choose from, with hours and minutes. One, two, three, four, five."

"I've got it! I've got it," she says with a small laugh. "There's all this activity going on around you, and you're not too concerned as to where you are and how you got there. Instead, you're giving nicknames to the people and cracking jokes about their names? Is that correct?"

"Yes, on my first trip there, that's about right. There were also those really awful-looking fish things May ate. She passed up the chocolate desserts, and they really looked good! That's why I had Ben buy that chocolate mousse cake for dinner a few nights back."

"I don't know how you manage it, Jena. Your brain goes in a hundred directions at once!"

"It's called multitasking! I'm quite good at it. Occasionally, I forget a thing or two, but usually I keep it all straight."

"Are you free for lunch tomorrow?"

"Lunch is good. Where? When? Noontime works for me, but then we'll need to deal with the lunch crowd."

"Faneuil Hall. Noon is best for me. Go on with your story."

"May had a sip of a really smooth red wine. I could have just gulped that entire glass down! She didn't finish it, though. When did all the publicity about not drinking while you're pregnant start up?"

"May was pregnant?" she asks.

"Yes. I thought that maybe she didn't finish her wine because she was pregnant. She just had this dainty sip. But anyhow . . . ." I stop myself. I was about to rub in that when I returned to May's memories on subsequent visits, I didn't allow myself so many of my own thoughts because of Katri's advice to listen more carefully, but I realize that this isn't a good time to tease her.

"Yes. But anyhow?"

"Anyhow, what I was complaining about during

kickboxing is that May is so gullible. She gets on really well with her brother and sister, August and April, and she senses that something is wrong, but she tries to argue it away. But earlier in the evening, she did notice something wrong with her sister, some unusual behavior. Oh. No, wait. That was me who didn't really trust her sister. Now I'm confusing my opinions with May's. May doesn't always get the same disconcerting feelings that I do. I didn't trust April earlier, but as the day progressed, I changed.

"This entire scene makes me think of a burning building. One guy sees a building on fire, flames shooting out, and he tells his friend to call the fire department. A more trusted friend says that he thinks it's nothing to bother about and another friend agrees. So the first guy feels the heat of the flames, but reasons that two of his good friends aren't concerned, so why should he be? He ignores his gut instinct and lets the house burn down even though his brother is screaming, 'Fire! Fire!' . . . ."

"I get the point!" she says, looking at me as if I just flew in from Mars and I'm jabbering in Martian.

"No, let me finish. Anyhow, the brother . . ."

"I have a better idea. Tell me what you saw in May's memory rather than making an analogy!"

"I'm getting there. August dances around in this jerky odd-ball fashion at the ball, so Jeffrey throws him out or tells him to leave or something. May finds it disturbing to see her brother behave so strangely. Ordinarily, they run to each other's aid, but May was waylaid by her sister and later by her mother and Jeffrey.

"It really irks me that May didn't put her foot down and trot off to talk to her brother. Nooo! She continues to allow herself to be pulled and pushed every which way. This one time, Sarah, May's mother, intentionally redirects May after Jeffrey signals to her that they're going the wrong way, and May just follows along. She even realized that her mother was manipulating her, but she always manages to come up with an explanation. She never noticed that her mother and Jeffrey were conspiring. Come on! How could she miss it? I saw it, and it was with her eyes."

"May must have also been looking at something else. What was she focusing on?"

"Hmmm. Not sure. I guess I wasn't really focusing on the same thing, so I saw something different. Oh, no, it was April. She was looking more at April, I think."

"Why do you say, 'Oh, no?' What's so terrible about looking at April?"

"Because May missed Jeffrey's hand gesture entirely. It gets much worse because then this businessman, Michael, comes over and starts talking to May! Oh, I forgot. Earlier in the day, Michael approached Jeffrey and May and was asking about August. May was surprised that Jeffrey and August would be doing business with the same person. She tried to ask about it, but Jeffrey cut her off and diverted the conversation away. So later, Michael saw May and Sarah and joined them. This time, when the slightest mention of business came up, Sarah diverted the conversation. May was clueless. She just found more excuses to explain away their behavior.

"At one point, May managed to escape her mother's watchful eye, and she saw April outside, at the edge of the clearing, arguing with a man whose face she couldn't see, so neither could I. Then she heard that April was seen walking with Jeffrey. Can you believe that she completely missed the connection? So much happened and so much of it connects to other pieces! Later, when April told May not to trust anyone, May suggested that they ask Jeffrey for help."

"Later?"

"Yes, she met up with April when she finally managed to sneak away from her captors."

"It's hard to listen and get through these trees and shrubs without banging myself up," says Katri as she battles with tree limbs and saplings. "How ever did you find this way?"

We've been off the gravel road for some time now and are following the markings I made on the trees through the woods. "I followed Sweetie Pie."

"You mean you were really serious about following the cat through the woods? I thought you were kidding!"

"Yes, he was hungry and it seemed natural to continue going this direction. Hey, I made it out and in good time. Oh, speaking of which, if you have a map of the conservation land with you, there's a shortcut from the side trail to Dirt Road. Since the side trail isn't on the map, just look for a trail that starts on Dirt Road and dead-ends around a stream. The stream is on the map. We won't have to walk back to Main Trail."

I wait while Katri pulls out her map to locate the side trail.

"Where was I?" I say as she folds up the map and puts it away, looking at me. "Yes, the buffet table. Did I mention that May ate these shrimp things? They were disgusting! Can you believe it? She passes by chocolate for cat food."

"You mentioned *fish* things."

The sounds of crunching tree limbs are suddenly gone. Alarmed, I spin around. Katri grins proudly, shaking her head, her eyes twinkling. "What did I do? What?"

"Listen to you! From danger to name jokes to shrimp to danger again to chocolate. But I'm not complaining. It's a good thing, really! Go on."

"It was a very busy party! Many twists and turns. Let's not forget, I had to follow May's thoughts, and what she sees, hears, and says, and deal with my own thoughts, too. When I think, I don't hear what's happening, so I'm interpreting on the fly! It really is a lot of work, you know." I stop, with my hands pressed firmly on my hips, awaiting an apology.

"You're right, Jena. That's a lot of information to process. It's no secret that we can't participate effectively in two conversations! Sorry. Go on. You were at the buffet table eating something you found unsavory."

"Exactly! And if it wasn't trauma enough that she ate those fishy things and put down that delicious glass of wine . . . Well!" I shake my head in indignation. "You know how I love chocolate?" I look back to see Katri slapping her hands to her face and mouthing "*No!*" in mock horror. I continue fuming, "Not one! She didn't eat one of those delicious-looking little chocolate desserts."

"You've mentioned the chocolate."

"It was important enough to repeat. Now, back to the Calendar family. May managed to escape her mother's watchful eye and was just about to chat with her sister when Jeffrey stopped her. He actually grabbed her arm to prevent her from going outside. Can you believe that? May fell and awoke in a room they referred to as the painting room. Her family rallied around her, promising to give her some room. Later, when she went outside to clear her head, this parking attendant told her that her brother wasn't drunk!"

"I'm confused. Who was in the painting room with May? Was it only Jeffrey and April?"

"Oh, did I skip that? When May regained consciousness,

Sarah, Jeffrey, April, and May's father, Wendel, were all sitting around her. April had a scratch on her face, too, no doubt from the struggle with Jeffrey, but April said that she tripped. He's a clever one! I have to give that to him!"

"Jeffrey?"

"Yes, Jeffrey. When he failed to control her actions, he changed his strategy. He told her that he thought their relationship couldn't withstand all the family pressures and that she put him last, blah, blah, blah. She fell for it! After all her worries, she fell for it. To make matters worse, she confided to him what April said to her in the painting room earlier. They rejoined the party, and just then August returned with his wife, Marlene. Marlene was just beautiful, wearing this red . . . ."

Bam! Katri slams right into a branch. I look over to find her rubbing her scratched cheek.

"I was looking at you," she explains.

"Trust me. I know how you feel!"

"You know, Jena, one of the reasons I ran into the tree was that I was amazed that your hands reached out in front of you removing obstacles, yet your eyes were staring off into the distance, as if you were seeing the story again."

"I have a good explanation for that. You see, the person speaking has the luxury of walking while their hands go on autopilot, clearing obstacles out of the way. The person listening has to pay attention—no autopilot for them!"

"Is that how it works?"

"Yes. Please make a note of it." I imitate the voice on the recording you hear when the phone number you dial has changed.

"And why do you trip when you're talking if you have this skill?"

"Oh, yes. Very complicated process. If I'm telling the story, my hands and feet go on autopilot, but if I'm only conjecturing, there's no autopilot."

"You said you saw Marlene. What was she wearing?"

"A red ball gown. It was gorgeous. She and August had to be the most stunning couple there. They danced splendidly together!"

Katri walks faster and moves ahead of me, so I call after her. "Do you know the way back?"

"Yes. Just follow the lipstick-lined trees. You must have

used an entire tube of lipstick marking all these trees."

Soon, we step out onto the side trail, and Katri leads us to the shortcut. I see her hands reach up to her face a number of times, and I hear sniffling. I notice that she's working hard to stay a step or two ahead of me.

"Katri? Are you okay?"

"Yes. My allergies are acting up. Tell me about Marlene's gown."

I describe the gown to the best of my ability. "Why are we walking so fast?"

"I need to get home and take my medication before my allergies get out of hand."

"Allergies, you say? I don't recall you ever mentioning allergies before."

"It's only this time of year and particular types of trees," she snaps, picking up the pace. "You don't know everything about me, Jena!"

We reach Dirt Road and I decide to walk silently behind her. Her pace is one step below a jog, and I don't feel any need to rush. We reach her car, and, without looking at me, she gives me a quick hug. "Lunch tomorrow." With that, she gets into her car and drives off! I would have declined an offer for a ride back to my house as it's such a short walk, but she didn't even offer one!

Chapter 13: Lunch and Chocolates

I purchased my lunch, and I'm waiting in Faneuil Hall for Katri, who's half an hour late. She's a doctor, so I understand that problems with her patients can prevent her from leaving. I know that she's a thoughtful person who never makes anyone wait unless she can't help it, and I've been late on occasion myself.

She runs over, holding a bag, and says with a huge smile, "Sorry I'm late! I had to stop at a particular store and wait in a long line. The service was horribly slow."

"Been a busy day for you?" I say, eyeing her bag.

"Oh, yes, very busy. I have something for you, Jena, and I think you'll be very pleased!" She removes a smaller bag from the large one, holding it in both hands and tilting it up and down. Her exuberance rubs off on me, and I begin to get excited about the bag. In spite of the seesawing action and my own growing enthusiasm, I manage to make out the words on the bag: "Delectable Delights—in business for fifty years."

"Chocolate?" I ask, looking at her hopefully. It's times like this that I really love my friends and family!

She beams, pulls out a small box, and offers it to me.

The box is daintily wrapped in silver foil paper, with silver ribbons tied in a neat little bow. No wonder service was slow! I pull it out and set it on the table. Katri is all smiles as she urges me on to open it. I decide that even if it tastes awful, I'll pretend it's the best ever and hope she doesn't make a regular gift of it. I tug at the ribbons and paper to find a little white box. I comfort myself knowing that if tastes awful, there isn't much of it! So like her to bring only one small piece of something. I open the box and gasp. Before me is the same sweet chocolate confection that I saw in May's memory. It's a little square dessert lightly iced with delicate chocolate shavings. The icing cascades like ocean waves, much more appealing than the smooth, flat fondant style. Unfortunately, it's so tiny that it can only serve as an appetizer dessert.

"How did you find this? It's just like the chocolate I saw in May's memory." In seconds, the miniature chocolate confection is gone.

Katri points to the bag and says, "'In business for fifty years'! Their first shop was in Betta. I remember it from my childhood. They moved to downtown Boston about twenty-five years ago. The company had made such a big name for themselves after hosting so many parties for wealthy people that they wanted a bigger, more upscale location. I was sad because my mother said that it was too far to drive to the new location. They have a huge selection of potential Jena desserts, let me tell you. But I was looking for what you might have seen, so I finally had to ask them if they could point out chocolate desserts that have been staples for the last forty years or so."

"Do you have more there?"

She tosses the bag over to me, "I bought others in case the one I gave you wasn't the right one."

"Thank you!"

After we finish our lunch, she says, "I did want to talk to you, too."

"Sure, I'm listening! The elusive Katri speaks. What? Did Jeffrey do it in the den with a hammer?"

She flinches and continues. "About what you said yesterday, you know, about how gullible you think May is. I wanted to say that it's human nature not only to trust the people we love, but also to need to trust them. May's mother supports Jeffrey, so that's a blood tie providing more support for May's need to trust Jeffrey. It sounds like May is close to her mother. It's possible that her pregnancy can affect her emotions. I'm saying this because I want you to understand how easy it is to be misled."

"When you said you had something more to say, I was expecting something else, something more informative. Do you plan on explaining yourself?"

"I will. In time, I will." She stands up, ready to leave, and asks quietly, "Are you going back soon?"

"Yes! And I won't lose myself, either!"

Chapter 14: No Way In

In spite my distraction when I was walking with Katri a few days back, I manage to remember where the side trail connects with Dirt Road. The trail is already overgrown, and as the summer progresses, it will seem even less like a trail.

As I reach the side trail my phone rings and I see Katri's name on my caller ID. "Hello, Katri."

"Hi, Jena. Are you going to the ballroom today?"

"Yes. I'm on my way there now."

"I want you to do me a favor right now. Hang up and call me back."

"Well, okay. Give me a minute." I end the call and call her back. "Surprise! It's Jena calling. Why did you need me to call you?"

"I wanted my number on your redial."

"Why? Are you worried that something will happen to me?"

"No, but if you need me, I want you to be able to call me easily. And can you do me one more favor?"

"I'm listening."

"Can you keep repeating to yourself, 'If I need help, call Katri'?"

"Are you serious? What is this, some sort of emergency response preparedness?"

"Yes?" she asks in a pleading way.

"You're serious."

"Please, just repeat it as much as you're willing?"

"If you're not worried about me, why are you asking me to do this?"

"Maybe I am, just a little. Come on. It isn't too much to ask. Say it quietly to yourself."

"It'll make me hungry. I'll need more of those chocolates."

"Done! Thanks, Jena. If you need help, call me."

"I'll call Katri, I'll call Katri," I say like a robot as I hang up, noting that she didn't lecture me on my chocolate obsession. Many times, I've insisted that quality chocolate can be a cure-all for ailments and part of a healthy, balanced diet. Some nuts, some fruit, some cookies and, voila! A balanced and delicious meal is ready.

Repeating Katri's mantra leaves me feeling very silly, but I do it. Mainly, I'm nervous about why she asked because I can think of only one reason why she would suggest something so odd. She's seriously worried that something else will happen, but what could it be? I know about the sense of self now, and I know what to do to make sure I don't lose it again. All this speculation helps the time to pass quickly; I soon find myself walking on the gravel road up to the ballroom.

I make my way to the lake since I didn't really have a chance to admire the view a few days ago. I wonder if Sonny is the one who tends this trail. Whatever could motivate him to come out here, clear the path, plant flowers, and pull weeds?

Signs of life are springing up all over the lake. I sit on the bench admiring the tranquility of this spot. What fun a costume ball on ice skates would be!

This bench, it dawns on me, is where I last left May! Shouldn't I be in May's memory right now? I try to think about May, hoping that doing so will shift me into her memory, but even as I attempt it, I realize it won't work since previous shifts didn't require this sort of effort. The memory usually resumes wherever I left May. I panic, thinking that this might be the end, that the memories may be gone. No! I promised Katri. There must be more, and I bound over to the ballroom to seek them out.

I hop through the window and run up the steps, heading for the ballroom. My thoughts jump around as I review the different times I left the ballroom. Once, I was lying down on the second floor. All the other times, I was standing, and I always entered her memory from the second floor, which is also where I left her memory. This is all so random! I mean, if there's really some deep mystery to solve, it's just by chance that I stumbled on it! If it weren't for Katri's encouraging—make that begging—me to return, I doubt I'd have done so. But, then again, I did mark the way back so I could return. Moreover, I think back to all those times when I walked along Dirt Road and I had to fight the desperate urge to explore the restricted land. Did I somehow always know this memory was here? Since I followed Sweetie Pie, could he have known, too? As bizarre as that idea seems, is it any more bizarre than being able to shift into someone else's memories in the first place? Is my cat a memory shifter, too? Now that's an amusing thought.

I walk around, covering every inch of the second floor. After an hour, I climb down the stairs, reciting my "call Katri" directive, more to amuse myself because I'm annoyed that May's memory is eluding me than because I think that calling Katri will solve this problem.

I walk into the pitch-black kitchen and feel along the right wall. I know this route because it's the same route that May took when she went to talk to her sister. I make my way to the hallway behind the staircase where slivers of light make it through the boards over the outside door, but they're so slender that they provide little help. I find the double doors on my right, the ones that I thought must lead to a stairway to the basement, to discover that it's only a pantry.

The door to the painting room is ajar, leading into more pitch-black space. I fumble along the wall to the right of the door in search of a light switch. Why didn't I bring a flashlight? In my defense, as if I really need to defend myself, to myself, if I had found May's memory, I wouldn't need a flashlight. That thought does make me feel less unhappy with myself.

Much to my relief, there's a switch and it works. The light is a little tulip-shaped thirty-watt bulb, not much light but enough for this little room. The bulb is in a crude fixture like those that I usually see in unfinished rooms or basements and is hanging out of a hole that was probably intended for the real fixture. The hole is wide enough that both the light and the crude fixture could fall back into the wall, making it a serious fire hazard!

This room isn't empty. On the floor, along the wall with the doorways into the entryway and closet room, I see piles of light fixtures. Different sizes and shapes of dusty, wall-mounted lights and ceiling fixtures lie scattered around the floor.

What I find when I turn toward the opposite wall is more shocking. Leaning against a couch (probably the same couch that May lay on so long ago) are the discarded paintings that once hung on these walls. The two paintings in the front lean against the two behind them. My sister Reena would have much to say about artwork being treated so carelessly.

I gaze sadly at the paintings. One is of the Calendar kids when they were children, and the other is the big family portrait. There's no memory to find in here except the memory I had when May looked at these paintings. How peculiar that these paintings were left behind.

I mope around the kitchen, then head to the dining room. My hopelessness makes each step I take seem heavier. It's gone. I'm sorry, Katri. I've failed. Then a new thought strikes me. Could my own sense of hopelessness be causing me to lose the ability to connect? How do I act happy when I really feel like crying? But that doesn't make sense; I don't remember acting happy in my visits to May's memory! No, if there's a memory to reconnect with, I can do it. As odd as it sounds, as hopeless as I feel, I don't consider leaving.

I hit the redial button on my phone and I hear Katri's frantic answer. "Jena, what's wrong? Do you need me to meet you?" Wow! The phone only rang once before she answered. Should I be alarmed that she's standing poised by her phone waiting for me to call her? "Jena?" she says urgently.

Oops. I spent so much time questioning why she answered her phone so quickly that I forgot to answer her. Why is she so worried? "Sorry about that. It's Jena calling Katri. Come in, Katri."

"What's wrong? What happened? Do you need help? Are you hurt?"

"No, no, nothing like that. I can't reconnect with May. Before, I just went to the last place I left her, but when I was here two days ago, I left her sitting by the lake with her sister. I was just by the lake, sitting on what's probably the very same bench, and nothing happened. That's when I got worried that I might not be able to reconnect, so I ran back to the ballroom. I went all around, in every room, on every floor. That reminds me—I saw the old paintings."

"Old paintings?"

"Yes, the ones in the painting room. I mentioned them before. There's one where all the Calendar kids were small; one with just May, April, August; and their parents; one with just August, Marlene, and Hannah; and. . . ."

"There's a painting with Marlene in it?"

"Yes. Actually there are two, the one I just mentioned and another one of the entire family: May, April, August, Sarah, Jeffrey, Marlene, and Hannah. How do they get babies to sit for paintings?"

"I don't know," Katri says impatiently. "Maybe they just paint the baby from a photograph. I wouldn't be surprised if most people get their painting done by giving the painter a photo. Jena, are you in the building now?"

"Yes. I'm on the first floor."

"Did you try entering the building from the front door?"

"Well, no . . . . It's a six-foot jump up since the steps to the front porch are gone. But that doesn't really matter. I was just by the front door and pretended I was walking through it. It's all boarded up, you know, so I can't open it and enter from outside. This is the front door, not the side entry where I entered through the window."

"You need to try to enter from the front."

"You aren't listening. There aren't any steps to the front door. I can't fly, you know."

"You're flexible! I've seen you climb trees before, I've heard stories, and you can figure it out. Call Katri if you need help," she says, hanging up on me.

The window by the front door isn't as long as the one I normally step through, so the sill is about five feet from the floor, a bit of a climb. Maybe it will easier to climb up from the outside. I run to the front of the house and view it from a distance of about fifteen feet. I see no place to climb or pull myself up. Given the options, going back in the building and climbing through the window to get onto the front porch is the best choice.

Back in the first floor of the ballroom, I survey the sill, checking for sharp objects, then I hoist myself up and through the window. I walk over to where the front porch stairs would have been to look down and confirm, yes, about six feet down. I pause to admire the charming view, and as I turn to face the ballroom, I feel the change.

I turn my head back to face the front yard, and I'm back to my own time. That was cool, so I slowly turn my head to face the door, and, yes, I can feel the change. Again, I turn my head to face the front yard, and I'm back to my time. I laugh. Naturally, I must experiment some more! Is it possible to face the door without moving into May's memory? I turn my head, and, yes, there's the boarded-up door. I'm bubbling over with excitement, moving between my perceptions and May's memory is far easier than I realized. I'm aware in the brief moments with May that she's having some extremely intense emotions, but, hey, I need to maintain my sense of self, and I reason that a bit of play is a good thing. She's not going anywhere. I notice that if I look at the yard, there's nothing I can do to draw out May's memory, but, poof, one turn of my head to the front door, and there it is; then one turn toward the yard and I'm back. Oh, wait. How about if I try this without turning my head? Yes, that works, too. As long as I'm facing the house, I can move back and forth between May's memory and myself. Oh, just one more time and I promise I'll stop.

Massive dizziness comes over me as I shift back to myself, and my body starts lurching forward. I manage to position my feet under me, which allows me to hit the ground feet first, but the impact is hard as I fall forward on my hands and knees. That was a valuable lesson to include in my Memory Shifting 101 handbooks! Don't, and I repeat don't, shift quickly between your own thoughts and the memory, especially if there's a steep drop nearby!

I look around as I dust myself off, thankful that no one witnessed my fall. When I face the house, wouldn't you know, I find myself, as May, standing on the steps. That was all I had to do? Come and stand in front of the house in the same location as the steps? No climbing through windows; no falling from porches; just come here and stand.

I'm not allowing myself to feel what May is feeling, I sense some intense emotions and I'm not sure I feel like playing this game right now. Then again, I'm also afraid to shift back given what just happened to me. Shifting in and out isn't a good thing: See rule one in my Memory Shifting 101 handbook. Oops, no, wait. That would be rule two. Rule one is maintaining my sense of self.

I take a few virtual deep breaths and remind myself: If I need help, call Katri.

Chapter 15: Distraught

I haven't even fully shifted into her memory yet because of the overwhelming sense of failure, of sorrow, of loss! May is distraught and I'm wary of shifting fully. Taking virtual deep breaths is useless. I really need my lungs so I can inhale and exhale and try to calm myself. I'm already finding it hard to remember that I'm merely an observer and that the pain she feels is hers, not mine. This one is for you, Katri.

"August?" she wails aloud. "August, I'm so sorry." May runs up to the front door porch and collapses by the railing near the steps. She's wearing a pair of bell-bottoms and a halter top. Her long, smooth black hair falls around her head. *"May? May? Why are you so tormented? May?"* Why do I bother trying to talk to her? Oh, yes. It helps me to maintain my sense of self. I really need it now, and I resolve to talk to her often! I know that something tragic has happened, but all I can sense is immense anguish.

Using the railing to pull herself up, she faces the yard with her head downcast and heavy. She doesn't want to lift her gaze to the horizon because something horrible looms before her. Floods of tears stream down her face, pattering on the porch like raindrops. She slowly raises her head, lifting her gaze, as dread consumes her. With a fresh burst of tears cascading down her face, she looks into the distance.

I see three towers of black smoke, with flames leaping up to catch the smoke from beneath. May takes hold of the railing and leans against it, wailing in anguish, "August? August? I'm sorry, so very sorry. Why, oh, why? It's too much! My brother? Hannah? Marlene?" She pounds her fist on the rail. I can feel that she's hurting herself, but she doesn't feel the pain in her hands. To some small degree, I welcome the throbbing pain in her hands, as it's more bearable than this feeling of loss, betrayal, sorrow, and overwhelming heartache. If grief alone can kill, then surely she'll die soon. Surely, she'll kill me!

"May? I talked to Katri about this. Please don't blame yourself. You were tricked." I'm desperate to reach her, to comfort her. Who could possibly watch someone so consumed by grief and not reach out? *"May, I'm here. Please don't blame yourself?"* I repeat these words to her. They're my only recourse.

She grips the railing, staring off into the distance and

remembering the ride home last night with Sarah.

"May, you've been quiet all the way home," Sarah said to her. "Tell me what's wrong."

"It's just the same worries about August. I've tried and I can't shake the feeling that something more is wrong. I saw . . . I, well . . . I don't know. I feel like I should go there."

"Darling, you're tired. You need your rest. Do you think August would be pleased if you visited him this late? They left the ball hours before us, and I'm sure they've long since gone to bed."

"I wish Daddy were here."

Sarah pulled over and turned the engine off. Cupping her daughter's face in her hands, she said, "May? I'm your mother and I'm here. If you're concerned about something, you need to tell me. What if, God forbid, there's a serious problem that might require your parents' help? Think of the consequences of keeping secrets! You know that I've always been there for you, my darling. You know you can trust me."

A few tears made their way down May's cheek as she shook her head out of her mother's gentle hands and looked out the passenger window.

"May? May? Look at me. I'm your mother and I love you. I love August. I love April. I love Wendel! We're family, and we have to stick together."

"Mother, I don't know who to trust or what to believe. I just don't know. This entire evening has been so confusing."

"Trust your parents, and trust that we can help you!" She took May's hands in her own. "Tell me what's bothering you, dear, and when I get home, even if Wendel is sleeping, I'll share it with him. We'll make sure that whatever troubles you, is all smoothed over tomorrow."

"Maybe we should go see Daddy now? If we turn around now, we might even see Jeffrey returning, and he can follow us back."

"Darling, Darling May! Jeffrey and your father agreed that I'd drive you home and make sure you're comfortable. It's been a rather stressful evening for you. Your father wouldn't be happy if I drove you to our house. He wants you to rest. This can wait until the morning. Sweetheart? Look at me."

May looked up while more tears trickled down her cheeks.

"May? Whatever is troubling you can't be so bad that we

have to stop what we're doing and wake everyone up. It really troubles me to see you like this. No one has died, so . . ." May shook her head and tears streamed down her face stopping Sarah. "If the lives of my child . . . my children are in danger I must know. Please don't keep me in the dark! Tell me!" She demanded frantically.

"April said . . . ."

"Yes, dear? Tell me what April said."

"April said that August might die tomorrow."

"Oh, no! That's an awful thing for April to say! I'll talk to her. May, think about it. Really, think about it. Why would August die tomorrow? What could possibly happen that would be so terrible that he would die?" She paused for a moment. "I'll talk to your father as soon as I get home. We'll get to the bottom of this." Smiling, she took May's face in her hands again. "May? Darling? Look at me. You know I love you! Yes? Good! Well, you can trust me to take care of this. I won't allow any harm to come to my child!"

May feels comforted by her mother's words, but she wonders why she said 'child.' Was it only August she would protect? Only May? Why not all of her children?

Sarah reaches into her bag and hands May a pill. "This will help you sleep. It's small and easy to swallow. You know I wouldn't want anything to happen to my grandchild, so you can rest assured that this is safe. You'll wake up tomorrow and find that your father and I have been hard at work making sure our family is protected!"

Much to my horror, May swallowed the pill.

May looks up from her memory of the previous night, sobs, "The key," and bolts down the steps from the front porch. She runs frantically around, looking for the key that she dropped the day before, too distraught to think straight as she runs haphazardly along the flowerbed. She dropped the key just below where she was standing last night, so she isn't looking in the right place, but no matter. She realizes that the key doesn't matter unless she knows the location of August's secret place.

She charges and stumbles up the stairs, throwing open the ballroom door. Her thoughts are racing around so much that I can't follow them, but her actions as she looks under shelves, in the fireplace, in every cabinet in the pantry and the kitchen, moving canned goods, throwing open all the closet doors, and running around rooms reveal that she's looking for the secret place. Finally, she collapses in a sobbing heap on the staircase in the main entryway.

She tenderly rubs her hand across the stair steps as she remembers sitting in this spot with August several years ago.

"May, they won't mind," August said.

"Yes, they will. You can't build a secret place in this building. They'll be angry that we're in here."

"No. I know Marlene's grandparents, and they love me! If they found out, they wouldn't mind. They'll probably think I'm clever and ask me to build another secret place for them. But never mind," he said, smiling sheepishly. "It's too late."

"Why? What have you done?"

His smile widened as he handed May a key. "I built it. No one even saw me! I know where the secret place is; you have the key. It shows how we trust each other and depend on each other. Family first always!"

She swatted at him playfully. "What's to stop me from searching around and finding this place? Or stop someone else from finding it?"

"Good luck!"

"I just get the key? That doesn't seem like a fair trade. Unless it's a bank vault, you can break in without the key!"

"This is about trust, May!"

"Can I tell April?"

"Sure, if you really want to. But April and I have our own little thing to do if we are scared and need help."

"April and I have our own little thing we do too when one of us needs to be cheered up."

"I know about that and I don't want to be left out. Now the circle is complete!"

"What about Mother and Father? Or even Jeffrey?"

"No! Especially don't tell Jeffrey. He isn't even family."

"We'll be married some day."

"Yes, when you're older! Even then, please just keep this between us, between blood! Promise?"

"Okay, August, but at least tell me; is it in the ballroom?"

"Yup."

"I'm going to find it. You think you're so clever."

"Ha!" August said smugly. "No one will find it! Go ahead

and look all you want!"

May's eyes refocus as she returns to her present time. "August, where? Where?" She remembers May Bear, the stuffed animal that she gave to Hannah, and sobs, "Not Hannah, too! Not Hannah!"

May hears the faint sound of sirens and returns to the first floor porch. The smoke and flames, tower higher, and she knows in her heart that the fire trucks will be too late. The road to August's home is still unpaved.

"May?" says April as she struggles to make her way up to the porch.

"April?" May is glad at first to see her sister, but then she sees that April is holding a cloth to her side, with blood seeping through it. "What's wrong with you?"

"What are you doing here? You have to leave. Go to the lake and . . . ."

May rushes to her sister's side on the porch. "No, April. What's happened to you? Don't tell me to leave."

"You can't be seen with me, May. You have to leave. I didn't realize you'd be here. Please go, go to . . . ." April grows pale and sways against the railing, pressing the wadded cloth tightly against her wound.

"April, don't start that again. You're bleeding. Why would you come here when you should see a doctor?" May tries to look at the wound, but April won't let her pull the cloth away.

"I wanted to find the secret place you told me about." Wincing, April tries to shift her weight and lean against the railing.

"What good does that do now?" asks May. Pointing toward August's house. "I came here to look for answers, too, answers to why he . . . ."

"Oh, May, August didn't . . . he didn't . . . . May, please, go to the lake. We can't allow anyone to see us together. Please leave before it's too late."

With fresh tears glistening in her eyes, May stays with her sister. "It's already too late, April. His home is burning. There'll be nothing left. I had no idea how distressed he was. How, April? How could he do this to his family?"

April battles to stand, biting her lip. "Jeffrey really loves you, May."

May is perplexed. What does Jeffrey's love have to do with

August?

April's strength ebbs, and she slowly slides down the railing until she's sitting on the porch. She says, "We thought that if we kept you out of the loop, if things blew up, he wouldn't suspect you and you wouldn't get hurt, but the more we learned, the more worried we became. It's all so wrong, May."

"We worried? Who are 'we'? You and August? And 'he.' Who is 'he'? You're in desperate need of a doctor, and instead you talk nonsense."

"Yes, August and I. We don't have the proof, May, the proof against Jeffrey. He can't know that we spoke. Never tell him that we spoke. You must leave and never let him know that you were here, or that you saw me. Go!"

"April, we've lost our brother, his wife, and our niece. It's unbearable! I can't lose my sister, too. You and I need to leave and get you to the hospital." May tries to help April up but she she's too weak to stand. Blood seeps through the cloth she holds against her wound.

I'm stunned! Even now, May thinks that Jeffrey is blameless. I hear what she hears, but we process the information differently. May's only focus is April's need to see a doctor. Maybe if April had agreed to go to the hospital, May might have had her wits about her and been able to hear what April was saying about Jeffrey.

"It's too late for me." April slumps into May's waiting arms.

"April? What happened? I can't lose you, too. No! No! We have to find a doctor! Please take my hand. I'll help."

April's eyes flicker open and then close. The wadded cloth, now soaked with blood, falls onto the porch. April weakly holds her sister's hand, murmuring, "Hannah," before she dies in May's arms.

Grief explodes in May; her tormented heart wails, "Not my sister, too! My God, what have I done wrong? What wrong? Why?" Cradling her sister's body, she rocks back and forth. "Noooo . . . ."

I shift out of May's memory working hard to inhale and exhale in long, slow, deep breaths. This is too traumatic. For my own sanity, I can't continue.

Chapter 16: Can't Go On

Trying to choke back tears, I push the redial button. When I hear Katri's voice, I say, "Calling Katri."

"Jena, what's wrong?"

Too late. The tears start rolling and I blurt out, "May's sister and brother, they . . . they . . . ."

"I know, Jena," she says softly. "They died. August and his family died in a fire."

"What?" I'm not sure which question to ask first. How does she know that they died? "August and his family died in the fire but not his sister," I say, still trying to calm myself by breathing deeply.

"What?"

"Why are you asking me 'what?' like you know something different? April died in May's arms on the porch. April was bleeding when she showed up at the ballroom. I don't know if she was shot, stabbed, or what. But she didn't die in a fire!"

Silence on the other end; I only hear my slow, controlled breathing. "Katri?"

"I'm here," she says quietly.

"Why did you think April died in the fire with August and his family?"

"That's what was reported."

"You knew? Why didn't you tell me? Why would you want me to go through this?" I wait, but no response. I'm appalled that Katri knew about the fire and didn't tell me. How could she allow me to suffer through this when she could have warned me? A feeling of betrayal and anger toward Katri displaces my lingering grief for May's losses. "Katri?"

There's a long pause. "Jena, I don't know. I don't know what I should say. I don't know if it will make a difference. What if I say something that biases your viewpoint? What if it prevents you from seeing the truth? I've already learned something different. What if I had told you what I thought? It might have changed what you saw."

"How could it change anything? It's a memory. I can't change a memory; I can only observe it. There's no fast-forward, you know. There's no rewind, and for heaven's sake, *don't* ask me to move quickly between her memory and my life. I took a fall doing that crazy number."

"A fall? From where?"

"Like I said, I'm fine. I fell from the front porch. Before I fell, I was bouncing between my life and May's memory with a turn of my head. It was cool. You should have seen it. And after I fell, I landed right in front of the house. Wouldn't you know, when I faced the house, there I was, on the stairs, in May's memory! Go figure!"

"Didn't I tell you to go around to the front?"

"I did. I climbed through a window by the front door."

"Oh."

"Katri, I'm sorry, but I can't go back. It's just too much for me. Do you realize that I feel what she feels? It's like surround sound, emotion-enhanced playback. What else can I learn? What good will it do?"

"Please, Jena. It's important to me, very important. Marlene . . . Marlene was my aunt. I know you're experiencing these memories for a reason. April's body was found in the fire, but you say that April died in May's arms on the ballroom porch. All the . . . all of August's family died that day. Hannah was my cousin. I know there's a reason you can shift to these memories. Just one last time. Go back one last time?"

"What do you think the reason is?"

"I don't know. I really don't. But I'm certain that the only way we'll know is if you go back. Will you?"

"I'll think about it."

"I can meet you there. I can get there quickly. Would that persuade you?"

"No, you don't need to meet me here. One last time, you say? To think that this all started as something enjoyable. Fancy dresses, delicate desserts, dancing, and now it's blood and mayhem. Would it be too much for me to ask to shift only into happy memories?"

"Happy memories don't beg to be heard. There's nothing to fix."

"I was hoping you'd agree with me on that, Katri."

"Call Katri if you need help. Repeat that to yourself."

Just before I hang up, I say, "I did call Katri. She's sending me back to the lions."

Chapter 17: The Clock Stops

I look out into the distance, none to eager to reenter May's memory. A melancholy feeling overwhelms me, and all my usual techniques to cheer myself fail. There's no smoke rising in the distance, but with May's memory so fresh in my mind, there might as well be.

Of all the times when fast forward or mute might be useful, now is the time I need it most. May sobs as she cradles her dead sister's body. April's long black hair, so much like May's, spills onto May's lap and onto the porch. Tears stream from May's eyes onto her sister's head as she alternates between pressing her cheek to April's and watching the flames and smoke billow in the distance.

As she holds her sister in her arms, she spots the key lying in the shrubs below. She feels that it's useless and stares at it blankly. What good is the key if she doesn't know where the secret place is? Over the years, she's searched in the ballroom, admittedly, not very hard, but at least she's tried. Why would August go to such pains to hide the room so thoroughly?

Below her, in the clearing, she sees Jeffrey approaching. To my horror, she's relieved to see him. She believes that he'll help; she hasn't processed any of April's warnings. She thinks that August is responsible for the fire. Maybe, in her bereaved state, she can hear me better, so I scream, *"Run, run, run for your life! Run!"* She waves to him. I feel like I'm inside a horror movie where the hapless victim waves her attacker over to finish her off.

"My sister!" she calls out as he climbs up the stairs and steps onto the front porch. "April died in my arms, and I'm lost. Lost! Can you tell me? Has anyone survived? By some miracle, has anyone survived the fire?"

"Let me take April," Jeffrey says quietly as he comes closer.

"Take April where? Why?" Still kneeling on the porch, May cradles April more closely and stares up in bewilderment at Jeffrey.

He pauses between each step. "My darling, I know this is terrible for you. April shouldn't have come here looking for you. It was thoughtless and selfish of her to involve you."

I fantasize being able to leap out of May's body and giving

Jeffrey a much-needed kick in the ass. Instead I yell, *"May, don't listen to him. Run! Look at him! He walks like a man who's inconvenienced because your sister dared to run for her life. Don't listen to him!"* Since Katri told me that April also died in the fire, I quickly gather how she got there. May is doomed if she doesn't play along. *"May, play the game. Play the game."* I know the true meaning of futility as I scream to May. I'm invisible. I'm just an observer of impending doom. I can't stand this.

"April was right to come here. Our brother is dead. She was looking for me. Jeffrey, what's wrong?"

"May, this is the time to play along. Tell him she was dead when you found her. How can you not see the danger he poses now?" I continue my futile efforts to communicate with May. Wasn't I the one who told Katri that you can't change a memory? Yet here I am, in this memory, this thing that was, and I continue my silent screams to change it. What else am I supposed to do? I have no other recourse.

Jeffrey sits beside May and puts his head in his hands. "This wasn't how it was supposed to happen. If only your brother hadn't interfered so much. He always had to play the hero."

"Hero?"

"Even when he was a kid, he always had to play the hero. Everyone looked up to August Lanlore. 'If August sees you doing that, he'll beat you up,'" Jeffrey sneers. "I hated hearing your brother's name. I hated the month of August. Do you know that some of his friends used to call me 'the dirty kid'?"

"It was you? You tormented April with the spider?"

"That's how I got perfect August all riled up! That's how he beat himself, too. Always playing the hero till finally he met his end!"

Sitting, still holding her sister's body, May struggles to move away from Jeffrey. He smiles and says, "What are you doing, May?"

"Jeffrey, I can't believe what you're saying. Did you have a part in my sister's death? And what about my brother?"

"Part? You act like you don't know."

"Know what?"

"Oh, please May, I'm not a fool. I know you spoke to your sister. I know she told you that Sarah is my mother."

Incredulous, May stops rocking her sister to stare at Jeffrey and asks, "Your mother? That can't be! How?"

"The clock has stopped for you, my dear. I saw from a distance how long you and April spoke before she died. But then." He looks down as if a thought, or a realization, has finally made itself clear to him. "I see. That explains why you didn't run. You really didn't know. How unfortunate. Your brother and your sister have killed you. They've murdered you. You see, May, your mother died when you were young, and my mother, Sarah, married your father and doted on you and the others. She was afraid that he wouldn't approve of an unwed mother, so she left me in the care of her parents. She promised me that one day I'd be a regular and central part of her life."

"My father was never like that. He would have loved you, too." May remembers that Sarah referred to her "child" and not her children. Sarah was looking out for Jeffrey. May feels a fresh surge of pain and guilt because she feels responsible for what has happened today. Now, only now, do all the pieces fall together in her mind. Now that it's too late.

"Does it matter now? Your infernal brother was forever poking his nose where it didn't belong. He wasted so much time with the hired help. We pay them, and that's all we owe them, their wages. Not August! He has to check the accounts, talk to clients, and butt his nose in where it doesn't belong. One sick little kid, what does it matter? They can have more children if she dies."

"What did you do to Annie?"

"Oh, is that her name? Annie?" Jeffrey sneers as he paces around the porch. "May, I have to take April. Time is running out." More sirens scream in the distance, causing Jeffrey to look nervously between the fire, May, April, and his watch. He wrenches April's body from May, carelessly shoving April's body aside. Taking a rope from his pocket, he ties May's hands to the rail.

May looks on in stunned disbelief. "What are you doing? If I'm going to die, let me die with April beside me. How can you do this?"

"I'm sorry, my darling. I have to get your sister back to August's house. She really shouldn't have left. I'll be back." He rolls April's body in a cloth he brought with him. He hoists her over his shoulders, making a face, as if he's carrying a sack of manure to the garden.

"Jeffrey?" she wails. "Jeffrey! Let me die with my sister!

Take me with you! I'll hold my sister's hand and walk with you. Jeffrey?"

He walks away quickly, without looking back, with April's body bouncing around on his shoulder.

She sobs violently as she watches Jeffrey carry her sister away. Once he's out of sight, she stops sobbing. I sense nothing from her; she's numb. I can tell that the rope is loose enough that she can wriggle out of it. *"May, don't just lie here. Fight! Try to undo these knots. They aren't that tight."* May is motionless; she's given up on life. Her brother, her sister, her sister-in-law, and her niece are all dead. Her husband has betrayed her, and her mother, her mother isn't even her mother. Now she understands why Sarah and Jeffrey look so much alike. They have the same black eyes and the same black heart.

The pain, Katri. I don't think I can take this pain. Loss and betrayal—how can May cope? She's given up. That's how she's coping. No, No, No. That's not how to cope with this loss. *"May, fight!"* Soon, I feel numb. Do I feel her numbness, or am I numb from my own frustration because I can only observe? That I'm helpless, I'm voiceless, I can do nothing—nothing but watch through her eyes, her own destruction.

It seems like an eternity has passed, but I know that it hasn't because the sun still looms high in the sky, adding to the irony as it forms a halo around Jeffrey's head as he stands over May.

"May," he says softly as he unties her hands. "I don't know what to do."

"Do? Kill me, too. I won't have your baby. What kind of child could have you as a father now that you've killed my brother? My sister? My sister-in-law? My three-year-old niece? And Annie. What did you do to her? Are you the reason she's sick? Do you think I'll remain silent? Do you? Do you? Answer me!"

A few tears trickle down his face as he listens to her cries of anguish. How laughable, I think. If I could laugh at a time like this, I would laugh now. How dare he grieve! He's the reason for her grief, and he has no right to grieve himself.

"You're crying? Why? Has a business deal failed? Are you going to lose a lot of money?"

"This wasn't my plan. Your brother is to blame." He shakes his head as if a fly is buzzing around, bothering him. "May, tell me where August's hiding place is."

"What are you talking about?"

"I heard you talking to April out by the lake. I know about the secret place. Where is it?"

"If you heard us, you know I don't know where it is."

"Well, my love, I have to go mourn the loss of my in-laws and join the others as we look for my missing wife. I have to leave you." He removes a small vial from his pocket and holds May's head steady with one hand. She doesn't fight him, but she stares into his black eyes. He opens the lid; she opens her mouth and willingly swallows the poison, still holding his gaze. "I'll stay with you, May."

"Leave me!" she spits out with all the venom she can muster against this man she once loved. "I'd rather die alone. Leave me now!"

Jeffrey walks away, leaving May to die alone. He looks back once and pauses. She shakes her head and shuts her eyes. I hear her thoughts. She doesn't want to die alone, and I feel her squeeze her hands together in despair.

Chapter 18: Patients X and Y

I feel oddly calm and numb, and my head feels like it is being held down. I hear the anxious voices of Katri, Ben, and Adam.

"She shouldn't have been here in the first place," Adam says. Only he would be lecturing at a time like this.

"What did you do to her?" Ben asks, his voice laced with poorly controlled anger.

I feel a small weight on my chest, and I hear purring. I struggle to open my heavy eyes. I'm lying on the ground in front of the ballroom. The source of the purring is Sweetie Pie, who is lying on me, watching me, with half-closed, contented eyes.

"Guys? Jena is awake." Katri moves forward to sit closer to me.

I'm trying to comprehend why I'm lying here, why all my friends are sitting around me, and why my cat is lying on me. I ask weakly, "What's Sweetie Pie doing here?" His unfocused gaze reflects the way I feel. It's unlike my cat to lounge around sleeping when he could be investigating. "Have we been drugged?"

Silence from everyone. I look at Katri. Who else would have drugs? Her guilty eyes are red and swollen. She slowly nods and throws her arms up and back down, leaving them resting limply on her lap. She sits slumped, very different from her usual upright posture.

I ask, "Why?"

"You . . . well . . .I . . . you . . .I was desperate." Her posture disintegrates even more so that Adam, who's sitting beside her, reaches over to rub her back and then hugs her with one arm. She brushes back a tear and makes an effort to correct her posture.

Adam and Katri are seated facing both the ballroom and me. Ben is sitting behind me, with his legs crossed and my head cradled in his lap. I feel a sudden panic. Poison? Will he pour poison down my throat?

He sees my alarm and hugs me, saying, "Jena, it's just me, Ben, your one true love." He smiles, and I feel silly thinking that he would poison me.

"What happened?" I ask.

"You were distraught, Jena. We couldn't calm you down; you couldn't hear us, so I had to give you a sedative."

"And Sweetie Pie?"

"I know the cats' purring soothes you."

I try to lift my hand to pet my cat, but it's heavy, so I let it drop. I can feel the vibration of his purring on my chest. The sky is blue. There's a gentle breeze. It's all soothing.

"He wasn't all that happy to be here, and your . . . um . . . your behavior upset him even more," Katri says. She lets out a long breath and looks down. Adam pats her back again.

Behavior? Why would my behavior upset my cat? Why are they here? "May?" I whisper trying to clear my head. "What happened to May?"

Katri holds up her hands to silence Adam and Ben. "Not now, guys. Please, not now. Jena, do you remember calling me?"

"I called you? No, I don't remember calling. Why is everyone here?"

"You called me, you were sobbing saying, 'It's me Jena. I'm here. You're not alone.' That was all you said, over and over. I was so scared; I thought we'd lost you. I called Ben and asked him to bring any cat he could get hold of, hoping their purring might soothe you, and I told him to meet me at Dirt Road Parking Lot."

"I called Adam," adds Ben helpfully. "Mainly, I wanted to know if he had any idea what the two of you were up to."

Katri continues, "When we got here, we found you balled up in front of the building here, crying and still repeating, 'It's me, Jena. I'm here. You're not alone.' You looked right through us." Katri shakes her head. "I'm sorry, Jena. I'm so sorry."

May, the ballroom, the memory of her talk with August, April, the poison, the fire—I remember them, and I thank God that I can't feel the pain anymore. I'm relieved that I'm numb. I feel something wet fall onto my cheek, and when I look up at Ben, I see him brushing another tear away. He's agreeing with Katri.

"Do they know?" I say to Katri.

"Not yet."

"We'd damn well better be told what's going on here!" Ben says angrily. "This is the second time now, Jena, that you've scared the beejeebees out of me in less than a week, and Katri has been the co-conspirator both times."

I drop my hand on Ben's and smile at him weakly. I feel like I've just lost all my family in one day, and it's devastating. I have three sisters and two brothers. Although they live on the opposite coast, we stay in contact by telephone and e-mail. How painful it would be to have my family wiped out in one day, and worse, to have them murdered by someone I loved. Again, I'm relieved that I feel so numb. Although I'm sympathetic to May's plight, I feel sad because she gave up and didn't fight back. I'm a fighter. I would want to avenge my family, and I certainly wouldn't want to help my would-be killer kill me! Not me. I wouldn't make it easy for him. Damn you, Jeffrey!

Katri moves closer to me, saying, "Jena? Stay with us in the here and now. Don't go back there." It's startling to see how concerned Katri is. I've never seen her so out of sorts.

"Hey," I say, waving my hand around weakly. "I can't go back. May is dead. Did you know that she would die, too, Katri? Or, should I say, I trust you knew that May would die, too? My God, Katri, why didn't . . . ?" I see her sitting slumped, her perfect posture gone, her face streaked with tears, and I stop. The damage is done; no point in going on about it now. Instead, I say, "I know how April's body got back to August's house. Jeffrey carried her there."

"Who the hell is Jeffrey?" demands Ben, his patience gone on hearing this other man's name again.

"Jeffrey was May's good-for-nothing, scumbag, low-life, murdering husband," I answer. "I suppose you also want to know who May is? Tell me, Katri; tell me how you think May died? Tell me?"

"She was found on the porch, right up there. She had a miscarriage and bled to death."

"Miscarriage? More lies. Lies, lies, lies, lies, lies."

"Jeffrey?" she asks, and I nod.

Ben says more cheerfully, "I guess I don't need to worry about this Jeffrey guy. He doesn't sound like my Jena's type!" He hugs me as if he thought he'd lost me.

"Ohhh," I say as my foggy mind tries to find the right words. "He's probably dead, anyway, or at least I hope so!"

Adam leans forward, slaps his hands down on the ground and stomps up—not stands up, but stomps up. He uncrosses one leg and slams his foot to the ground, then the other leg follows as Katri's eyes grow increasingly wider. Before he can speak, I burst out laughing, not a simple "ha, ha, ha" but a stomach-aching, tear-shedding, floor-rolling laugh.

What is Adam having a fit about, exactly? Is it because Jeffrey killed the Calendar family and I find it distressing? As I realize that Adam doesn't know what happened, I laugh harder, especially when I think of what it will sound like when I try to explain it. Then I laugh again, realizing that Katri will be backing me and imagining Adam's shock and horror when he learns that Jena has finally corrupted Katri. I laugh, because if we don't give them the real explanation, we'll need to provide some other explanation for my behavior. That explanation, however, will probably have some equally unbelievable parts. Does Katri also appreciate the irony? I don't know, but now she's laughing, too. She's free to roll around on the lawn while I remain caged in Ben's loving arms. Katri and I look at each other and then look at our husbands, whose faces alternate between rage, anguish, and fear, and we laugh. And that song, that '60s song by Napoleon XIV, "They're Coming to Take Me Away," keeps going through my head, causing me to laugh still more. I fight the urge to burst out singing, but that song fills my head, and I can't stop laughing.

Adam is still stomping around the yard with his hands waving in the air. Finally, he stops and puts his hands on his hips. "Well, Ben? Well? What do you have to say for yourself?"

Ben sits in stunned silence. Laughter is supposed to be infectious, right? It hasn't infected our husbands! I almost feel sorry for them. They must think we're crazy, and we haven't even told our story yet. I realize that I must stop laughing, and I grudgingly allow the sad memories to surface. Katri's laughter fades, and we look at Ben as he defends himself for a crime he hasn't committed.

"What? Why are you blaming me? I'm not a part of this! I don't know any more than you do."

"Look what you allowed Jena to do! Look what she did to Katri!"

"Excuse me?" Although my mind is still foggy, I don't appreciate this accusation. "Adam, I think for myself, thank you very much, and I don't need Ben's permission to walk and talk." Both Katri and Ben back me! "As for Katri, I did nothing to her! Nothing! She . . . ." Katri shakes her head slowly and deliberately, indicating not yet.

"Blimey, Adam, why are you blaming me? It's unreasonable. Be thankful that Jena is half-drugged or she'd have jumped up and punched you."

That's my Ben. I give him my best smile, which, given how I feel, probably looks like my cats' "Hi, I'm high" look because he's been over medicated.

Adam flops down on the ground where he was sitting before his outburst. "I'm sorry. I've never seen Katri so upset. When I got here, she told me, 'I think I killed Jena. I sent her to the lions and they ate her up.' I've never, ever seen her so anxious and worried." He shakes his head, muttering "never" several more times; Katri puts her arm around his shoulders to comfort him.

I don't want to be the one who explains what happened here today. Already, Adam thinks the blame lies with me. I want to make sure that he and Ben know that Katri is an equal partner in crime, and I might even argue that she's the mastermind. I may have stumbled on the memory, but she pleaded with me to go back even after I told her I couldn't.

"Well, Katri, I think you owe us all an explanation," I say.

She pauses, and then lets out a long, drawn-out sigh. It doesn't stop us; we sit quietly and wait for her to speak. At last, she says, "Where to begin? I'll start with my profession. It makes more sense if I start there. I've worked with some seriously disturbed patients, so trust me when I say that Jena really isn't nuts."

"You're trying to help me—right?"

Somehow, my questioning her motives puts her more at ease, and she smiles. "Yes, I am. You'll see."

Looking at the men, Katri takes another deep breath and resumes her explanation. "I noticed a trend in some patients who heard voices and were delusional. Not all of them, of course, just some who spoke of things they heard that made some sense. But their condition seemed to worsen with drugs, or, possibly, the drugs clouded over what they actually saw and heard.

"One patient, I'll call him X, told me details about a kidnapped child that he insisted was alive and needed his help to be reunited with his real family. He told the story as if he was that little boy, that is, from the little boy's point of view. I did some research, and X was describing what happened to a little boy who had been missing since he, himself, was a child."

She shrugs and looks off into the trees shaking her head. Another deep breath. "He could have looked it up or heard about it. In any case, his condition rapidly deteriorated as he became more agitated because we were preventing him from helping. Later, another patient, I'll call her Y, came in. We struggled to get her to take her medications, and, finally, we were forced to give them to her by IV. But before the IV, she told me about a jewelry heist that happened more than a hundred years ago. She insisted that the rightful owners, or, rather, their heirs, should have that jewelry, but if she didn't do something now, the jewelry would be lost forever. We had to sedate her because she became extremely agitated when we didn't act on her demands to do something about it.

"Not even a day after her most violent outburst, I heard about a family boating trip in which an accident caused the boat to explode and sink, killing the family. A family member filed a claim on an antique necklace, thought to be over a hundred years old, and said to be lost in the accident. The hubbub was about the insensitivity of someone filing the claim so soon after losing five members of their family.

"I did more research and learned that many years ago, a wealthy family had reported the theft of a ruby and diamond necklace, much like the one described in the claim.

"The families of these two patients said that before their lapse into delirium, they had been happy, charismatic, intelligent people, fascinated by history and what might have happened here and there, in this time and that time, just like you know who."

Unable to contain myself, I clap my hands and loudly proclaim, "There are more people like me? We can have a party."

"Those people aren't staying in a luxury hotel, you know!" she says, arching one eyebrow and tilting her head.

At this point, I'm bouncing with excitement, but the men clearly aren't looking at the situation in the same happy way. They're horrified. I don't think they understood that the stories were true; instead, they apparently interpret Katri's words to mean that Jena is insane. "Katri," I say. "You need to repeat that comment about Jena not being crazy. The guys aren't connecting all the pieces."

She looks at the men's horrified expressions and says, "Guys? Guys? You aren't following what I'm saying. I saw something real in those patients, an ability of some kind. Jena has it, too. She can see into someone else's memory, a memory that has lingered because of something lost, something undone."

"Oh, she time travels?" Ben asks in laughable disbelief.

Frustrated, I burst out, "For heaven's sake! I mean—duh! You *can't* travel through time. That makes no sense! Ben, please pay attention."

Ben sticks his face just two inches from mine and says, "And hearing memories does?"

"You have some valid points," I say, pointing my hand up in the air for theatrical effect, but given my drugged state, it flops around as if I were drunk. "However, there's a big difference between hearing and seeing someone's memories and time traveling." I try to sit up, but I can't, so I lie back down. "When we memory shifters—that's what I call us—move into another person's mind, or into their memory, we have no control over the memory we're observing. We hear, smell, taste, think, and feel as the person we're observing does, but the person is unaware of us. And let me add a stern, very stern warning."

Adam's eyebrows arched what I hope is a thoughtful look, and I continue. "One: Maintain your sense of self by not allowing your own thoughts to be consumed by the memories that you're observing. Two: Don't attempt to move in and out of a memory too quickly, especially when something steep is nearby."

Adam looks at Ben, Ben looks at Adam, and now it's their turn for fits of laughter. The disadvantage is that my head is still on Ben's lap so his laughter jostles my drugged kitty and me around. Sweetie Pie is oblivious to all the commotion and continues purring. With a great effort, I push myself upright and move Sweetie Pie to my lap. Katri sighs several times, looking at me. "What?" I ask. "What did I say? I don't get it; I just provided a very thoughtful and detailed explanation, with the added benefit of the lessons I learned."

"You just had to add your commentary? I was doing just fine without you." She imitates my handclap, shaking her head again.

"Excuse me? What's that supposed to mean? It's okay if you talk about patients X and Y and how you've met others like me, and that's credible? But if I add details, it becomes a joke?"

"They weren't ready for that sort of detail yet," Katri says loudly, trying to speak over the men's laughter.

"Yes. You have a point. They're sl-o-o-o-w."

Red-faced from laughter, Adam squeaks out, "Quick, Jena Tell me what I just thought."

"That isn't how it works, Adam. I would first need to murder you, and then, later, a memory shifter would happen by this spot, see your memory of being murdered, and know that you didn't accidentally fall on your head from the first floor porch, as I told the police. When the memory shifter realizes how skeptical you were about our abilities, he or she won't feel compelled to help you."

"Ohhh, that's how it works," Adam says as he and Ben fall into another round of laughter.

This won't do at all! Katri says it, and it's credible; I say it and time to laugh. "Okay, Katri," I say. "Why don't you tell the guys why I kept coming back here? Better yet, tell them what you told me at dinner Saturday night. And don't forget to tell them about the chocolate."

Adam stops laughing to glare at Katri with a tell-me-it-isn't-true expression on his face. He stands with his arms crossed, waiting for an explanation.

Katri, however, has other plans, and she snaps to attention at the magic word "chocolate." She reaches behind her, holding up a big bag of chocolates from Delectable Delights. "I had my Jena-disaster-relief strategy all laid out," she says. "Ben, cats, and chocolate. Maybe this will keep you quiet." She tosses the bag over to me, but Adam intercepts it.

"Hey, those are for me," I protest.

"They're for all of us," Adam says reaching into the bag.

"No, she said they were for me. If you're eating them, how will that keep me quiet?"

Ben nudges me, saying, "That's enough. Let Katri talk."

"Wait a minute," says Adam, looking at my bruised and scraped knees. "Are those scratches related to the no-head-turning rule you mentioned earlier?"

"Well, yes. I fell."

"From where?"

I point up above me, and Adam's eyes grow huge. "Jeez, Jena! Are you crazy?" Seeing Ben look up and shrug, he says, "Ben, that's six feet up."

"The stories I could tell you about Jena and climbing trees, especially the ones about her younger brother," Ben says resignedly. "Jena has jumped from that height many times before." Kissing my forehead, he adds, "And from what I hear, she's broken a few bones and torn some really nice dresses."

"I do," counters Adam.

"Later, then. Katri has more to say and I want to hear," I protest more firmly.

"I agree," Ben says. "Katri, please continue."

"Thank you, Ben," Katri says. "And, Jena, I have more chocolates, so don't worry about running out. As I was saying, after I met Jena, I learned about the personality of certain patients and noticed the similarity to Jena's personality. One important thing I observed in Jena was a quality that I didn't see in any of the patients. Jena deals with tragedies well, especially her own. I think that cracking jokes and making light of serious situations allows her to bounce back quickly from huge traumas. She doesn't take anything too seriously and is quite adapt at explaining away bizarre or scary situations—like the first time she experienced a memory. Other people would have rushed off in search of treatment, but Jena shrugged it off, complaining about the music, admiring the dresses, and wanting chocolate instead of 'fish things.'"

"Again, you *are* trying to help me, right?"

Katri ignores me. "I saw hope that if Jena had this gift, it might not drive her insane. She's different. Or it could be that the medical community, which was trying to help the other patients, drove them mad. The fact that they never resolved the problems that they witnessed in the memories they visited probably made their condition worse.

"I knew that I could stay close to Jena and be ready to help her if she entered a memory. At dinner Saturday night, when she told me about the ballroom, she told me things that weren't the typical Jena's imagination gone wild but more as if she saw the ballroom and it was real. I knew that she was entering a memory, and I encouraged her to go back."

Adam fumes at these words, but she silences him with a look and a wave of her hand. "I must confess that I also had personal reasons to ask her to go back."

Katri takes several deep breaths, clearly trying to calm herself and fight the tears I see forming in her eyes.

I say, "You already look like a raccoon, so what are a few more tears to smudge your makeup?"

She laughs, and the tears stop. "I know about some of the people Jena met. Jena mentioned May—it was May's memory that

Jena shifted into. Jeffrey was May's husband. May had a sister named April and a brother named August."

"And it should be no surprise why I called them the Calendar family."

Katri smiles at my interruption, but the men aren't amused. Katri rises to my defense. "Guys, that's why Jena was successful. Her flippancy, her ability to throw in sarcasm and humor, that's what saves her."

Naturally, I pause and look around as if I'm looking at my subjects who adore me. The subjects, however, are rolling their eyes and eating my chocolates. At least the cat is looking at me adoringly, even though he's drugged. I'll take what adulation I can get at this point.

Ben puts his hand on my shoulder and says to Katri, "Jena doesn't need any more praise."

"Can't have too much praise," I say, shaking my head while I munch on chocolates. "Please, more praise. I think it's safe to interpret Katri's words to mean, 'Jena is perfect just the way she is.'"

Katri clears her throat and forces a smile. My previous joke stopped her tears, but now I see them forming again. "I'm truly glad you're the way you are. What you've found means so much to me, and I appreciate that you allowed me to slide on occasions when you could have pushed for further explanation. I'll provide that explanation now. August was married and had a child, a little girl named Hannah. His wife's name was Marlene." She pauses. "Marlene was my mother's twin."

Of course, Katri has already told me that Marlene was her aunt, but she didn't mention that other small detail. Sometimes I think she holds back information just for a dramatic delivery later. In any case, the men seem impressed by how all the pieces fit together.

"Jena brought back information. Although it won't allow me to personally clear Uncle August's good name, it counters what I was told happened that day. You see, it was rumored that August was enraged because he was financially ruined and Marlene was going to leave him, and that was why he torched his house and held his wife, his daughter, and his sister April captive in his burning home. It was also believed that May died of a miscarriage brought on by the trauma of losing so many family members." She pauses and turns to me. "Jena can take it from here."

"April actually died in May's arms, right up there." I point behind me to the front porch. "She came here looking for August's secret place—which reminds me, we need to look for that later. She was bleeding. I don't know if she was stabbed or shot or what, but I'm sure she bled to death. She knew that August was in danger. The night before, she told May he might die. Jeffrey tied May's hands to the railing and took April's body back to the burning house. He came back to May and poured a small vial of some nasty-tasting stuff down May's throat. She didn't even fight; she wanted to die. I was there when she died. I was with her. She was alone, she was thinking that she didn't want to die alone, and I was saying, 'It's Jena. I'm here. You're not alone. I'm here.' So April died in my arms and I died with May." The drugs aren't working anymore, and May's anguish resurfaces.

"Okay, battle stations, battle stations! Operation Cheer Jena, activate now," says Katri, jumping up.

"Don't eat my chocolate." I'm not sure what they're up to, but I'm not letting them eat my chocolate.

Adam mumbles, "Is that it?" He grabs my bag of chocolates and stuffs piece after piece into his mouth, tossing the wrappers around.

My tears dry up quickly, and with renewed energy, I put down the cat and lunge at the bag. Ben jumps in and pulls me away but not before I grab the bag. "Oh, Adam, this is a low blow."

"It was better than the alternative," he mumbles through a mouth stuffed with my chocolates.

"Meaning?" I ask, placing my bag of chocolates safely behind my back.

Ben chimes in, "Well, I for one thank you, Adam." Looking at me, he says, "Katri told us that you could relapse when you started remembering what happened. Not many people live through their own death."

"Oh, you don't say?"

He rolls his eyes and explains, "She told us we had to sing and dance some stupid song. That was what she expected us to do. I thought it was a really far-fetched plan, but I didn't want to argue with her when she proposed it, especially given her state of mind at the time. That's why Adam grabbed your chocolates as an alternative."

"I feel like I'm relapsing now, so go on with your routine." I look at Adam, who's choking on my chocolates because he's laughing at the same time. "Yeah, that's right, Adam. Spit out perfectly good chocolates."

"But, Jena, you're wrong! I didn't kick you when you're down. I used my quick wit to save you," he says grinning from ear to ear, with chocolate on his teeth and smudged all around his mouth. "I wasn't planning on following Katri's plan, either. You're a good friend and all, but that was a bit much. But when I realized that stealing chocolate was such a huge offense, I jumped at the chance to help you."

"Anyhow," I say glaring at Adam, "the next order of business. Somewhere in this building is a secret place, where August hid away some papers or something. There's also a key to this room, well maybe it's still there, underneath this dirt around here." I point to where I think May dropped the key. "We need to find those papers. May and April thought they were important, and Jeffrey wanted them enough to ask May about the room before he killed her. My plan is for the three of you to do some investigating. I need to relax for a bit, so I'm going to sit by the lake. If you're still searching, I'll join you later."

They all nod and scamper off to the building and don't give me any grief about wanting some time alone to pull myself together. I feel as if the lake is the only place for me to be right now. I put a huge rock on the end of Sweetie Pie's leash to keep him from running away although he's so doped up that he won't likely be doing anything other than purring and sleeping.

Chapter 19: The Lake

I walk to the side of the house where the renovations would have been, and I try to picture what life might have been like for the Calendars with a happily-ever-after ending. As I walk, I theorize that the fault lay in Sarah since her deceit helped to foster Jeffrey's rage and determination to succeed. Wondering whether Jeffrey was motivated by revenge only, success only, or a combination, I surmise that it must have been both since he hated August and yet he loved May. What sort of turmoil must have existed in Jeffrey to love one person and hate another who was so close to her?

Pausing in front of the large rock that May saw April sitting on, I ponder the oddity of these memories. I feel like they're my own, but they aren't. Or, at least, they weren't my memories, but maybe they're mine now. After all, I remember them.

Enough with the memory stuff! I make my way to the trail, sauntering down to the lake and enjoying the peaceful sights and sounds. I take a few deep breaths to allow the beauty of my surroundings to relax me. My forever-active mind starts to daydream about buying the ballroom. It would be a heavenly location for events. Remove some of the trees, so the lake is visible from the ballroom; renovate the second floor, so it has windows looking out on both sides. This building could be "Dream Events" headquarters. Now that's a welcome diversion.

Looking at the bench where May and April talked about childhood memories touches me, causing me to turn away from it, as if it's somehow to blame. I feel guilty wanting to walk away from it, as if I'm turning my back on something important. I walk over to it, deciding to allow myself just a few more thoughts of May. Gliding my hand over the seat saddens me since I no longer can touch her memory. The Calendars died years ago, but, for me, it was just hours ago. "Good-bye, Calendar family."

I sit down and the feeling comes over me, the same feeling I had when I was shifting into May's mind. I allow it to take hold. It isn't May's memory. The person looking out over a lake awash in sunlight is smaller, much smaller—a child around three years old. Maybe it's May's childhood memory, I think hopefully, but my hopes are dashed as I realize that May's memories have all been in sequence. My excitement ebbs, but I remind myself that I'm not listening to this person, so I can't hear what she' thinking. Well, don't I feel foolish? I sit here speculating about who she is, when all the while, all I needed to do was listen.

She's so terrified that she's trembling as she remembers. April placed her firmly down on the bench, and leaned in just inches from her face and said, "You must remain quiet until I come back or someone mean will give you a boo-boo as bad as mine. You must not cry out or leave this spot!" April pulled a wad of cloth away from her blood-soaked blouse and lifted it a few inches to reveal a deep gash in her side. I would have been speechless with terror if I were really that little girl. How could she speak to a child that way? April handed her a stuffed animal and continued, "Never, ever, give up May Bear. Do you hear me, Hannah! Never, ever, ever."

Hannah? She's alive? Fear grips me as I realize that Jeffrey will arrive at the ballroom soon. My silence is maddening as I again find myself a helpless observer of doom.

Little Hannah whispered, "Never ever," as she watched her aunt run down the trail and out of sight. She sits here now, too terrified to make a sound, so she muffles her sobbing by burying her face into May Bear. The poor little thing is worried that if she's bad, she'll get a big boo-boo like her Aunt Pril's. She'll be good; she'll be quiet, and she holds May Bear tightly against her, sobbing quietly into the fake fur.

I can't stand this. It was painful enough being inside May, but this little child is suffering. I want to hold her and tell her it will be all right and let her sob as loudly as she wants to on my shoulder. This is too cruel. I sit in helpless horror with this child, this sweet child, and fume that Jeffrey got away with his crimes. Then, my thoughts snap back to Hannah. She feels a hand on her shoulder. Oh, no! Oh, no! Not Jeffrey! Not Jeffrey! No. I've had it. I'm just about to snap myself out of Hannah's memory, since I know I can't bear to be with this dying child, when she looks up. Standing before her, looking kindly down at her, is Jameson.

"Hannah, sweetheart. Oh, Hannah," he says soothingly as he brushes back her pooling tears.

How sad her little tear-stricken face must be. Jameson scoops her up in his arms and hugs her tightly. Thank you, Jameson. Holding Hannah was just what I wanted to do. Hannah knows who Jameson is and finds comfort in his arms as she locks her little arms around his neck, sobbing. Her face is wedged in the crook of his neck, and she can feel his whiskers, but she doesn't think about that. It's something I notice, something to distract me.

"Pril had a big boo-boo. She was sad."

"It's okay, Hannah. Everything is okay. Don't you worry about anything. It's okay."

"I'll get a big boo-boo, too," she sobs, holding Jameson tighter.

"No, sweetie. No, sweetie. April sent me to protect you from boo-boos, and I will. I'm your protector." He holds her in his left arm and uses his right arm as if he's in a sword fight, and she smiles. "Back, boo-boo, back," he continues, jabbing at the air beating the boo-boos away from Hannah. He hurries along the lake, moving away from the ballroom as he keeps the imaginary villain away from Hannah.

"Can I play with Annie?"

"No, darling. Annie is gone. We can call you Annie."

"I'm Hannah."

"Okay."

He tries to reposition May Bear and Hannah shrieks, "No! Pril said no. My May Bear!"

"It's okay. You're safe now; you can keep your toy. She'll always be yours."

I run to the building, shouting, "Hannah! Hannah! Hannah is alive. She's alive! Ben? Katri? Adam? Hannah is alive. We have to find her."

I run to the kitchen door, forgetting that it's boarded up. Then I run around to the other side in time to see the rest of the troops climbing out the window.

"She's alive! She's alive!"

"How do you know?" asks Katri.

Pointing toward the lake, I say, "I was at the lake behind the house. It's huge. If they cleared out some of the trees, the view would be gorgeous." Seeing their confusion, I shift back to my reason for returning. "I shifted into Hannah's memory. Her Aunt April carried her to the lake and sat her on the bench. Come on. I'll show you."

I turn and run back to the lake, waiting impatiently while they meander over. I hear Adam questioning why they need to walk to the lake to hear the details. I suppose he has a point.

When they're close enough to see where I'm pointing, I say, "There, right there. April sat Hannah down right there and scared her into silence. What she did was horribly shocking! April must have saved Hannah from the fire and was trying to save her from Jeffrey. Thank God, Jeffrey never came back here. Jameson, Jameson found her. He has a daughter Hannah's age . . . . Oh, dear!"

"What?"

"Annie, Jameson's daughter, must have died. I forgot to mention that earlier. When Jeffrey was confessing to May, before he murdered her, he said something about August interfering with some business deal and Jeffrey commented about August doing something to save Annie. Annie was very sick; I don't know why. Jeffrey never said she was dead, though. And, and, and . . . Hannah or Annie has May Bear or had May Bear. If we can find Hannah, she may still have that bear. April made her promise to keep it. I think August hid something in the bear that reveals the location of the secret place. We need to find a man named Jameson with a daughter named Annie." Looking at Katri I ask, "Do you happen to remember anyone named Jameson or Annie?"

"No."

"Oh, well, worth a try. Say, did anyone have any luck finding the secret place August built?"

Ben answers, "No such luck, but Katri found the paintings. We sat in there as she told what few stories she could remember about her aunt."

"We'll find the room later," I say. First, let's look for Hannah or this child named Annie, who will be an adult now. Maybe we can clear August's good name, after all? Did anyone find the key?"

Ben shows me his dirty hands. "I tried."

"Let's all look for it. After May's death, this ballroom was never used again," explains Katri. "I'm betting that whoever owns it hasn't done much gardening or anything here, and it's just under piles of dirt."

"Why bother?" asks Adam as he follows Katri and me. "If we find the room, we can just break in."

Katri shoots him a silencing look.

I mark a big circular area under the spot where I believe May dropped the key and divide it into quarters. "I'll take this spot and you three can each take one of those. Sift through carefully." I look around and find a rock for digging. "Well, let's go."

Sweetie Pie tries to stagger over, looking rather drunk, and Adam starts to imitate him. "That's not very nice, Adam. Katri, I think you drugged him too much."

"Oh, he's fine. He's probably feeling really woozy."

We commence our careful excavation of the ground. Well, some of us do. Adam looks around for tools to speed up the digging, so he ends up doing none. Katri gingerly pokes around with a stick, trying to avoid messing up her freshly manicured nails. Ben, of whom I'm very proud, digs with gusto.

It's no surprise that Ben announces, holding up the key, "I found it!" More important, he's looking at me, obviously amazed that it's all true.

I jump up. "Great! Let's go. We need to find May Bear."

"Jena," he calls after me. "Where are you bounding off to?"

"Home! Come on, guys. We need to find Hannah—I mean Annie. Gosh, I don't know whether I should call her Hannah or Annie."

"This is a workday. Some of us need to go back to work, you know," Ben yells after me as he scoops up Sweetie Pie.

Jogging backwards, I say, "It's hard, though. I know her as Hannah. It seems wrong and sad, too, since Annie is dead. In any case, workday or not, you still need to go home, so let's move it. You can walk faster than that carrying Sweetie Pie." Then, smack! I fall right down on my butt. "I did that for your entertainment only! It was purely intentional and scripted."

Adam stands stiff-backed with his chest puffed out, lightly rocking his head and clapping like a king at the royal concert hall, and says in a laughable attempt at imitating Ben's accent, "Oh, bravo, bravo."

Katri chimes in, "Encore, encore."

"Hey, guys. The last time you asked me for an encore, all of you went swimming in a river in the wintertime. Have you forgotten?"

Looking sternly at Katri, Ben says, "Don't point out any deer to Jena, or at least wait until we're safely away from any harmful obstacles."

"I see lots of obstacles at my disposal here," I retort.

"Lots! You're never safe."

As we walk back, Adam says, "Say, Jena, how do you know where the memories are? You know, the ones to be read, or shifted to, or whatever it is that you do. How do you know?"

"I don't know. I just stumbled into May's mind while I was walking Sweetie Pie."

"Oh, come on. You must have received a message or something."

"Yes, I have an answering service that picks up messages! I confess that I've been drawn to the conservation land. For years, I've longed to walk around here. On the other hand, I've always been intrigued by new locations to explore. It isn't like I was provided a set of rules to follow."

"You mentioned those two rules. How did you know those?"

"Trial and big error! I learned about losing my 'sense of self,' Katri's words, by the way, because I stayed in May's memory without allowing many of my own thoughts, and, um, well, Ben can explain what happened then. The other rule about shifting quickly came up when I changed too quickly from May's memory to my own world, and I got a bit dizzy and fell."

"What?" Adam teasingly asks, swinging his head quickly from front to back. "You didn't swing your head this way and that way, did you?"

He is shocked when I respond, "Yes, I did something rather like that but I turned my body, too. It was cool. I was having fun with it. Hey, what did Katri say about how I make jokes and that saves me? Go ahead, Katri. Tell them again."

"I remember that," Ben chimes in. "Something about being a perfect nut just the way you are."

"Whatever. Let's map out our plan for finding Jameson. When we get home we can . . . ."

"I have a better plan for the rest of the day, which involves a beer, a couch, and a TV," says Ben.

Adam slaps Ben on the back. "I like Ben's plan. Count me in."

"What about 'some of us have to work'?" I ask.

Katri rolls her eyes at that the men. "You know I'm in," she says to me.

"I thought so. Say, I'm ready for a chocolate now. Who

has the bag?"

Adam starts running in front of us and calls back, "I was hungry."

"So you ate all my chocolates, repeat, *my* chocolates?" I call after him.

"I'm surprised you didn't sense it," he replies as he keeps his distance from me.

Chapter 20: The Gown

The men sit zoned out in front of the TV, each with a beer in one hand and chips in the other. After all, it's been a trying day for them, what with witnessing their distraught wife or friend going through an emotionally crippling experience, where she witnessed four members of the same family die and then feeling as if she nearly died herself. Well, no wonder they need to relax! Teasing aside, I really don't mind. They had to digest some really bizarre information today, and I think they handled it well.

Katri is driving us to the library. I suggested Web surfing from home, but Katri has her heart set on going to the library. She convinced me to go by telling me that she'll sort through the books and I can go online there. The downside is that the library hasn't acted on any of my numerous suggestions to build a coffee shop.

The quiet time as we ride allows me to think, and I remember that Katri's great-grandparents at one point owned the ballroom, so I ask her, "Katri, what was your mother's maiden name?"

"Tolass. Why do you ask?"

"I remembered that May bought the ballroom from Marlene's grandparents. I believe their last name was Streemings. Does that ring any bells?" She shakes her head. "Did you know that the ballroom was owned by your family?"

"Not really. I remember playing in it once or twice. Maybe it was a wedding. I'm not sure. What I remember most was skating on the lake. That was really something."

"May and her family skated on the lake, too. That was how August and Marlene met!"

"Oh!" Katri says. "I just remembered something I need to show you. Let's do the library later, okay?"

"Sure, it's early. We have plenty of time."

As we drive in silence to Katri's house, I remind myself that she's hurting. This is her family, or some of her family, that we're discussing. I look at her, expecting to see a pained expression that she's attempting to hide, but I don't see any sign of masked feelings; instead, she looks quite pleased with herself. No, wait. I remember that expression. She's plotting something, like she was the day she drove me to my surprise birthday party. A devious smile lurks underneath that mask.

We pull up to her house and she jumps out, bounding up to the door and waiting there impatiently. Peculiar behavior since Katri isn't a bounder; that's something I do. It irks me that she has still more information that she's kept from me. I saunter up, watching her bounce around, signaling with her hands for me to hurry up.

Inside, she plants me on a chair and cheerfully commands, "Wait for me here."

It feels like I'm sitting in an episode of *The Twilight Zone*, witnessing Katri morph into a bouncing, bubbly person. Will she burst at any moment and return to the Katri I knew before?

Katri's home is immaculate. Everything has its place. Both she and Adam like a minimalist modern decor, with neat corners and subtle colors. There are magazines, perfectly stacked, on the coffee table, so I move them around.

"Jena? Shut your eyes," she says, hidden from my view. "Tell me when they're closed."

Good heavens! What could she possibly have to warrant so much trouble? "Closed," I say.

I hear a rustling sound. "Open."

I gasp and sit with my mouth hanging open before I remember to breathe and close it. Katri is wearing the same lovely red dress that Marlene was wearing the evening of the ball.

I surmise that Katri must have been a lot closer to her Aunt Marlene than I suspected. I do the math. Katri is forty-two now; the date on the sign was 1970; that would make her only six when Marlene died. I'm surprised that Katri would remember her at all.

"It was worth it just to see you gasp! A reminder for me that you were really there."

"How do you know I wasn't just gasping because it's such a lovely dress? Gee, with a nip and tuck and some liposuction I could fit into it!"

She laughs and twirls around. "I've never put this on. Well, wait, I did try it on when my mother sized it to fit me. She talked about her memories of Aunt Marlene while she did the alterations. I never wore it to a party. My mother and Aunt Marlene were close. She was angry and bitter for many years. I always thought the bitterness was directed at August. Now I think that maybe, just maybe, she blamed Jeffrey. I find comfort in thinking she knew

August wasn't capable of killing his family. Let me change out of this; I'll be right back."

Katri returns with the kind of large white box that's used for storing wedding dresses. Her steps have so much energy that she nearly bounces over to me. "Here, I want you to have this."

"The dress? I can't possibly take something so valuable. Besides, it won't fit me!"

"It can be sized; you can't be more than one size bigger than I am. I'm also taller than you with more muscle tone . . . ."

"Oh, and I have a lot of cushy tushy? Thanks!"

"I didn't mean it that way. It's just that I'm not really that much smaller than you. I just carry my weight differently. The point is that this dress is meant for you. I've always considered giving it to you. That first time we walked together on Dirt Road and you commented about a woman in a *billowing* dress, I envisioned you as that woman."

Her eyes dart quickly to the coffee table, and she smiles contentedly as she reaches down to realign the magazines.

"Are you all right? I can't believe how long it took for you to notice that!"

She shrugs and reaches down again, and this time she shifts the magazines around. To my amazement, she leaves them that way and says, "Jena, this is just a dress, a dress that connected me to my mother, and the moments we shared when she talked about Aunt Marlene. Your willingness to go back to the ballroom each time, even as it became more and more intense and depressing for you, meant more than I can say, but I can show you. This dress really is you, and I know you'll enjoy it. I'm relieved that you stumbled on the memory at the ball. I know you don't care for '70s clothing, so you might not have hung around."

I nod my head vigorously. "Yup, that's true. I didn't much care for what May was wearing the day she died." I put up my hand to stop what protest I think I'll hear. "Not that I'm speaking ill of the dead or making light of a very sad situation, but that was one hideous outfit. Her emotions were so extreme that I couldn't even hear myself noticing how awful it was. It didn't even match!"

Katri walks over to me, looks me squarely in the eye, and smiles as she wipes away a tear, "You're making light of a sad situation, and that's why you made it through it. That's what saves you! You can laugh. When everyone else is crying and they throw their hands up in despair, you laugh!" She gives me a big hug then steps back. "For so long I've felt tormented that my mother hurt for so many years, and now I feel free to believe that she didn't blame Uncle August for Aunt Marlene's death and in turn blame herself."

"Why would she blame herself?"

"I know that Aunt Marlene and Uncle August met while they were ice-skating on the lake." She takes a few slow, long, deep breaths and battles more tears. "Mother told me how they met. Mother and Aunt Marlene had seen August on the lake many times before. He was always helping the children learn to skate, or fixing their skates, or just pulling them around and having fun. Aunt Marlene noticed him, but he was so busy helping others that he didn't notice her. Well, she was an excellent ice skater; actually, she was excellent at what ever she did. Mother suggested that Marlene could meet August by offering to help him: 'After all, he can't teach all those children himself.' Aunt Marlene took my mother's advice. All these years, Jena, all these years, I thought that my mother felt like she was Aunt Marlene's killer, but I don't believe that now. So, you see, you have to take this dress!"

"How did they manage to save the dress from the fire?"

"Oh!" Katri's eyes grow wide. "Mother picked up Aunt Marlene's . . . ." She stops, and then with a serene smile she continues, "It feels so good to speak her name to someone who's met her. As I was starting to say, Mother picked up the dress on her way home from the party. Aunt Marlene had another party to attend soon afterward and wanted some alterations. Mother also made May's and April's dresses. They wanted different colors but the same design. Say, Mother was there, you know, at the ball. You may have seen her!"

"No way. Really? What are your parents' names?"

"My mother's name was Marla and my father was Michael."

The blood drains from my face as I recollect that Michael had some business dealings with August and Jeffrey. I never did find out what was going on, but Jeffrey wanted August out of the loop. Maybe Michael's wanting to talk to August meant that Michael was one of the good guys and not part of the plot to hurt the Calendars.

"What's wrong? Do you remember them?"

"Nothing's wrong! I do remember them. It was a fond memory. April and May were bouncing around the dance floor doing a ridiculous dance routine. Some of the other guests looked on in disdain, but when Michael and Marla joined the girls in their silly dancing, the other guests finally joined in the mayhem. It seemed like everyone was having lots of fun. You should have seen all the hats flying around."

"My mother told me about that dance. She was one of the ones who had to chase after her flying hat!"

"The Michael I mentioned earlier, the one that I said had some business dealings with Jeffrey, that was the same Michael." Too late, I thought. I already blurted that out!

Katri's face hardens, and her tears stop falling. She stands stiffly with her arms crossed. "My father wouldn't do business with Jeffrey. Why are you so sure that the Michael you mention was my father? Michael is a common name!"

"But how many Michaels have wives named Marla and are attending the same party? In any case, Michael was nice. Please don't be so defensive. I'm not . . . ."

"Well, Jena," she interrupts me, moving her hands to her hips, "You did just tell me Jeffrey killed, what, one, two, three, four, and probably five people? Wouldn't you be defensive if someone told you that your parents did business with a killer, and you suspect that the murders were partly related to shady business dealings?"

"I'm sorry. My comment was poorly worded. Michael was a good man. I'm sure he wasn't a party to Jeffrey's scheming. But this brings to mind something else I forgot to mention earlier." Katri is still glaring at me. "I don't that think Jeffrey killed the Calendars just because of a business-related problem. I think it was more because he was worried that they would tell their father that Sarah was actually Jeffrey's mother."

"No, how could something like that be kept a secret?"

"I think that was all part of the problem. May's mother must have died when she was young and Wendel, her father, remarried and allowed Sarah to raise his children as her own. I suspect that August found out about Jeffrey being her real son, and August was going to expose it."

"Are you saying that you believe Sarah was part of it? Part of the murders?"

"Yup, she sure was."

On our way to the library, I realize that I don't know what sort of work Michael was involved with and, given how defensive Katri was earlier, I don't want to ask her directly. But I'm curious as to why Jeffrey would want to conduct business with Michael.

"You know, I'm fortunate that I found a friend with your occupation," I say. "Where would I be now if I didn't have you?"

"Yes, and I'm fortunate to have found a friend with your gift!"

"So true. So true. But I'm serious. It was a lucky day for me when you decided to become a doctor! How did you arrive at that decision?"

"I always wanted to help people. My father was in pharmaceuticals, so I pretended to receive a shipment of medication, naturally in the form of assorted chocolate bars. Of course, I needed patients to give my medication to, so I used my dolls. My poor dolls. I cut a hole in their mouths so I could make them take their medication. Well, after a while, some of the dolls got rather smelly and my mother threatened to stop buying me dolls if I continued giving them candy of any form. Instead, I provided therapy to my dolls. Eventually, I graduated to real people." Katri laughs and I laugh, too, because I can so vividly imagine Katri as a little girl providing advice to her dolls.

"I see. You realized as a child how well chocolate works as a form of therapy. How perfect that you met me."

The silence for the remaining drive isn't awkward, so I can get away with looking out of the window and occasionally commenting about a flowering tree. But I'm struggling to keep my heart from jumping out of my mouth. I worry that she might hear it pumping wildly as my thoughts race and I work to beat them down. Pharmaceuticals? Shipping? Procuring medical supplies?

Oh, May, I finally understand! I understand how we can find reasons that explain how something that appears to be wrong, isn't wrong. There's no way I can allow myself to believe that Katri's father was involved. It hurts too much to think it's even possible! I won't speak another word of what I know to Katri. Her parents are dead; let her keep her memories of them. Even if Michael was involved, there's nothing to gain by exposing it now other than hurting my friend. Nothing! I vow to remain silent.

Chapter 21: The Library

It's a relief when we arrive at the library and Katri and I head off in separate directions. Alone, in the computer room, I no longer have to worry that she might see the fear and doubt spreading on my face.

I start my search for Jameson, but I'm quickly discouraged when I realize that a last name is required with the online directory. That blows that idea! For the hell of it, I also search to see if Jameson is a name in a business, but that doesn't help, either. In a desperate attempt to make my search produce something useful, I try searching with Jameson as the last name, but no one with that last name lives in Betta, Massachusetts. Next, I search for anyone with that last name in all of Massachusetts. It's disheartening when one hundred hits pop up on the screen. A hundred isn't an impossible number, but then I slump in my seat and accept that kindly, sweet May, wouldn't have called Jameson by his last name without a proper prefix. It would have been Mr. Jameson.

Katri soon joins me. "You know, finding someone with just a first name is pretty difficult."

Pointing to the screen, I explain my dilemma to Katri.

She looks at the screen, looks at me, looks at the screen, and then pulls up a chair. "No. Tell me more about how Hannah knows Jameson. Who is he? For that matter, how did you know that was his name?"

"Hannah knows Jameson because she used to play with his daughter, Annie. And Jameson told May at the ball that the Lanlore kids had done a lot for him."

"Jameson was at the ball?"

"Yes, sort of. He was working. Remember when May went outside to get away from everyone? He was the attendant who spoke to her."

"What was he attending?"

"The cars. I think he was like the lead or head attendant. He managed the keys. When a guest needed his car, he gave the keys to another man, who fetched the car. He was a kind man."

"What did he look like?"

I have to think for a minute before I can answer. "Hmmm, a big, teddy-bear-looking man with sandy-blond hair. He was wearing sunglasses, so I couldn't see his eyes. Which reminds me.

Did I ever tell you about the pretty blue eyes that all the Calendar kids had? They must have gotten it from their father because he had the same beautiful eyes. Sarah had black eyes like her son's." I stop talking because Katri's lips are pursed and her face looks like it's about to explode. "What?" I ask her.

"How does that piece of knowledge help us find Jameson?"

"Well . . . ."

"Oh, who are you kidding, Jena? You got sidetracked!"

"Whatever! He was really tall."

"Really tall teddy-bear-looking man, you say? How old?"

"I'm not very good at ages, but I think he might have been in his thirties or forties. He was a tanned, good-looking man. If it helps, I remember that he had a deep, powerful voice that was somehow soothing."

"Powerful deep voice! Yes! Someone comes to mind, vaguely. I'll call Adam. He grew up around here, too." She takes her cell phone from her purse.

"They don't like you to use your phone in here," I say, looking around warily for a librarian.

She runs outside to make her call and I follow. "Adam," she says after she dials the number. "Do you remember a guy from the seventies who had a deep voice and had a business relating to renting or moving cars? Big guy, sandy-blond hair?" Pause. "Thanks." Looking at me, she says, "'Park It' or something like that, some business. Adam said he remembers some nice guy helping him with one of his projects."

"Let's check to see if a business with 'Park It' in the name is still around!"

Excited, we run into the library in opposite directions, with me heading straight to a phone book and her to the archives. She looks back, sees me at the phone book, and returns. "That's probably a better place to start. Do you see anything?"

"Yes!" I'm thrilled. "Park It, Buy It, Sell It Auto—what a name!" I jot down the telephone number and address. "Let's call."

We run back outside and I pull out my phone and dial the number. I hear gum chomping on the other end. "Hello. Park it"—chomp, chomp—"Buy it"—chomp, chomp—"Sell it."

"Hi. I'm looking for a 'Park it' business that might have been around in the '70s. Do you know how long your company has been in business?"

Chomp, chomp. "Been here a month. Don't know."

"Is there someone there you can ask?"

Chomp, chomp. "Yee's gone for the day." Chomp, chomp. "He'll be back tomorrow." Chomp, snap, chomp. "Call back then."

"The chomper hung up on me!" I tell Katri.

"Chomper?"

"She chomped on her gum the entire time. She said that 'Yee,' or something like that—she was chomping so much, it was hard to understand what she was saying—would be back tomorrow. Can you go there tomorrow?"

"Not tomorrow. In a couple of days or, better yet, next week."

"Didn't you tell me once that your patients who memory shifted had a sense of urgency?"

"Yes, but you don't, do you?"

"Well, what if my sense of urgency is broken?"

"You're hypersensitive, Jena. You'd know, I'm sure. I think a break from all this emotion will do us all good. How about next week?"

"Fine. Next week, then."

147   Lisa Nevin

Chapter 22: Meeting Jeffrey

The next day it dawns on me that Jeffrey might still be alive, and because I know his first and last name, I can find him. Since I'm worried about his business dealings with Michael, I don't want Katri to know of my plans.

I'm pleased that there's only one Jeffrey Dellner in the online directory. Although the listing isn't in Betta, it's close enough so that I believe it could be the same Dellner.

I call the number and a young voice answers, so I ask, "May I speak to Jeffrey Dellner?"

"I'm Jeffrey."

I take a chance that, with all the Calendar children dead, Jeffrey's mother would have managed a way to maintain her connection with her son. I could even imagine Sarah insisting to Wendel that Jeffrey was like a son to her. "Oh. You sound younger than I would have expected. Is your mother's name Sarah?"

"No, that was my grandmother. She died many years ago. You must want my father. He's in a retirement villa. Are you a friend of his?"

"I'm a friend of a friend. He told me to drop by if I was ever around."

"Really? Who?"

"It was someone who knew Jeffrey from way back when. He was . . ." I hesitate. What if this young man doesn't know about his father's first wife? What right do I have to interrupt his life just because he has the misfortune of having a killer for a father?

He saves me by providing the answer in an oddly hopeful way. "Are you a friend of the Lanlore family?"

"Yes."

"Oh. I'm sure my dad would want to talk to you. Please do visit him. You probably know what happened to his first wife and her family," Jeffrey adds sadly.

Boy, do I! But I control the urge to let him know.

"Yes," I reply, with equal sadness. "How has your father been all these years? I'm glad he was able to rebuild his happiness," I lie. I'm not at all happy for him; numerous foul curse words come to mind as I think of him.

"My mother and father divorced when I was young. Mother thought Father never stopped loving May. I guess it would be hard to let go of someone who died so tragically. Please visit him and let him know how I helped you find him."

How unusual that this young man is so willing to share so much with a stranger. And even more peculiar, when he thought I knew the Lanlores, his tone softened. He seems hopeful that his father will show him gratitude for helping me. I want to confess to this man that nothing I can say to his father would make Jeffrey senior glad he had divulged his father's address to me, but I keep quiet. "I'll be sure to do that," I lie again. "How can I find him?"

"West Bendel Retirement Villa."

"Thank you." We exchange good-byes and hang up.

West Bendel is an hour's drive! At least this gives me time to think of what I might say to Jeffrey. I hadn't considered that, which might explain my anxious feeling. Nevertheless, I get in the car and head in that direction, figuring that I can turn back at any time. I want to see his face and prove to myself that there's no harm in contacting him. Even though the urge to turn around grows stronger, I continue, determined to meet this man in person.

I arrive at the retirement villa and get instructions to his apartment. At least I know why they call this a "villa" and not a retirement home! Jeffrey must have done well for himself. The entryway has marble floors, and a large flower arrangement in a Vientiane vase sits on a sculpted cherry table in the center of the room. Three hallways diverge from the center room. Neatly carved wooden signs hang above each hallway. They read: Luxury Living, Luxury Assistance, and Gentle Care. Jeffrey's apartment isn't far down the Luxury Assistance hall. He should be living in prison, not a retirement villa, I think as I walk toward it.

He opens the door and barks at me, "Did you come to change the linen? I called an hour ago."

"No, sir. I don't work here. I came because I'm researching old ballrooms, and I want to ask you questions about the Dellner Ballroom. It . . . ."

"You stay away from that ballroom!" he growls, with his face contorted in an ugly scowl.

"I saw it on the Betta Conservation Land . . . ."

"What? That ballroom isn't part of the conservation land. They were supposed to fence off that area. That should have been part of the agreement. Have you gone into the ballroom?"

"No, sir. It's boarded up. I had in my notes the ballroom

was owned by the Betta Conservation Land and that they were going to open it up."

"Open? Impossible! Come in here! Tell me who you are again," he demands as he walks away, leaving the door open behind him.

His apartment has a cathedral ceiling that peeks over the joined space of the kitchen, dining room, and great room. A sculpted ivory crown molding dotted with gold berries edges all the walls. The front door opens into the great room, which is separated from the dining room by a cherry half wall. On my left, above a masonry fireplace with a granite ledge, hangs a painting of the younger Jeffrey, the one I met in May's memory, and his mother standing behind him, with her hand resting on his shoulder. Farther from the fireplace are French doors leading out from the dining room leading onto a terrace that overlooks a lake. The entire apartment is a gaudy show of wealth.

I follow him to a couch in the great room and sit across from him. "I'm an event planner, and I've been looking at old ballrooms around the state. I came by the Dellner Ballroom a while ago . . . ."

"That ballroom should have been fenced off," Jeffrey repeats. "How did you find it? The road doesn't even connect to the driveway anymore."

"To be honest, sir, I stumbled onto it when my cat got free of his harness."

Scowling, he sneers, "How stupid! Never heard of such a thing as walking a cat."

Jeffrey's face hasn't aged well. Bitterness has formed deep creases on his brow and around his lips. Maybe he felt guilty for murdering May but I doubt that he suffered remorse because the man I see before me is filled with hate and rage. Ironic, if I'm right. Does he shake his fist to the heavens at night, cursing God's injustice in making him kill all those people? He doesn't speak; he barks. He doesn't look; he glares. He doesn't even breathe; he snorts.

"Did you say it was boarded up when you saw it?" he barks again. I'm surprised that he doesn't growl after he speaks like an angry dog.

"Yes, it was."

"All boarded up?"

"Yes." I snicker to myself at how much he would snarl and growl if he knew that there are two open windows and how much worse he'd growl if he knew I had been inside.

"Good. Get out of here and stay away from that ballroom," he demands, whacking the air with the back of his hand.

"Wouldn't that have been May's ballroom?" I ask. "It was sold to her, wasn't it?" I could kick myself for saying that aloud, but this heap of hatred just flames the angry feelings in me.

Taken aback by my comment, he leans forward and growls at me, "What do you want?" His stare beats into me and I'm half-afraid that he can read my mind.

"I want to know about the ballroom, that's all."

"I still get those damn electric bills. I've been telling them and telling them to shut off that damn electricity, but they say that only May can order it turned off. Well, May is dead and has been for thirty years. I don't even pay the damn bill; I just throw them out!"

"Thirty? I thought she died in 1970."

"What do you know about May?"

"I was told that she died on the front porch of the ballroom in 1970. The night after the costume ball she held."

"Look here, Missy. You got some wrong information. You stay out of that ballroom."

"I have all the right information, Jeffrey." I stand up to leave because I don't feel like I can contain my own rage any more. He acts as if the world has wronged him and he's angry for it. This lump of flesh and loathing fathered a child? How cruel to the child.

"I didn't say you could leave. Sit down."

"I don't need your permission."

"I'm sorry," he says more quietly. "I can be rough around the edges. I've had a rough life." He points to an oxygen tank. "And you've probably heard how I lost my first wife and what would have been my firstborn child." His shoulders slump, and he shakes his head. "She died in my arms at the ballroom, and when I hear that place mentioned, all the pain resurfaces." He sits shaking his head as if he remembers the suffering.

If I didn't know the truth, I'd be filled with pity. Now, though, I feel only anger. I burst out, "That woe-is-me song and dance may have worked on manipulating May so that she wouldn't go to her brother, but it won't work on me. I know you're a sly, deceitful bastard." With my own evil smile, I add, "Both figuratively and literally." Many times, in the past few days, I've been pleased with myself, and I again find myself pleased at how my clever pun has caused a shock wave across Jeffrey's face. My self-congratulatory feelings cause me to stand taller and prouder and hold my head up higher. Ripples of glee cascade through me as I see that my small comments have angered him.

We stand up, glaring at each other, but I break the spell and run for the door. When I look back, he's holding his hand to his chest, laboring to suck in air. He motions to me to help him. Dream on! I remain standing comfortably by the door, fervently hoping that I'm seeing his last moments on earth. He finally sits down, grabs the oxygen line, and pulls it to his nose. His raspy breathing stops. How fitting that his meanness has taken its toll on him and aged him beyond his years. I didn't notice any problems with breathing when he opened the door, but do I dare to hope that it was just me who upset him? Well, good! Maybe that was my reason for coming here, to upset him.

"Lady, let's talk."

Given his labored breathing, I'm not afraid that he'll chase me around the room and stab me a hundred times. Still, I no longer want to be behind closed doors with this man. I don't know quite what he's capable of doing. "Not in your apartment. Over there in that opening." He can't see where I'm pointing but he lives here and he should be familiar with the seating area down the hall from his apartment.

I maintain a safe distance from him as we walk. I'm curious about this villa and hope to rile him more; I get a perverse pleasure from seeing how my words affect him.

"How long have you lived in this nursing home?"

"It's a retirement villa," he says, looking down at me.

"Looks like a nursing home to me," I say, knowing that I hit a nerve. Bendel Retirement Villa is no ordinary nursing home; it has lavish suites with as many lounges as a five-star hotel.

As we walk, Jeffrey struggles with his breathing. He pauses occasionally and leans against the wall.

He sits on a couch and I make a point to sit on the chair opposite him. He leans forward. "You can't prove anything."

"I'm not trying to prove anything. I just want to know why."

"Even if you could prove it, I'm a sick man." He leans back and his face softens for a moment before returning to its habitual scowl. "Damn August! He was always poking his nose into other people's business. He never could keep to himself. What I had planned was good for the business."

I'm momentarily stunned as I recall what he said to May before he killed her, so I blurt out, "It wasn't good for Annie."

"That was an accident. What do you know about Annie?"

I'm working hard to keep my voice muffled. "It wasn't good for May when you poured that poison down her throat." There, that should get his attention.

His eyes open wide, his shoulders slump, he tilts his head down, and a lone tear makes its way down his cheek. He brushes it angrily aside as he recovers his hostile posture. "I loved May," he says defiantly.

Surely, my eyes must be popping out of my head. I feel like they are. This man sickens me. His reaction is unbelievable. Our conversation, for lack of a better word, is more along the lines of throwing sentences back and forth, given that our retorts jump from one topic to the next. It's hard for me to respond in a civil manner to a killer who blames his victims for their deaths. "That's a sick way to love someone."

"I'm a businessman. Annie was an accident."

"How do you accidentally kill someone? Oh, oh, oh, better yet, how do you accidentally torch someone's home? How do you live with yourself? What was it? Your revenge because your mother abandoned you?"

"She never abandoned me. She always made sure that I was well looked after, and I knew she was looking out for me. Look where I live now." He sits forward in his chair, and although there's a coffee table between us, I find myself recoiling against my chair. "How do you know about this?"

"Does it really matter how I know? I know. And you're right; I can't prove a damn thing. Not a thing! But I wanted to meet the man who was capable of so much destruction. I wanted to know why you left May to die alone."

"She told me to leave."

"Well, duh, of course. If someone pours poison down your throat while you're staring into their eyes, would you really want them to hang around and hold your hand? She begged to die beside her sister."

"It was August's fault." He waves his hand dismissively.

This man's moral values are so corrupt, so nonexistent, that he believes what he says. Seething, I ask, "How was it August's fault? How?"

"He shouldn't have involved her. He shouldn't have involved April. He should never have gone to the party. He should have minded his own business." He speaks deliberately, as if he's explaining facts to an ignorant simpleton. He looks at my like he is expecting me to agree that August's interference was unprovoked.

My rage grows. "And little Annie? How did she get in your way?"

"Stupid kid!" He spits the words out of his mouth as if he'd sipped sour milk.

"She was how old? Two? Three? They aren't often doing calculus at that age, you know?" My hands are aching from holding the armrest in a death grip.

"Stupid kid," he repeats and stands up.

I get up so I can escape him. "I really don't know why I came here. I really don't, but I feel a little bit better. All I see is a miserable, sick, lonely man that hasn't aged well. I have some small satisfaction in seeing that you weren't capable of denying all the guilt for what you've done. Maybe that was why I came here because you're right, I can't prove a damn thing. And if I could? I wouldn't because it would only cause more people to be hurt. Marlene's sister . . . ."

"Marla?" he spits out venomously. "That woman derailed a plan of mine that would have transformed that puny Lanlore business into a global monopoly. I hope I brought some misery to that meddlesome woman's life."

As I look at this hate-filled man, I understand how right Katri is. Bitterness is no way to live. At first, I had an overwhelming urge to hurt him, but now I only want to be free of him. "Well, Mr. Dellner, I appreciate your taking the time to speak to me. You serve as a fine example of how hatred and bitterness can eat away the soul, leaving nothing but decay. I'm sorry for you." With these parting words, I walk quickly to my car, glad that I never gave him my name.

Although I don't feel threatened, I watch my rearview mirror as I drive away, checking to see if he followed me outside to discover my license plate number.

    As I drive along the freeway on my way home, my heart starts racing and my palms feel sweaty. I pull over quickly to recover. My mind is rushing and unfocused. What's wrong with me? A heart attack? Call Katri! Call Katri! Something deep inside suggests that calling for an ambulance might be the correct choice. After all, I reason with myself, Katri can't do CPR over the phone. I nearly laugh at myself, but fear grips me again. The deal is, if I need help, call Katri.

Chapter 23: Panic

My hands trembling, I cry frantically into the phone, "Katri? Katri? Oh, my God. Katri?"

"Jena? What's wrong? Where are you?"

"I . . . I . . . don't know," I wail. "Help me!" My anxiety is mounting. Dizziness and nausea consume me. My heart is beating frantically; I can feel it pounding inside me. I'm afraid that if I look, I'll see it beating beneath my skin. I struggle to take slow, deep breaths as a crushing feeling overwhelms me, and I gulp down air instead.

"I will, Jena. What are you feeling? Tell me what you're feeling."

"Heart racing . . . either I'm spinning or the world is spinning. Oh, God. Dizzy, did I mention dizzy? I feel, I feel, I feel like I'm going to die. I feel like getting out of my car and screaming and screaming and . . . Oh, no! Make it stop!"

"Jena, try to breathe. Breathe slowly and tell me your husband's name." I don't respond quickly enough, and she repeats, "Tell me!"

"Ben." My heart is going to leap out of my throat. Why does she want his name?

"What's your cat's name?"

"Are you trying to help me?" I yell frantically, in tears, into the phone.

"Yes! Tell me! Answer quickly."

"Which cat? I have four." I take in a few slow, deep breaths and wonder why she's asking me these stupid questions. I'm about to die, and she wants me to give her the name of one of my cats? And why just one? What about the others? As I manage to gain some control over my breathing, I ponder why she only wants one name, but soon my wildly beating heart overwhelms me.

"Oh, Jena, all four!" She pauses, then repeats in an equally frantic yell, "Jena, all four!"

I yell back, "Pookachoo, Sweetie Pie, Fluffy, and Fooffula!"

"Does Ben love all those names?"

"He hates them all. Why are you asking me these idiotic questions?" I fight the urge to run around screaming, but even so, I find myself getting more and more annoyed with Katri.

"Tell me all your sisters' names," she says.

"Valerie, Reena, and Deedee. You want my brothers' names, too?" I feel antsy, as if I'm in the wrong place. I should be doing something, going somewhere, getting something done.

"Yes."

"Why?"

Katri speaks quickly, decisively, as if any pause could spell the end of me, so she can't allow any dead air. "I'm trying to get you to talk. Where are you?"

"I'm in my car." I manage to slow my breaths as I contemplate her silly questions. I'm not sure why I called her in the first place.

"Are you still driving? Pull over!"

"Of course not! I pulled over before I called." Oh, that does it. First, she asks me dumb questions, and now she insults me! She actually thinks I'd call her in such a state, on a cell phone while I'm driving. My energies are focused now on my complete annoyance with Katri.

"Where is your car? What city?"

"Oh, I'm just outside of West Bendel."

"West Bendel? That's an hour's drive! Why did you drive out there?"

"To see Jeffrey. Oh, *no!* It's happening again." It all surges at once: the heart, the palms, an immense feeling of unease, and a need to move, but I don't know where.

"Sing!" she bellows into the phone.

"Sing what?" She wants me to sing? Tears gush from my eyes. "Make it stop. Make it stop. Make it stop."

"Oh, 'Home on the Range,'" she says and then adds, "Sing with me," so I join her, if only to humor her, and together we sing the chorus.

"Can't we sing a more interesting song?" I ask, feeling oddly calm.

"Sure. Like what?"

"Milkshake!" I then cheerfully recite the lyrics.

"I'm writing it down. Jena, are you playing with me here?"

"What do you mean? You said you wanted to sing, so I'm suggesting a song from this century."

"I never heard this before. What is it?"

"'Milkshake.' It's a hip-hop song by Kelis, much more

interesting than 'Home on the Range.'"

"Jena, we need to call 911."

"Because I like hip-hop? Don't you think that's a little extreme?" My head feels clear. I continue my deep breathing and wonder what's wrong with Katri.

"No. I think you're having panic attacks. If it starts again, breathe deeply. You shouldn't drive yourself home."

It's starting again. I can feel it: the racing heart, the sweaty palms, the intense need to do something. I start to gulp down air, and I try to focus on breathing slowly, but I'm struggling. Bless her heart, I can hear her, quietly and off key, singing the lyrics I just recited. Listening to her makes me laugh, and I manage to take slow, deep breaths.

"I can call 911 and send them to you. Where are you?"

"I think I know. I know why I feel this way. The ballroom! We have to go to that shop. The shop. Yes, the shop. I'm sure the answer is at the shop. You said you thought it would be an overwhelming urge? Right? I have an overwhelming need to go to the ballroom, and that shop is the key!"

"Don't drive right now."

"I feel fine."

"Wait for a little bit. Don't drive just yet. I'll wait here with you."

"Don't send an emergency squad here."

"I won't. So tell me about something. Anything."

"I really do feel better. Didn't I call you? Didn't I pull over?"

"That you did. Can you put the phone on speaker and put it on the passenger seat?"

"Sure, I can do that." I look at the time. "Damn! That shop will be closed by the time I get home. Tomorrow, I'll go tomorrow, with or without you. I'm sorry, but this is important. I can't wait till next week."

"I'll pick you up tomorrow. Don't disconnect the call until you pull into your driveway."

"I won't. Do you want to sing?"

"No!"

"What if I feel another attack coming on?"

"You sing it. I can be backup."

Chapter 24: Finding Jameson

Katri pulls up in Adam's red BMW convertible, waving at me and looking like she's escaped with the loot from a jewelry heist.

"Wow! You sure are driving in style today. How did you convince Adam to hand over the keys? Isn't this his baby?"

"It's my car, too," Katri replies firmly.

I hand her the address, looking around the car and remembering Ben's words to me when he first saw it: "Time to get that business of yours hopping so I can live in the manner I should be accustomed to."

The next morning, he provided an example of what he meant. As on most mornings, I made coffee and I told him it was ready. He was up in the loft where he could see the kitchen counter, so he looked over the railing and said, "I don't see any coffee."

"It's right in the pot," I said, pointing to the coffee pot.

"No, proper coffee is in a mug in my hand. That there," pointing to the coffee pot, "is called pre-coffee. If I were living in the manner I should be accustomed to, the coffee would be in a mug, sitting up here beside me."

"Oh, brother!"

"Coffee," he whined.

"Ben, the only way you're getting coffee today is if you come down here and pour yourself a cup. Either that or you can lick it off your face after I pour it over your head."

"Well, if you bring a mug with some cream and sugar in it, I might be able to catch some of the runoff."

I smile at the memory as Katri pulls up to Park It, Buy It, Sell It Auto, which isn't in the best part of Betta. It's an old, run-down, dirty, red brick building with black and gray mortar. The window trim is cracked, and the paint, or what's left of the paint, is badly chipping. Cardboard and duct tape cover the door's broken windowpane. There are some beat-up cars with "For Sale" signs in the lot. Katri and I eye each other warily.

As we walk in, Super Chomper is talking on her cell phone and doesn't look up. Chomp, chomp. "No way." Pause. Chomp, chomp. "Then what?" Pause. Chomp, snap, chomp. "No way." We hear many more "no ways" before she finally looks at us as if we couldn't have been any more of a burden on her oh-so-busy day. "I gotta go. Some people just walked in."

Just? We've been standing here a good three minutes!

She says nothing, just looking at us.

Katri begins, "Hi. Can we see Mr. Yee?"

"No Yee"—chomp, chomp—"here."

"I called a few days ago and you told me that someone named Yee was out for the day," I explain. "I'm looking for him."

"No Yee here." Chomper actually said that entire sentence without chomping, but she makes up for it with a few bubbles and snaps.

Katri and I exchange concerned glances while Chomper chomps away, filing her nails. Her blond hair with purple tips is in a messy ponytail, and she has a nose ring, a tongue ring, and a dime-sized hole in each ear.

Katri says, "We called a few days ago; we were told that the owner was out. What's his name?"

Chomper says clearly, slowly, without any chomps, "It's *Sonny*. You must have misheard me." She rolls her eyes and resumes filing her nails.

Katri shoots me a questioning look. I whisper to her, "I told you that I had I trouble understanding her through all the gum chomping."

Then, it hits. Sonny? Wasn't Sonny the name of the man who helped me at the ballroom? Could it be the same man?

Chomper goes to the back door and yells, "Sonny, some ladies here to see you."

After a moment, in walks Sonny, the same kindly man who helped me at the ballroom. He gives Katri a bewildered smile. "May I help you?"

"Actually, you can help both of us." Apparently realizing that she now stands between him and me, she moves to one side. "Is this the same man, Jena?"

A warm smile spreads across his face as he recognizes me. "I wasn't sure if you'd come around or not! I hope you're feeling better."

I realize now why he was familiar when I saw him days ago. Although he must be in his seventies now, he doesn't look it. He still stands straight and strong, the same warm smile as when he reached down and scooped up Hannah. Her impression of him burned his features into my mind. If I had seen Hannah's memory before I met him days back, I'd have known then who he was. Sonny is Jameson.

"Thank you. I'm fine now."

He motions for us to follow him out the back door. He leads us through an empty storeroom nearly the same size as his shop. We pass through a door in the back of the room and then turn right down a hallway. A big, thick window on the left side of the wall looks out into an empty garage. At the end of the hall is another door, which we follow him through.

He maintains his home better than his shop. It's simple and neat. We enter a room with a plain beige couch and a coffee table on the left side and a nicely polished grand piano on the right. The room isn't very big, and the piano takes up a large percentage of the space. Sonny notices me admiring the piano and asks, "Do you play?"

"No, I'm afraid not although I'd love to. My younger sister, Deedee, is a concert pianist."

"Deedee, you say? And does she go by Deedee when she plays?"

"Yes, she does!"

"I've heard her play, then. My daughter, Annie, who plays well, likes going to concerts, and I often go to them with her."

Sonny motions for us to sit on the couch.

Still smiling, I explain, "You're a difficult man to find, Sonny. I was looking for Jameson."

His expression goes flat and cold as he asks cautiously, "Where did you hear that name?"

What am I supposed to say? That I heard May use it? At a loss for words, I sit silently, staring at him.

His face softens as he studies Katri's face, tilting his head from side to side. "You look familiar."

I can see that she's hatching a bright idea. She says, "You might have known my parents. I remember them using the name Jameson when I was a child. And I think you probably knew my Aunt Marlene. Marlene Lanlore."

Sonny takes a short, rapid breath, then nods. His eyes revert to me, no longer cold but amused. "But you? I'm not sure what to make of you. Still shifting in and out of memories?"

Both Katri and I gasp. I stammer, "Wh-wh-what?"

"It was something you said into the darkness of the ballroom. That you didn't have time for robbers and murderers because you had May's memories to shift to."

"That was you? You were in the ballroom that day, in the dining room?"

"Yes, that was me. I stayed behind that day because I didn't think you were, were . . . ."

Katri winks at me, then chimes in, saying, "I understand! Trust me. I've been friends with Jena for almost ten years, and she often evokes that sort of reaction."

I scrunch my face up to demonstrate my displeasure, but my glare only prompts chuckles from Sonny and Katri. It's the cherub cheeks. I vow again to practice stern looks in the mirror!

Sonny continues to eye me, studying my face as if he's looking for something that he's sure must be there, but he can't find it. He finally asks, "What was your name again?"

"Jena."

"Jena," he says thoughtfully. Then again, "Jena. When I first saw you walking around the ballroom, I had a good feeling. You seemed like a nice young woman. You had a cat you were fussing with. I was there that day. I had just cleared the trail to the lake and planted some pansies, and then I saw you with your cat. I had more work to do, so I returned a few days later. Yes, I was in the dining room when you were at the ballroom that day." He inhales and exhales slowly many times, shaking his head. "You seemed like a friendly person, but when you wanted to know where Jeffrey was and you called yourself May, I didn't know what to make of it. I couldn't figure out whether you were there to help or hurt Annie."

"Help!" I quickly interrupt, nodding my head vigorously. "Really! It's help! I'm no friend of Jeffrey's! He's a sad, angry, bitter man!"

"That he is. That he is. I hear the two packs a day smoking habit caught up with him too."

"Sonny, I can't explain how this all makes sense, but I need to find something."

He raises his hand as if to silence me, slowly shaking his head, and says softly, "Jena, I think I understand. 'Jena's here. I'm not alone. Jena's here.'"

I gasp. "It was you who called Katri a few days ago?"

"No, I never called Katri. No. Those were May's last words. She had her hands clasped together, as if she was praying. Her arms were outstretched in front her when I found her, and her eyes were closed. I don't think she knew that I was there. I took her hands tightly in mine and held her, and her last words were, 'Jena's here. I'm not alone. Jena's here.'"

Both Katri and I gasp, and a lump forms in my throat. No, no more raccoon eyes for me! No! "I'm counting blue sheep!" I announce firmly.

"What?" Katri asks, staring at me.

"I've had enough crying for this week. I put on mascara this morning and I'm counting blue sheep so it won't smear! My diversion!" I look off into the distance as I picture blue sheep and kick myself for wearing mascara. I really thought all this boohooing nonsense was over!

"Why blue? Why sheep?"

"What, Katri? Do you think that they should be multicolored, or is it the animal you object to?"

"I think multicolored could be more of a distraction."

I think for a minute and realize that she has a point. Blue sheep jumping a fence does get a little boring, but pink, green, yellow, blue, orange, red, and purple makes it more distracting. As I ponder multicolored sheep, Katri says to Sonny, "We get this all the time."

"I'm right here, Katri, right here!" I say, giving her my most disapproving look. The look only causes her to laugh, so I explain, "I didn't want to cry, and it was a pleasant distraction!"

"What? Counting blue sheep?"

"Well, no. I like the idea of the multicolored ones, actually."

"Ha!" she says nodding at Sonny, "See what I mean?"

"What do you mean, 'see what I mean'? Did you hear what he said? May heard me. She heard me! Aren't you even a little bit touched?"

"Yes, but only you would interrupt at such a poignant moment and bring up blue sheep!"

"Yes, and only you would point out that they should be multicolored, which, as I said, is a pretty good idea."

"Well, thank you."

"You're welcome," I respond, and we both turn our heads

back to an amused Sonny, who followed us the entire time, with his head rapidly turning to watch whoever was talking.

"Sonny, I . . ."

He stops me, laughing, and says, "You're two peas in a pod! And, Jena, I don't know how you did it, but I believe you provided comfort for May in her last moments. How can I help you?"

"Annie, or, well, actually, Hannah. Hannah is Annie—right?"

"Yes, Hannah is Annie," he replies sadly. "After May died, I went to the lake and found Hannah sitting there alone, sobbing quietly. The firemen thought that Hannah had died in the fire. I suspect you know the truth of what happened to her parents."

"That Jeffrey killed May, April, August, and Marlene, and that he'd planned for Hannah to be there, too. That truth?"

"That's right. I didn't have any proof, and I was afraid that if he knew Hannah survived, he'd kill both of us. The man was ruthless. My little Annie had died the night before. Annie and Hannah had the same blue eyes. It was painful for me, pretending that Hannah was Annie and not being able to bury my daughter properly, but it was the least I could do. The least I could do for August!" His voice trails off.

I start to speak, and Katri says so quietly that I struggle to hear her, "It works for you! Suggesting it to others may well sound flippant and insensitive. Especially now."

I whisper back, "I know! That wasn't what I was about to say!"

With a twinkle in his eyes and a hint of a smile, he says, "Counting multicolored sheep works. Do yours only jump fences?"

"Well," I respond seriously, "because it's important to avoid having my appearance ruined by running mascara, not to mention that crying makes my eyes swell, I maximize the distracting effect by having them dance and sing, as well as jump fences. Let your imagination run wild."

Katri is smiling, and I get the feeling that she's proud of my unique style of handling grief and trauma. Maybe what I see is her relief that my methods can work for others. Or possibly, she's just relieved that I didn't deeply offend Sonny. To my credit, he did ask me!

He is already talking about something else as I come out of

my own thoughts. ". . . and tearing around the ballroom. He tore down the wall in the front and moved it out to the balcony, walled in the doors from the entryway and closet room to the back room, and tore up the floorboards. He wouldn't allow anyone in there. He saw me on the property once and flew into a rage. The next thing I knew, he framed my company for some serious transportation violations and nearly ruined me. I stayed clear of him, mostly because I was afraid that he would see Hannah and realize who she really was. But I got back at him in small ways." He grins widely. "I kept the trail cleared that went to the lake. He hated it, I know, because he would tear out the flowers I planted!

"I made sure that the power remained on in the ballroom. You see, the ballroom was in May's name, and when she died, it wasn't Jeffrey's to sell. It was built into the contract. He called the electric company to demand that they turn the power off, but I had a friend there who told me that Jeffrey would call, fuming and cursing, but my friend told him that only May could shut it off. He was at the ballroom nearly every day for a year, searching for something. I don't know what he was looking for."

"I do! That's why we're here! The bear, a stuffed teddy bear that Hannah had. Do you still have it?"

My heart sinks as Sonny shakes his head slowly. "Sonny," I remind him. "When you found Hannah by the lake, she was holding a stuffed animal. You tried to move it, so it wouldn't fall, but she wouldn't let you. She called it 'May Bear.'"

Recognition spreads across his face. "May Bear? How did you . . . ? Never mind. May Bear wasn't actually a teddy bear; it was a floppy, brown stuffed dog. I can see why some people might have thought it was a bear. Annie called it her May Bear and slept with it until she was ten. She was always very careful with it."

"Please, Sonny. Please tell me that you still have May Bear."

"I'm not sure. I'll have to ask Annie. Please, ladies, remember to call her Annie. She doesn't know who she is."

Oh, dear. How are we going to tell Annie about Hannah? It will be traumatic to learn about her real parents, and if we don't share the full details with her, she'll believe that her father killed her mother. This is complicated. "Does Annie remember anything about what happened?" I ask.

"Maybe. I'm not sure. We never spoke about it. For the

first few months, she insisted that her name was Hannah, so I called her Ann, and over time, she accepted Annie. She had nightmares for years. She would scream, 'No, free, no!' and 'My May Bear!'"

"'Free'? She said, 'free'?" I ask. "Katri, could she remember anything from thirty-six years ago?"

"Thirty-six? That was thirty years ago," Sonny clarifies.

"But I saw a sign on the property that said 1970."

"That was actually Jeffrey's error! He blamed the sign company and put them out of business."

"Sonny, does Annie still live around here? Can we call her?"

"She's vacationing. Can't this wait till she gets back?"

My heart starts racing, panic wells up inside me, and I breathe. Deeply, slowly, I inhale, then exhale. I think of blue, green, and yellow sheep singing "Milkshake," and that does the trick. I let out a cleansing exhale. Sonny and Katri are staring at me. "No! It can't wait. We only have a few days. I should never have spoken to Jeffrey. I think that started it."

"Started what?" Sonny asks.

"The urgency to get this done. The fear that something will happen to the ballroom."

"No! Don't blame yourself. If you talked to Jeffrey, you only reminded him of the clause in the sale of the ballroom. It would have only been a matter of time before he remembered."

"Clause?"

"The thirty-year clause. He couldn't sell the building or change it for thirty years."

"Change it. But didn't you say that he made changes by extending the top floor to the balcony and walling off the doors to the painting room?"

"Yup, and when the chandeliers went missing, Marla and Michael Nearlen got wind of the thefts. They went to the ballroom and saw what he had done. Oh, there was a blowup that day," he says, smiling. "I was at the lake. They told him that he had no right to make changes and showed him a copy of the contract. Jeffrey tried to be Jeffrey, with his 'my beloved wife' bologna, saying that he wanted to fulfill her dream and on and on. But the Nearlens didn't believe anything Jeffrey had to say, and they warned him that if he made further changes, he would lose the rights to the ballroom. That's when he ripped out the lights and boarded it up. Later, when I noticed that he didn't come around anymore, I opened up a few windows and put in some crude lights. He had rights to some of the surrounding land, and later he lent rights to Betta Conservation Land, with the agreement that no one could enter his property and that they would fence it off." Sonny smiles slyly. "Yeah, I forgot. I took care of that fence!"

"When does this thirty-year agreement end?"

"In two days."

"When does Annie return?"

"Next week. I was planning on joining her tomorrow."

"You have to call Annie and ask her where May Bear is. I'm sure she still has it somewhere. And, Sonny, it wouldn't be a bad idea to suggest that she cut her vacation short, at least for now. I think she'll want to know what's been hidden away for thirty years."

Sonny looks confused, and I continue, "Maybe I didn't quite explain it all. I do that sometimes. August built a secret place in the ballroom. He wrote down the location and hid it inside May Bear when he realized that he was in danger, and he told May, in so many words, what he did. May told April about May Bear. When April put Hannah on the bench by the lake, she told her never to give up May Bear."

Frozen, Sonny stares at me. I realize that it isn't usual for a perfect stranger to know so much detail. I innocently ask, "Do you have any questions?"

"I, well, yes. I don't know what to ask first. April died in the fire. How could she have brought Hannah to the lake? And the bigger question: how do you know this?"

I've said too much to this man, so instead of explaining how I know so much about April, I say, "Memory shifting has its benefits."

"Weren't they suspicious when they never found Hannah's body?" I blurt out. I'm immediately sorry for saying it.

Sonny's teddy bear statue slumps, his eyes droop, his lips tremble, he sighs deeply, and nearly collapses on the chair beside the phone.

"I'm sorry, Sonny. That was insensitive of me." This kind soul of a man sacrificed his own daughter's burial to save August's daughter. Katri and I remain silent, allowing Sonny time to grieve for Annie.

    "No, Jena. I appreciate your asking. I had blocked it out all these years, and I've finally dealt with it. Now we're going to find May Bear. Annie is just under three-hour's drive up north, so she can come back quickly. I'll call her."

Chapter 25: Finding the Bear

Sonny says, "Annie? Hi, darling. It's your dad." Pause. "I could be better." Pause. "Yes, I do. I'm calling because I need to know if you still have May Bear." Pause. "Oh, I see." Pause. "Well, I'll explain it to you, but I think you really should come home first." Pause. "I really need to find that May Bear, so I can't stay on the phone to explain it." Pause. "No, I'm not hurt, nothing like that, but this is something important. Something you should come back for." Pause. "Nightmares? You still have them?" Pause. "Well, then, it probably does have something to do with the nightmares. Yup, probably does." Pause. "See you tomorrow." Pause. "And, Annie, if I'm not home, go to our lake spot. You'll find me around there." Pause. "Good-bye, darling. I love you, too." He puts the phone down, "May Bear is in a box in the attic. Annie isn't sure which box. Come on. I'll help you look."

We follow him down a short hallway into a bedroom. It doesn't look used anymore, probably a guest room now, but it might have even been Hannah's old room. It has only a bed with a plain beige comforter, a nightstand, and a dresser. The furniture looks much like the assemble-it-yourself furniture sold at discount stores.

Sonny sees me looking at the furniture and says, "Annie doesn't like this room, either. She thinks I should have flowered bedspreads and painted walls with pretty murals. I'm a simple man. I like simple things. When she moved out and took her things, I furnished it with what it needed."

"Oh, no, really! I wasn't thinking that at all!" Ben always tells me that I wear what I'm thinking on my face. It's hard to hide anything from Ben, but Sonny has misread me. What he thinks is dislike for his furniture is my sorrow for what Jeffrey has done to his life.

Sonny pulls down a ladder, secures it, and then motions to us to follow him. Katri climbs up before me. She looks at me wide-eyed as I climb the ladder, causing me to feel nervous about what she sees in the attic. We look at each other and then at the attic several times and sigh. The unfinished attic covers the entire house, and the bedroom we just walked through is at one end of the house. Starting three feet from the ladder is a stack of boxes, between two and four feet high, spanning the width of the attic and reaching all the way to the other end.

"You say you think it's in one of these boxes?" I ask.

"Yup," says Sonny, reaching for the first box.

"Any idea when she put it away?"

"She said it was five or so years ago"

"Do I dare to hope they've been stacked up here chronologically?"

"Well, yes," he begins, to which Katri and I let out a sigh of relief. But we're too quick, and he continues, "But a few days ago, I was searching for something, actually for Annie's trip up north, and I moved most of them around."

I guess my "urgent need" to solve the mystery doesn't cover a huge inconvenience! If only we'd come a few days ago. Definitely, some flaws that need to be worked out with shifting memories.

"Jena?" Katri calls out to me.

"Yes? What? I'm right here. Don't yell."

"I beg to differ on that. Sonny moved the boxes he knows he looked in before and put them against that wall," she says pointing behind her. "He's sure that he would have seen May Bear." My eyes follow her hand to the four boxes sitting against the back and then back to the sea of boxes in front of us.

"Sonny? Can I have a glass of water?"

"Sure! How about you? That's Katri, right?"

"Yes. My apologies. I should have introduced myself. I'm Katri Evers. And I'd love a glass of water, too."

Sonny makes his way down the steps.

I turn to Katri, saying, "I felt just awful asking about Annie's missing body. It just didn't dawn on me that he'd put his daughter's body in the fire."

"Yes, I hear you. I was also wondering why there was no report of a missing body. I figured it was such an inferno that the investigators determined the remains were incinerated."

I nod and continue, "He's a sweet man, so I don't mean this the wrong way, but do you think he also, just maybe, kept Hannah to replace Annie? I mean, he could have handed Hannah over to your parents!"

"I kind of wondered that myself, but I think that he was really scared for Hannah and trying to protect her. Given what Jeffrey did to her family, they were well-warranted fears."

We hear Sonny's footsteps on the ladder. First, we see his head, then we see three bottles of water. He hands one to each of us and wipes the sweat from his brow. It's a little warm up here. Thankfully, he opens the window behind us.

As he starts sorting through boxes again, he says, "As I mentioned before, I was there when May died. I heard some of Jeffrey's confession. I knew about Marla and Michael. You must be their daughter. I always liked them! I know that Hannah could have had a better life with Marla and Michael, if she had a life. But I have no doubt that Jeffrey would have killed Hannah if he knew she was alive, so I hid her. I've wondered for years what to say to Hannah if she learns the truth. I still don't know. I understand how the two of you question it. I have to admit; having Hannah with me did help to fill the void that Annie left."

He walks over to the boxes, puts three on the floor, and waves us over. "Come on, ladies. Let's find May Bear."

We work our way through the sea of boxes filled with school reports, class papers, report cards, stamp collections, and every kind of memento known to man. I find it all fascinating as I slowly make my way through the boxes. On my tenth box, I find some black-and-white photos of a sickly little girl. Sonny notices me studying them and walks over. "That's Annie a few months before she died." He sorts through the pictures and stops at a snapshot of a happy little Hannah hugging a smiling, healthier-looking Annie.

"Here," he says. "This was three days before Annie fell ill. It feels good speaking Annie's name and actually referring to Annie."

I work hard to mask my emotions. I'm disgusted with the injustice that Sonny has suffered while Jeffrey has spent all these years living in luxury. One picture of Sonny's once neat and well-maintained business has a date written on the back: 1975. A limo is parked in front of a sign on the building that reads, "Park It, Drive it, Limo Service." The younger Sonny, the Jameson I met in May's memory, is seated wearing a nice suit and smiling. Annie is in his arms, hugging him, and his lovely wife, smartly dressed, is beaming beside him, with her hands on his shoulder and her cheek pressed next to his.

"Sonny, what happened to your wife?"

Again, I instantly regret my hastily spoken words as his

shoulders slump and he stares at the boxes. "I'm sorry. I really shouldn't ask so many questions. I just, well, I just . . . . I just need to keep my mouth shut."

"No, Jena. I don't mind you asking. It just hurts, that's all. Not because you're asking but because no one was asking anything after the Lanlore kids died. The world fell apart after that. You see, my wife shot herself. She was angry with me for not going to the police about Jeffrey. She loved Hannah, but she didn't believe that Hannah was at risk and she wanted me to expose Jeffrey. He didn't think much of working people or their property. He disposed of some drugs behind our building; it was a field back then. Annie must have found them. When August heard how sick she was, he visited us. He was the one who found the drugs. He was suspicious of something, so he walked around the property. I think that's what got him killed; he started snooping around and Jeffrey found out that August knew the truth. I owed it to him to save and protect his daughter! I owed it to the Lanlore kids. They were good kids, good kids."

Sonny composes himself and continues, "I owed it to August to protect his daughter. I knew that nothing would end the grief my wife felt when we lost Annie. She just couldn't take it. It took her five years and two miscarriages before we finally had Annie. She just couldn't take it." Sonny turns away and picks up another box.

Katri whispers to me, "Stop looking at the photos and just focus on finding May Bear! You won't find it in between the pictures."

Is she insane? Does she think I can take a handful of pictures and not look through and wonder about them? She rolls her eyes, shaking her head. Then she takes a box, swishes things around, and hands it to me.

"Here, take this one. If I find you looking at more pictures, I'm sending you downstairs."

"Checking my boxes before I look in them is hardly an efficient way to search."

"Whatever."

I spit out my water, coughing. The firsts keep mounting. "You just 'whatevered' me."

"Yes, I know what 'whatever' means! You're not the only one who can say it. Look in these boxes here, then" Katri says as she pushes some boxes she just scanned toward me and takes the one full of pictures away from me.

"So you're admitting you're wrong?" I ask.

"Oh, is that what you always mean when you say it?"

"No, not always. Sometimes it means 'be quiet.'"

"Okay! Whatever! Start searching!"

I notice Sonny watching us, laughing, so I explain, "Yes, she's always this bossy. I don't know how I stand it. Do this, do that. She even tries to ration my chocolate!"

"You like chocolate?"

"Yes!" I perk up, eager to encourage the sharing of chocolate. "Do you have some?"

"Yes, I do," says Sonny as he makes his way toward the ladder. "I bought a supply to take with me up north for Annie. They're her favorites from a shop that used to be here in town."

The lights come on, and at the same time we both say, "Delectable Delights."

"You've heard of them?" he asks.

"Yes. Katri here introduced them to me. Now don't be stingy with them. Well, you can be stingy with Katri's. She thinks one is enough, but not me."

Katri shakes her head in what I guess is dismay at my audacity as Sonny disappears down the ladder, but I don't care—it's chocolate!

After a few minutes, Sonny rejoins us in the attic. He has a little bag full of candies for each of us. My bag looks heavier than Katri's, so I'm happy.

We continue searching quietly through the boxes, with the occasional sound of candy wrappers, mainly from me, crinkling into the air. Katri, who is quickly scanning boxes for me, sees May Bear first. She pulls it out and asks, "Is this it?"

May Bear is worn but still intact. It seems surreal that the little stuffed toy that I saw only a few days ago is now over thirty years old. How can this be happening? How can I see a memory? And not just any memory, but a memory with a mystery, and my friend has a stake in the memory.

"Katri, I just remembered something that Jeffrey said that will make you very pleased with your parents!"

"Yes?" she says as she uncharacteristically dances around with May Bear.

"Jeffrey really hated your parents. I guess your mother had a hand in preventing some lucrative business deal for him, probably between him and your father."

"My mother worked in the business too, Jena. She started it! I suspect the biggest problem with Jeffrey was that he didn't want to deal with a woman." Katri laughs. "My mother was a force to be reckoned with!"

"As is her daughter," I say proudly.

Looking at May Bear, Sonny asks, "Do we need to cut it open?"

"Yes."

"Annie isn't going to like that."

"We can sew May Bear back together. And, besides, the reason Hannah was drilled to keep this toy was so we could find the note inside."

Sonny closes the lid on the box he was sorting through, looks up, and says thoughtfully, "Her name is Annie now."

"Sonny, I'm sorry for the losses you've suffered, but soon she'll have to find out that she's Hannah."

"Well, I was thinking. Maybe we can work things so she never needs to know?"

"She needs to know that she . . . ."

"Look, miss. She's my daughter . . . ."

"No, Sonny, she isn't. You're . . . ."

Katri, shocked at our exchange, raises her hands. "Stop, please, both of you. This is very emotional for everyone involved. Sonny, Jeffrey can't hurt Hannah now. She can only gain. But whatever there is to gain will be for Hannah Lanlore, not Annie. She'll have to know who she is. It's inevitable that she'll learn the truth. She might prefer to go by Annie because she's used to it; she might change her name back to Hannah. Who knows? Jena here knows her as Hannah; you've been calling her Annie." Looking at Sonny, she says, "You realize that she's my first cousin?"

"You're right. Well, I guess I should fetch some scissors."

"None of us need to be up here anymore," I say, getting up to wipe the dust off my clothes. "Let's all go down."

We regroup in the front room. Sonny hands me the scissors, and I carefully cut four inches along the seam on May Bear's back. I put my hand in, feel around and around, and then proclaim, "I can't find anything. I'll need to dump the contents out."

We all move to the kitchen table, and I wait while Katri and Sonny clear it off. I slowly pour and pull the stuffing from the toy onto the table while Katri and Sonny sift through it.

Sonny is the first to spot a tiny, folded-up piece of paper, no bigger than a piece of the stuffing. He looks at it and turns to me with a twinkle in his eyes, saying, "You're contagious."

Katri and I look at each other. I'm confused. She's concerned. Neither of us understands what he means.

He lets out a jovial, Santalike laugh and says, "The inspector on the boat with a beer. You know, like from the game Clue but played on a boat."

I arch an eyebrow, Katri tilts her head, and we exchange quizzical glances.

Sonny watches our bemused looks and hurriedly defends himself. "Oh, come on. I was making a joke."

"What did he do with a beer?" Katri asks.

"Well he drank it, of course!"

"Clue is a murder mystery game," she informs Sonny.

"Joke, Katri! Sonny is just joking." Looking at Sonny snickering, I say, "Well, I appreciate your humor. I might have been slow about getting it, but I appreciate it."

"Sonny, you've only been around Jena a few hours and already you've been Jenafied."

"I'm proud of you, Sonny," I say. "For her to say that you're Jenafied is a compliment, but tell us, what does it really say?"

"'Basement.'"

"That's it? Basement? I don't recall there being a basement."

Sonny looks worried. "There isn't."

"Poppycock," I say firmly. Although Katri and Sonny are crestfallen, believing that the clue is useless, I'm optimistic—no, confident—that this clue is our answer.

Katri looks at her watch. "It's getting late now. We'll need to look tomorrow. Shall we meet at Dirt Road Parking Lot?"

Chapter 26: Demolition

Katri starts out sullen as we drive back to my house. She glances at me frequently. I suspect that she notices how optimistic I am because with each glance, her mood improves.

Katri's cell phone rings. I answer it.

"Hi, Jena. Just as well you answered," says Adam's voice. "They're going to raze the ballroom tomorrow."

"What? No! Katri? Didn't Sonny say we had a few days?"

"Yes, why?"

"Adam just said they're going to raze it tomorrow. Adam, there's no way they can get machinery in there by tomorrow. There aren't any roads. They'll have to cut down some trees first."

"They aren't going to bulldoze; they're going to burn and blow," explains Adam.

A sick feeling starts to rise up in me. "We have to go there tonight, now! Adam, bring flashlights. Katri and I know where the secret place is. We'll meet you either at Dirt Road or at the ballroom. Are you in?"

"I'm in, and Ben is here beside me. We'll meet you at Dirt Road Parking Lot."

"Okay, bye." I hang up and say to Katri, "I need to call Sonny."

Chomper answers the phone.

"This is Jena," I say. "I was just visiting with Sonny a little bit ago, and I need to speak to him." I'm kicking myself for not getting his home phone number.

She chomps away. "He doesn't want to be disturbed."

My patience is ready to burst. I say urgently to Chomper, "He knows who I am, and he'll want to hear this. Please tell him I'm on the phone."

She chomps for a little bit, then I hear her walk off and yell, "Sonny, some lady named Jena is on the phone. Says she has to talk to you."

"Hi, Jena," he says, with his voice cracking.

"Sonny, we just learned that Jeffrey is having the building destroyed tomorrow. We're heading there now. Can you meet us there?"

"Yes. I'll leave right now."

"Oh. One last thing?"

"Yes?"

"That girl. Why ever do you have her working there?" Katri smacks me, I smack her back, and we glare at each other. I, however, have the last glare since she has to watch the road.

"Yeah, I know," says Sonny chuckling.

We pull into the parking lot to find Ben and Adam waiting. Ben comes running over to the car, not to greet me but to admire the BMW. His eyes are thirsty as he walks beside it, caressing the hood. I roll my eyes; I've never understood the car fixation!

"Did you guys bring flashlights?" I ask.

"Yes, we did. Four of them," says Ben smiling. He hands us each a flashlight. I run off toward the ballroom, with them trailing me.

"So where is this secret place?" ask Adam.

"The basement," I say.

"That's it? The basement? Where in the basement are we supposed to look?"

To which Katri adds, as we make rapid progress through the woods. "Oh, that isn't half the problem. The ballroom doesn't have a basement."

The men, who previously had a kid-on-a-treasure-hunt air of excitement, both stop. Adam asks, "Well, then, why are we going there?"

I don't stop; I keep walking. No time to lose. Katri is right behind me. I call back, "There must be a basement! August must have built one."

Incredulous, Adam calls after me, "He added a basement to an existing building? No way."

"Come on, Adam. I'm not going to wait for you," I say. "August was very talented. If he said 'basement,' then there's a basement. I'm going."

Katri follows me.

"Guys, if you can't handle it, no problem. Jena and I will let you know later."

I hear them trampling after us, cursing and breaking twigs. Forget a sneak attack, that's for sure.

"I have an idea," I say. "There's a pantry off the hallway in the kitchen. When I first saw the closed door, I assumed it led to a basement." They nod as they remember the door. "It's there, somehow, behind the shelves. I'm sure of it."

"Jena, there's just no way that this guy poured a basement under a pantry in an existing building and no one noticed."

My hands move deftly through the trees, clearing debris, jumping across obstacles, ducking under limbs. I move rapidly, effortlessly. "Adam," I explain impatiently. "He didn't have to create a complete basement, but to him it's a basement, or maybe it was a code word for something under the first floor. Whatever! I'm sure it's somewhere in that pantry."

"Well, I'm telling you, you're wrong."

I just laugh. I know it. I can feel it. It's there. We have to find it tonight. I feel the urgency, so I pick up the pace.

"Jena, we have all night," says Ben breathlessly. "Why are you running?"

Running, am I? I realize that all of them, even Katri, are breathless. Not me. I could run for miles. Never mind. If they can't keep up now, they can catch up later. I chalk up my increased energy to my urgent need to get to the ballroom, and I push forward quickly, easily, through the forest.

At our pace, it doesn't take long to get to the ballroom. Sonny, surprisingly, is already waiting. As I pass by, I tell him what I believe. He's equally unconvinced that I'm right, but he follows us.

We step through the window, where all five of us turn on our flashlights, and I lead the way to the pantry. I open one of the doors, Katri opens the other, and we peer into the pantry, shining our flashlights into it. It's ten feet wide, with five shelves, each about three feet deep.

"Let's take the shelves out," I say, tugging on the closest one.

Adam stops me. "If this guy added something when these shelves were already here, and he was trying to keep what he was up to a secret, it must have been on the lower shelves. Let's start at the bottom."

Ben reaches down and yanks. Since there's only a small amount of give, Sonny and Adam help. They're all tugging and yanking when the shelf finally releases, sending all three of them hurtling against the boarded-up back door. Five hundred plus pounds of men ramming the door loosens the boards. We all pitch in and remove the remaining boards. Now we can take advantage of the remaining natural light and get some fresh air.

I kneel down, and as I'm looking and feeling for a keyhole, Adam asks, "Now what are we looking for again?"

"A keyhole," I say holding up the key.

All of us kneel side by side, tapping, poking, searching, and occasionally bumping heads as we search for the elusive keyhole.

Adam lightly taps the wood. "There's something here. Let's remove the next shelf." The rest of us look at each other with arched eyebrows. We didn't hear anything significant.

The men tug and fight with the next shelf, but it doesn't budge, so they stop and rest. Katri and I offer to help and they laugh, which, of course, annoys us. We kneel closer to the shelf, studying it. This shelf is different from the bottom one. It has a wide, rounded end like a bull nose on a step. All the remaining shelves look like this one. I point to it, and motion to Katri to try to slide it out. It gives a little, but it's old, and it sticks. Ben sees what we're up to, removes a small cloth from his pocket, wraps it around his hand, gives the wood slider a good hard tug, and manages to slide it out part way on both sides. The men grab hold of the shelf, and it comes out with a great deal of effort.

Adam slowly shines his flashlight along the wood below the place where the shelf was attached to the wall. Gliding his fingertips over the wood while we follow his hand movements with our flashlights. He takes a penknife from his pocket and begins to fiddle in the wood. A small piece pops out, exposing a keyhole. We applaud!

Excited, I put the key in the hole, and although it fits, it won't turn. Ben takes the key and carefully starts to jiggle it as he squirts oil into the keyhole. Clever Ben to bring a little can of oil! That works, the key turns, and parts of what once looked like an ordinary wall start to separate, revealing the outline of a door about two feet wide and as high as the distance between the two shelves. Ben works it, and it pops out a little more from the wall, tilting up toward us, like a flap with the hinge on top. With my flashlight, I follow the seam of the door. Where the door seam stops, a vertical-cut like pattern that looks like the door seam, continues up and down from the seam, making it appear it is a natural part of the wood. There's a similar vertical pattern at a parallel location on the left side of the pantry wall. The horizontal seams of the door are covered by the shelves.

Ben manages to wiggle the door up, breaking the rusty

hinges. He tosses the door aside. Eagerly, we all shine our lights into an empty space.

Clearly, this is a big letdown for all of us. My friends give up and start packing up their things. Ben puts his hand gently on my back and says, "Jena, there's nothing there. Let's go."

Not budging, I say, "The basement. He said the basement, and basements are usually below ground. It's here, I tell you. I know it's here."

"Yes," Sonny says, coming to my aid. "August was very clever and a skilled carpenter. He didn't trust Jeffrey, and he knew how impatient and arrogant Jeffrey was. August would have worked hard to conceal the real hiding place just in case Jeffrey found it. Jeffrey would have given up at this point."

"Oh," I add cheerfully. "Do only arrogant people give up easily?" I feel around inside. "Adam, can you feel around and see if you can find another keyhole cover thingy?"

"Sure, I'll look for the thingy."

Adam feels around, slowly moving his hand. Finding something, he works his other hand in. He pulls out a piece of wood, tosses it aside, and then opens his hand up to me, so I hand him the key. He tries the key and then reaches back for the oil, which Ben is holding ready for him. Someone watching us would think that he's a surgeon and Ben and I his brilliant, mind-reading assistants. The shelf platform hinges down. We all scramble for viewing positions, but Adam, being closest, squeezes his head in and shines the flashlight down the hole. "There's something down there, about five feet down."

"Is there a rope?" I ask.

Adam pops his head out to make sure that I see him and rolls his eyes. "If this guy was so clever, there must be a better way." He continues to feel around until we hear a scratching sound, soon followed by a grinding sound.

A strong sense of foreboding comes over me. A little like the anxiety attack I had when I drove home after my visit with Jeffrey, but it's not as severe. "I'm feeling really antsy, guys," I say. "Can you move any faster?"

"Chill. I almost have it."

The antsy feeling is getting worse, Katri notices the change and signals to me that I should go out and get air, which only adds to the uneasiness. I urge him on. "Adam, if there's anything you can do to go any faster, please do it."

"I've got it," he says, pulling out a leather bag.

From outside, we faintly hear someone say, "Dad, this building is really something. Why do you want to destroy it?"

We all turn off our flashlights and Katri whispers, "We should hide."

"We don't need to hide," I say. "We have it now. It's too late, too late for Jeffrey. Game over, asshole. Let's just walk out the door and go to the lake." I feel confident that we're safe.

"He did kill five people. We should hide!" demands Ben.

"We're safe." Logic would argue that we should hide, but I march right out of the kitchen door, looking right and left. As I cross the yard, I'm vaguely aware that the owner of the voice isn't visible. Everyone follows, quickly and quietly.

"Sonny, do you know a different way back?" I ask. "I remember when you walked me out days ago, you took a path directly to Main Trail."

Sonny signals for us to follow him, and he leads us away.

Ben runs up to Sonny and whispers, "Hi, Sonny. We haven't really been introduced. We spoke on the phone. I want to thank you for helping Jena." Sonny stops to face Ben and they shake hands, exchanging light pleasantries.

"I'm sorry," I say. "I forgot to introduce everyone. Sonny . . ."

Adam interrupts, whispering, "There's a psycho killer back there, on the other side of the trees," he says pointing back toward the ballroom, "And you guys want to stop and have introductions? We need to keep walking and remain silent."

"Sonny, that's Adam, my husband," says Katri. "He gets like that when he hasn't had dinner. Have you eaten anything, dear?"

"Why am I the only one who's worried about Mr. Psycho?"

"First of all, Jena isn't worried." Katri says calmly, and Ben nods. "She has a pretty good sense of things. Second, we're a good distance from the ballroom. If they didn't hear us walking to the lake, they aren't going to hear us now."

Adam mumbles, "Maybe they're following us." He walks ahead of Sonny, thrashing and cursing into the trees. Since he doesn't know the way out, he has to stop and wait for Sonny to confirm that he's going the right direction. I lightly touch Katri, Sonny, and Ben and give them a naughty smile—they'll figure it out!

I inhale deeply and loudly. Adam whirls around. "What? What?"

"I sense something." I stop and look fearfully both ways. Katri, Sonny, and Ben join in the game as we stand frozen. "All the thrashing around and swearing has drawn attention to us. Jeffrey is coming."

Adam whirls around, trying to peer through the trees now covered in darkness then he stops and glares at me. "Some tree rustling draws attention, but all that chatty nonsense back there, exchanging introductions and offers of tea and cookies, doesn't? Oh, please." We all burst out laughing.

185   Lisa Nevin

Chapter 27: What's Inside

It's late by the time we pull up to our house, which is the closest to the ballroom. Sonny is with us since his car wasn't in the Dirt Road Parking Lot. I don't know where his car is, and no one asked. At this point, everyone is eager to know what's in the bag.

The air is crisp with excitement as we scurry from our cars into the house. I go to the kitchen to get a pitcher of water and some glasses while the others follow Ben to the dining room.

Sweetie Pie watches as I join the others, fortunately and uncharacteristically not demanding his devotional.

Adam places the bag on the table, and we all take a seat, staring silently at the cracked, faded, black leather bag. I want to reach for it, but I believe that those who lost family members should check the contents. It was Katri's aunt and uncle who died in the fire, and her first cousin who will be affected by whatever is in that bag. Sonny's daughter died, but he raised Hannah as his daughter, so maybe he should open it. I don't want to make suggestions as to who has the most right to check inside, so, instead, I sit wishing that someone would do something.

Adam saves the day, saying, "Why is everyone just sitting here? We go through all this trouble to find this bag, nearly getting killed, and you just look at it?" He grabs the bag and pulls out the contents, placing them on the table. There are two letter-size envelopes, one addressed to May and the other to Hannah, along with a bulging eight-by-ten-inch envelope.

Without looking at anyone, Adam opens the letter to May and reads:

My Dearest Sister,

I apologize for failing you. The more I investigated, the more I learned, and the more dangerous it became. I had hoped that I could protect you by keeping you in the dark, but today, at your party, I learned something that leaves me believing that there's no amicable fix and that your relationship with Jeffrey cannot continue. He's not who you think he is.

As you know, several months ago, Jameson's daughter, Annie, fell seriously ill. Her symptoms were so sudden and severe that I didn't believe they were from natural causes. Michael told me about an exclusive deal that Jeffrey was trying to negotiate with him. Jeffrey even discouraged Michael from sharing information with me. I'm confident that Jeffrey was in over his head and desperate for undamaged prescription drugs.

I know that Jeffrey has been to Jameson's shop and is aware of the large property. I told Jameson what I suspected, so we searched his property and we found haphazardly discarded drugs. I couldn't take my findings to the police because Jeffrey had forged records to make it look like I had handled the shipment. Fortunately, Jameson believed me and agreed to keep quiet until I could find more evidence linking Jeffrey to the tainted drugs.

I didn't find the evidence I was looking for, but I did find more disturbing information. Did you ever think it was odd that Mother encouraged you to get married so young? It was Father who put his foot down and insisted that you wait until you were older! Have you noticed that Mother always seems to bristle with pride when she sees Jeffrey?

Our real mother died when we were very young. You were only a year old. I couldn't speak to Father about our real mother because Mother, or, I should say, Sarah was always by his side. Later, I discovered that Sarah had a nine-year-old son when she met Father. She was unmarried and trying to hide her son from our father, so she allowed her parents to raise her son as their own. I discovered this while I was searching birth records. It was no easy feat, either; she didn't use her real name on Jeffrey's birth certificate, so a copy of it wouldn't have been enough proof to convince Father that she'd lied to him all these years.

While I was looking through birth certificates, I learned that Jameson is Father's brother. I confronted Jameson; he explained that they'd had a falling out when Father wanted to marry Sarah. Jameson didn't trust Sarah and told Wendel so. The rift between them grew when Sarah insisted on raising us as "her own" and was angry with Jameson for suggesting that she shouldn't.

It pains me to know that, as I write this, April thinks that I'm the one who dumped the drugs. Annie is very ill and not likely to live through the day, but Jameson will still be tending his post to avoid drawing attention to himself.

You've probably heard about my financial "ruin." This rumor is, to some degree, true from the perspective of Jeffrey and Sarah. I was concerned about what would happen to the family business when word got out of what Jeffrey had done with the illegally purchased and tainted drugs. I liquidated my business assets and invested in U.S.

Savings bonds. There are one million dollars in bonds in the envelope.

I'm so sorry that Jeffrey has not lived up to your expectations. Forgive me, May. Forgive me. Sarah is quite skilled at creating lasting rifts between family members and without proof, I would only look like an angry and vindictive brother if I'd come to you. I'm afraid of what they might do if they find out I know the truth. I fear for my life and for my family. For your own sake and Hannah's, don't speak to Jeffrey or Sarah. You must go straight to Father and to the police. If Jeffrey even suspects that you know, it's the end, the end of all of us. Take good care of Hannah, and let her know that her parents loved her.

I'm sorry it has come to this.

Love,

August

Adam puts down the letter. Katri and I look at Sonny while Adam and Ben look at us. Ben is the first to speak. "Who is Jameson?"

Arching an eyebrow, I point at Sonny, who sits staring blankly at the letter. "Sonny, some reason you didn't mention anything about the brother thing?"

He sighs, starts to speak, then stops, shaking his head ever so slightly. With a long sigh, he finally says, "Like the letter said, Wendel and I had an argument. The rift never healed, and I stopped looking at him as my brother. All his kids died, and he still had his head in the sand about Sarah. Watching him take on Jeffrey like he was a savior made me ill."

"Is Wendel still alive?" I ask, even though I realize that Wendel would be well into his eighties.

"No, he died fifteen years ago. I wouldn't be surprised if Sarah helped him along."

We all sit quietly out of consideration for Sonny, who has dealt with so much loss and pain over the years.

Adam picks up the second letter. "Is everyone ready for the letter to Hannah?"

Ben objects, "I don't think we should read her letter, Adam. She's alive. She can read it herself."

I, for one, really want to know what the letter says, so I'm pleased when Katri responds, "Hannah doesn't know who she is yet," with emphasis on "yet," and then looks at Sonny, who nods back. "So it's better for us to know what it says. Please read the letter, Adam."

Adam reads:

My Darling, Sweet Hannah—my sunshine,

How it pains me to write this, as I know you'll only read it if your mother and I are dead. There's so much that we wanted to teach you. We looked forward to the next winter when we could take you out ice-skating on the lake. How special it would have been for each of us to hold your hand on the very lake where the two of us first met.

Whatever you might have heard, or you might hear, your mom and I have always been deeply in love. Your birth was a happy and joyous occasion. My precious little girl, how I wish I could have been there to walk you down the aisle on your wedding day.

I told your Aunt May in my letter to her, but I want to be the one to tell you that the loving man you call Sonny is your great-uncle. He's a wonderful, warmhearted man and if you need help, he'll help you.

All our love, hugs, and kisses,
Daddy and Mom

Adam's voice wavers as he reads. The note has a few smudged ink spots, and I picture August brushing back tears as he writes. I wonder if August knew that April had escaped with Hannah that day—I hope so. I hope his last thought was the belief that his daughter was safe in May's care.

Adam opens the larger envelope. "There's a lot of money here." He holds up a document. "Bank statement." He thumbs through the papers and holds up another. "This one is the deed to the Dellner Ballroom. The thirty-year clause ends tomorrow! Hannah needs to claim the ballroom tomorrow to prevent Jeffrey from destroying it. Oh, wait." He pulls out a letter-size envelope. "It has 'Sonny' written on it!" He hands it to Sonny.

"We'll understand if you want to read it privately," I say.

"No. I'll read it aloud. But, Jena, if you see me starting to raccoon my eyes, you start the multicolored sheep count. Deal?"

I grin and Sonny reads:

Dear Uncle Sonny,

I hope you don't mind my calling you the same name that Hannah uses.

I want to thank you for all you've done for my family and me. There's so much I'd like to say about what you've taught me, but I don't have the time as I need to finish this letter and hide it away before the ballroom gets busy.

If you're reading this, it means that Jeffrey has won—for now. I know that Annie isn't doing well and isn't expected to make it through the day. She was a wonderful little girl and will be missed by everyone who knew her. As we agreed, I'll take her body for an autopsy. Rest assured that she'll be treated gently. I'll have the results mailed to you, just in case Jeffrey tries to intercept my mail. You should have them in two weeks.

Love from your nephew,
August

Sonny's eyes are misty but he smiles. "What are your sheep doing, Jena?"

"Oh, they're break dancing now. How about yours?" I appreciate Sonny's bringing up the sheep because I was starting to battle the pain and frustration again. August wrote these letters thirty years ago, but for me, only a few days have gone by.

He takes in a deep breath and nods while Adam and Ben continue to glance suspiciously between us.

"Sonny, you've only been around Jena a few hours and she already has you doing her anti-raccoon tactics?" Ben asks

"Yup. Works, too!"

I clap my hands together, stand up, and say, "Okay! First thing tomorrow, let's all go to the ballroom and stop this guy once and for all!"

191   Lisa Nevin

Chapter 28: Speaking Up

Ben and I arrive at the Dirt Road Parking Lot at dawn, having left super-early in hopes of getting to the ballroom before Jeffrey.

The Everses pull up and fuss around inside their car before getting out and looking around. "Any word from Sonny?" Adam asks.

"Sonny knows a shortcut to the ballroom," I say. "He got there before us yesterday, remember? We should plan on meeting him there."

"I agree with Jena," says Katri.

Along the way, Adam says, "I've been thinking. How, exactly, are we planning to stop Jeffrey? Let's not forget that the guy's a psycho. I'm not inclined to put my body between him and the ballroom."

"The blast crew will be there; he's not going to kill us with them around," I answer. "Besides, I think his killing days are over."

"I really think we need to discuss this more! Look what the guy has done; he's not going to let it go." Adam's pace slows as he mumbles about the need for a better plan, or at least a plan.

"He's not very healthy. There isn't really much he can do. I met him. I'm not worried."

"A sick person can easily fire a gun! And if Jeffrey does get there before us, he'll know we found the secret place, and he'll feel more threatened."

Although I really don't care whether we walk at a leisurely pace or a faster one, I suggest, "Then we should walk faster!"

We make speedy progress to the ballroom, arriving before Sonny.

"No Sonny yet," says Ben. "How odd. When I dropped him off at his car last night, he told me he'd be here by dawn. Oh, well," he shrugs. "Glad we beat Psycho here."

We make ourselves comfortable on the steps on the side entrance, waiting for signs of Jeffrey or Sonny.

We hear a clicking sound, like a gun cocking. In unison, our heads turn left toward the sound. The half wall around the porch blocks our view, but soon we see Jeffrey slowly making his way around from behind the building.

Sitting on the step above me, Adam huffs and puffs while his face grows bright red. I work to stifle my laughter but small peeps escape me. Without moving his head, Adam eyes me and mumbles through clenched teeth, "And why didn't you sense the danger?"

"Why would I?"

"Well, you sensed that we had to get here in a hurry yesterday, sensed that we needed to leave, sensed that we were fine by the lake, and now this madman has a gun pointing at us. You should have sensed it."

"Enough," Katri hisses.

"Guess her senses can't be trusted after all."

By now, Jeffrey is in front of us, glaring at me. "How did you find it?" he growls.

Helping Jeffrey is a younger man that I suspect is his son even though he resembles Jeffrey only in hair color and height.

His eyes dart nervously between the gun, Jeffrey, and us, as his chest rises and falls quickly.

I pause before responding, mainly to annoy Jeffrey but also because I'm still battling laughter and the urge to make flippant comments. I speak slowly and thoughtfully, as if I'm not entirely sure what he's talking about, "I gather you're talking about the secret place August built?"

"Answer me." he says waving the gun around at us.

Adam mutters, "Jena, don't egg him on."

"What are you planning to do, Jeffrey?" I ask. "This ballroom belongs to Hannah."

"Hannah died thirty years ago. This place is mine."

"Hannah is very much alive; she knows what you've been up to."

"Rubbish! If someone's claiming to be Hannah, she's lying. Give me the papers, now! I know August squirreled away money. I know you have it."

"Dad, this is wrong," Jeffrey's son says, looking pale and horrified. "Please put that gun away. You can't hurt these people. We don't need this place, we don't need . . . ." He reaches halfheartedly for the gun.

"Shut up," Jeffrey snarls. "You've always been weak like your mother. This is business. Watch and learn as I did from my mother."

The urge to laugh vanishes. Torrents of rage consume me, and I stand up. This man not only bears the blame, but he blames others for his crimes, and he hopes to pass on this legacy of learning to his son. "Business? Killing five people is business?" I say, approaching him.

Ben quietly calls after me, "Jena, no."

I'm not stopping. This hate-filled man has lived comfortably, unpunished for his crimes. What other crimes has he committed along the way in the name of business? As for that pittance of sorrow that I saw trickle down his cheek two days ago, it was more for a business deal that failed than for his wife. And his son. Is this the Jeffrey that I spoke to on the phone? Do I dare stop and request introductions? I laugh out loud, thinking what Adam would say to that. Jeffrey threatens me now? He threatens my husband? He threatens my friends? Enough, now; I've had enough! I helplessly watched his cruelty to May and her sister. I won't watch helplessly now.

"What?" he says mocking me. "You speak of business? What's that little business of yours, Dream Events? What do you know of business? Sacrifices have to be made that only a shrewd businessman can carry out."

"Oh, I'm so sorry. Have I misunderstood you all this time? You're just business savvy? Well, no, wait. You're sly. The way you manipulated May on the balcony the night of the ball and managed to work up a fake tear, telling her how you needed her support and how hurt you were and blah, blah, blah."

His eyes bore into me as he asks, "How do you know that?"

I don't look away. "How do I know? Ask yourself why this person that you're holding a gun on approaches you without fear."

I smile as I hear Adam say faintly in the background, "She's gone mad, that's why."

Ben whispers, "Maybe with her ability she can stop bullets."

"Oh, not likely, Ben. Be real."

"I *am* being real, Adam. Look what she's done so far."

Annoyed, I look back at them. "Do you mind? You're distracting me. I forgot what I was about to say."

"Oh, sorry, love!" says Ben. "You were about to explain to the killer why you approach him without fear."

"Oh, yes. Thank you." At last my chance to speak freely has come, and I turn my attention back to Jeffrey. "How do I know that you and your mother stood right up there," I say, pointing up to the boarded-up window, "and spied on May as she relaxed over there on that bench? Tell me, Jeffrey. What did you see that day? The clock has stopped for you, Jeffrey."

Jeffrey continues looking at me in stunned silence, no doubt wondering if it's merely a coincidence that I use the same words that he said to May. "How do I know? Well, the one thing you missed, the one thing you couldn't hear, the one bond you never broke was the bond between May and her brother and sister. You didn't hear what August whispered to May as he left the ballroom or see what he handed to her." I hold up the key. "And you didn't hear what May said to April as she walked away into the night. You thought you were clever to spy on them, but May whispered, for April's ears only, 'May Bear!'"

Jeffrey jolts to attention on hearing that name.

"Oh, so you know what May Bear is? How ironic! When you torched August's home, you nearly destroyed the only clue to the location of the secret place. As I said, Jeffrey, Hannah is alive. Why do you think April was here that day you found May holding her body? Your own greed and arrogance prevented you from seeing it. She could have saved herself, but she saved Hannah, instead. You were a fool to come here today. Isn't it amusing that your ultimate downfall came because you tried one last time to cover up your crime?"

Behind Jeffrey, Sonny is quietly approaching from the bushes, flanked by Betta Police officers. Jeffrey's horrified son also sees them, but he does nothing. Whether he's too stunned to speak or too stunned by his father's actions to warn him, I don't know.

"You can't prove anything about this fantasy. Hannah sat on a bench. Then what? She walked to a nearby house and they raised her as their own? You really think that some child showing up unexpectedly wouldn't have been noticed and reported?"

"No, Jeffrey. Jameson found her. He found Hannah and her stuffed toy." At the mention of Jameson's name, Jeffrey's face goes white, then red with rage. With great joy, I continue, "Yes, Jameson saved Hannah. He was the one person who could bring in a little fair-haired, blue-eyed child and raise her as his own by calling her Annie."

Jeffrey fumes, "Annie! That little brat of the hired help. That stupid kid cost me millions."

As Jeffrey and I speak, Sonny continues to creep up and is now standing behind Jeffrey. Jeffrey's son says nothing. A lump forms in my throat as I look at the young man. Does he worry that his father will turn the gun on him, too, if he doesn't support his "business plan?"

"Annie," booms Sonny, causing Jeffrey to whirl around, "was an angel." Every ounce of Sonny's strength goes into his arm as he plants his fist on the side of Jeffrey's face. In spite of his fitness, he can't quite muster enough of a swing to knock Jeffrey over, so Jeffrey manages to avert some of the blow. I jump forward, bending my knee into my chest, and plant a sidekick against Jeffrey's back that sends him hurtling forwards. How nice that all those kickboxing classes have paid off.

He quickly rolls over, pointing the gun at Sonny, but Jeffrey's son, already in position, lunges for the gun. It fires.

We all stop and look down at the father-and-son pair. We wait anxiously, wondering who will stand. After a moment, Jeffrey's dazed son stands up with the gun in his hand.

Astonished that his son shot him, Jeffrey stares at him, holding his bloody chest, and then looks at me. "How did you know?"

Oh, what poetic justice for me to deliver the words he last hears. To a man who has escaped justice for so long I say, "I'm your conscience."

Jeffrey's son lets out a long, sad sigh and shakes his head, looking at his father, then at Sonny, and finally at us. "I'm sorry. I'm so sorry. I would never have brought him here if I . . . if I . . . I'm sorry."

Sonny puts his hand on the son's shoulder and says gently, "A son's worthiness is defined by his own actions, not by his father's. You have a good mother, Jay; she's raised you well."

"Jay?" I ask. "Did Jeffrey have two sons?" I work hard to mask rising panic at the thought that the second son may not have turned out so well.

"No. Jay is a nickname," he says, looking at his father, whose vacant eyes stare up at the ballroom. "I was named after him."

Ben runs over to me. "Seriously, Jena. Are you crazy?

What were you thinking?"

Adam answers for me, "Well, she had a sense that she should speak to him."

Katri gives him a good whack across the back of his head.

A young woman with reddish blond hair appears through the trees. She looks quietly at Sonny, who is smiling at me, then walks up to me and hugs me, with tears glistening in her eyes. "Thank you, Jena, thank you. I finally understand now what the nightmares mean, and why I was always so attached to May Bear."

August's, May's, and April's eyes stare back at me. I look into her face, and I think of that terrified little girl sitting on the bench. I remember the anguish I felt at being unable to hold her, so I give her a hearty hug in return. Hannah is alive, and she stands before me.

To Katri she says, "I hear we're cousins?"

Katri nods, beaming. "Yes. My mother was your mother's sister. They were twins."

I walk away from the others, not so much because I want them to have their quiet time, even though that's part of my reason, but because this experience has taken a huge amount of emotion out of me. I don't want to witness any more tears, whether they're from sorrow or joy.

I leave them to their friendly banter and walk around to the front of the ballroom, looking up, trying to remember what I saw in May's memory. The grand ballroom, the stairs, the balcony, and the freshly trimmed hedges are still vivid in my mind. After all, it's only days since I saw the ballroom in its finest.

Ben walks up and hugs me from behind. "We're ready to leave, Jena."

"So soon?"

"Soon? It's been an hour. The police have already taken Jeffrey's body away. You, darling," he says kissing my cheek, "have been lost in thought."

We rejoin Katri and Adam, who are sitting on the steps by the side entry. Katri approaches me with a rolled-up sheet of paper, which she hands to me, saying, "The deed to the ballroom. Hannah wants you to have it."

At first I'm elated, but it doesn't feel right. I explain to Katri, "I'll have to decline. Although I'd like to see this ballroom put back into use, I'll always see May on the front porch watching

Jeffrey walk away with her sister's body thrown nonchalantly on his shoulders."

Katri takes my hand and places the deed in it. "It's your decision what to do with it, but regardless, it's yours. Think about it, Jena. You're an event planner. Now you'll have the perfect location for events. Ice-skating on the lake in the winter, boating in the summer, and spectacular parties all year round. You can stand on the front porch and see the tragedy that occurred there years ago, or you can build new memories, happy ones."

"I'll think about it, but it'll cost a small fortune to renovate this place."

Katri smiles. "Friend, you don't need to worry about that!"

We start down the gravel road and I look back. Yes, this place could do with some new memories. The painting room could be my office. I start to mull over all the changes I'd like to make.

Adam asks me, "So, do you have a sense for what I want to eat tonight?"

I just sigh, and I hear him say, "Ouch! What?"

Ben asks, "Now what? How will you know the next mystery to be solved?"

"I don't know! But I do know not to turn my head rapidly back and forth once I'm there!"

Katri begins, "Thank you, Jena. I know I put you at risk when I asked you to return to the ballroom, and I'm .. .."

I stop dead and look at her, shaking my head. "No, don't tell me you're sorry. You were looking out for me. What if I'd gone back or witnessed other memories and you weren't there? I could have had one of those attacks; I wouldn't have known what to do. No, Katri, you encouraged me to do what needed to be done. You helped me, and I should thank you!"

"You're welcome. And if you need help?"

"I'll call Katri!"

Author's Favorite Links

(The author favors the following businesses, however, the businesses listed below do not endorse this novel.)

Zephyr Adventures www.zephyradventures.com
Skiboards.com www.skiboards.com
STRUB Sports Designs www.strub.ca
CentreSki and Bike www.centreskiandbike.net
Phoenix Inline www.phxinline.com
Pro-Skate Inline School www.proskateinlineschool.com
Miami's Great EsSkate www.skatemiamibeach.com
Empire Skate Club of New York www.empireskate.org
Inline Club of Boston www.sk8net.com
Skate Boston www.skate-boston.com
Diann Izzie www.diannizzie.com

Contact the author:
www.lisanevin.com